Murder in Wasilla

Mary Wasche

mary Wasche

This book is dedicated to Jacob, Michael, Natalie, Andrew, Katrina, Nicholas, Cindy, Matt, Ken, Koren, Marty, and Maren.

Special thanks to Jesica Sartell, sister and editor extraordinaire, who put her heart into helping tell the tale in the best way possible.

Chapter 1

IF NOT FOR the full moon dominating the sky like a huge spotlight, Gary might have missed the ghostly shape that lay shimmering on the shoulder of the isolated Knik-Goose Bay Road just north of Wasilla, Alaska.

"What the hell?" Gary muttered as he passed. "Goddamn! Is that somebody layin' there?"

He jerked his pickup onto the edge of the road and yanked the steering wheel until the truck spun back the way he'd come. There was never much traffic this far north after midnight. Even if there had been, he would've done the same thing and to hell with anybody who didn't like it.

There it was again, highlighted by the radiant moonlight, right where he'd seen it. Gary drove up closer, killed the engine, and sat for a moment, staring. "Holy shit! It's a woman. A naked woman...what the hell...?" His voice trailed off. He pried the grungy black baseball cap from his head, scratched the hair plastered beneath it and peered through the windshield.

He rolled down his window and leaned out. "Hey, there, lady! Hey! You okay?" He studied her for signs of breathing or movement. There was nothing.

Gary climbed out and took a tentative step closer. Dazzling moonlight reflected from the body, setting it off from the gravel where it laid serenely, limbs perfectly aligned, face upturned toward the inky sky. For a moment, Gary imagined he was looking at an ivory statue of a sleeping woman. But the tangled halo of blond hair that pillowed her head told him she was real.

He walked over and touched her hip with the toe of his boot, then jerked back at the clay-like thud. A shudder rippled through him. His thoughts raced and he muttered, "She got rigga mortis or whatever they call it? Musta been here for a while if it is."

He took a step back, suddenly light-headed, and bent over to fight a rush of nausea. He'd never seen a dead woman. Much less a naked one. After a few gulps of frigid air, he straightened up and looked toward his truck, wishing he had a blanket to cover her. "Poor thing. Left all alone on the highway on such a cold night. Lucky some animal didn't come along," he mumbled.

He moved another step backward, legs beginning to tremble. It was impossible to tear his eyes away. Not old, he figured. Not a teenager, either. Thirties maybe. Real pretty face. Nice knockers. He couldn't help letting his eyes trail down to the cleft between her legs. He tore his gaze away, ashamed.

Giving in to morbid curiosity and a desire to somehow take care of her, he walked back to the body, reached down and gingerly wiped away a trickle of blood that trailed from the corner of her mouth. He shuddered at the feel of her stiff, cold flesh, and brushed the blood off across his pant leg with a hasty swipe.

He stared down at her face, unsettled. Why did it seem like he'd seen that face before? Did he know her? Then it hit him. He stumbled backward, gasping. She'd been at the bar earlier that night. Her and her three friends. Pretty women, nice women, not the kind who usually hung around the Buck Shot. They'd only stayed a short while, nursing their cherry red girlie drinks in tall-stemmed glasses, whispering to each other, giggling. He'd noticed this woman because she was so innocent looking, with her fluffy blond hair and soft blue sweater. Now here she was naked on the side of the road, dead! His knees grew weak.

He stepped away, shocked, mesmerized by the pearly body gleaming in the moonlight, then began backing toward his truck, arms wrapped against his chest in an effort to stop the shivering that threatened to overcome him. He needed to sit down. Needed the familiar warmth and comfort of his truck seat. Wished he'd bought that cell phone he promised his daughter he'd get.

The prick of headlights in the distance caught his eye while he reached for the door handle. He turned toward the lights with relief. When the car didn't look like it would slow down, he dashed to the center of the highway and began a frantic wind-milling of his arms above his head. He was forced to jump all over the road, arms flailing, while a filthy low-slung sedan that had seen better days tried to maneuver around him.

Gary ran to the driver's window when the car rolled to a stop. "There's a dead woman! Call the troopers! There's a dead woman over there!"

A wizened old man peered through the smudged window, fear playing across his narrow, craggy face. He kept the engine on and studied Gary with bleary eyes before cranking down his window with obvious reluctance. His face turned ashen when his gaze followed Gary's pointing finger. "What the...? That a body? She dead?" His eyes widened. "Whaddya want me to do? Ain't got no cell phone. Goddamn..." he stammered through the whiskey breath that floated between them.

"Go get help!" Gary ordered. "Fast! Call the troopers."

The old man tore his gaze from the body, nodded to Gary and rolled up his window. His car coughed and screeched before it lurched ahead, leaving a sputter of oily smoke hanging low over the pavement and disappeared into the darkness.

Gary ducked away from the stench of the car's fumes. Shivering against the November night's numbing cold, he sunk his neck into his collar and hurried back to his truck. Even with the heater on full blast, it took a long while for the trembling to stop. He hunched behind the wheel of his truck, huddled into his jacket. Despite the gusts of wind that seeped through the crack in his windshield, it stayed comfortable enough in the cab if he turned the heater on every ten minutes and the defroster kicked in just enough to keep the windows clear.

He'd been fretting ever since the old guy left. *Really couldn't blame the old man if he just kept going. Probably scared to get involved.* Gary didn't like the idea of sitting here all night, but didn't dare take off or he might end up in trouble for leaving the scene. He wished he hadn't had all those beers and the extra swigs of Jack. It would be bad if the cops smelled booze on his breath. He blew into his palm, grimaced, then rolled the window down and sucked deep breaths of fresh air through his mouth. Maybe that would help take the smell away. He couldn't pull his gaze from the body, and was sure he'd never forget this night. Maybe he should move her because she could draw wolves or coyotes. No, better to just leave her where she was and wait. He shuddered, agonized. She'd been so alive earlier, so pretty, so happy with her friends.

It was now close to two in the morning and not a single car had come along since the old man left. This section of the highway didn't lead anywhere folks would need to go this late at night unless they were on their way home, and homes were few and far between so far out of Wasilla. Gary shifted around, trying to get his protesting muscles and bones comfortable. He hunkered into his seat, feeling sorry for himself, wishing he hadn't noticed the body at all and was home in bed where he belonged.

By now, the moon had glided to the middle of his rear window and illuminated the dials on the dashboard. Bone-tired, worried that the old man had just gone home without making the call, Gary's muscles began to react to all those bumpy hours on the grader. The six beers that had gone down so easily at the saloon made him drowsy and he wished again he hadn't had that much to drink. It would be serious trouble for sure if the cops figured out he'd been drinking. But staying was the right thing to do. His eyes drooped shut.

The high-pitched whine of a siren in the distance jerked him awake. While he rubbed his hands over his eyes, dots of blue light drew swiftly closer and the whoop of the siren increased. A white sedan with *Alaska State Troopers* in blue lettering along the side pulled up across the highway, lights flashing blue and red into the night. The siren died while Gary shook himself awake, stretched the kinks out of his shoulders and tried to stay calm. Always got this way around the law. Even though he hadn't done anything this time, he needed a few deep, calming breaths before he could pull open the door handle and step out to meet the officers.

Chapter 2

ALASKA STATE TROOPER Nick Kerrans sized up the man who started across the highway toward them. From the looks of the dirt-smudged clothing he wore, Nick judged him to be a construction worker of some kind. The slightly faltering gait was that of a man around sixty. The ragged cuffs of his jeans puddled over mud-stained leather boots and a greasy black baseball cap fit his head like it never came off. Shaggy, graying whiskers surrounded a tight mouth, and tufted eyebrows tinged with glints of gray hung over his eyes. From the man's demeanor, Nick recognized that he was no stranger to the law.

"Know him?" he mouthed to the fellow officer at his side.

Matt murmured an answer, "Nope, not off-hand."

The man stopped when he got near them, and without greeting, turned and pointed. Nick blanched at the sight. He heard Matt gulp.

THE MOON HAD diminished to a pale illusion on the distant horizon and a hint of pink and yellow shimmered over the eastern mountaintops by the time the medical examiner peeled the latex gloves from his hands, flexed his fingers, and motioned to the attendants to load the body. Nick tipped the wide-brimmed trooper's hat up off his forehead and stepped back. The air had a keen bite this time of year, as if it had been cleaned and refreshed by the frosty autumn days that brought snow and biting winds to Alaska so early every fall. Even on a day like this, the sting of the wind made his eyes water and the penetrating cold numbed his cheeks and fingers, but it didn't bother him. Twenty above was just fine. This was what was best about being a trooper – being able to spend most of his working hours outside. And he never tired of the vast, jagged mountains that were visible no matter where he was.

He watched Matt help the attendants load the body bag and secure the door of the coroner's van. Matt walked toward Nick and pointed toward the man who sat slumped in the cab of his pickup on the shoulder of the highway. "Should we let him be on his way? The guy's been here all night."

"Guess we better," Nick replied. "He's been cooperative and we've got all his info."

Matt scrunched deeper into his jacket at a piercing blast of wind. "Man, that's a strong wind. Snow's coming." He gave a shiver. "You feel okay about letting him go?"

"Yeah, I believe him. I think he does work for Northwoods Construction on the new hospital, like he said." Nick eyed the man in the pickup. "We have no reason to hold him. He's not actually a witness, if what he told us is true. He says he knows nothing, that he was just the one who spotted the body. And he did the right thing, waiting for us like he did."

Matt pounded his gloves together, gave a shake, and turned to Nick. "Well, let's make it clear he needs to come in to the station and give a statement. He's the only lead we have right now." He paused. "He sure looks beat."

Matt walked over, spoke to the man in the truck, and turned back. Gary revved up his truck, spit gravel with a hasty illegal U-turn across the highway and sped away.

Nick shook his head. "God, they're dumb asses sometimes. We could've ticketed him right there. Do you think he even realizes that?"

"No," Matt answered. "He's an Alaskan, that's for sure. Pretty much does what he wants."

Four other law enforcement vehicles had arrived during the past few hours, and the highway was now cordoned off. A uniformed officer directed the sparse morning traffic through a single open lane around the scene. Every passing driver's head craned, curious eyes focused on the patch of ground where the authorities were gathered. The vehicles crawled along until the impatient officer forced them along with vigorous motions.

Nick and Matt helped secure the area while a search crew began combing the surrounding ditches and pavement now that it was light. Streamers of yellow tape flapped and snapped between the trees. Fine, dry snowflakes began to skitter across the highway.

"The snow's starting already," Matt said. "Is there anything else you think we need to do here?" He looked longingly toward the car and sniffed his reddening nose.

Nick shrugged. "It's been a long night and we have the report to do. Let's head back to Wasilla and see if we can find out who she is. Do you have the pictures?"

"Yeah." Matt waved at the camera in the back seat.

They pulled off their gloves, shrugged out of their heavy uniform jackets, and tossed them in the back seat. Matt took the wheel, giving the heater's dial a quick twist to high. Nick slid his hat off and swiped his hand over his close-cropped hair before folding his long legs into the passenger's seat. He reached back and brought the digital camera to his lap. "Look at how she was arranged so neatly. Whoever put her there posed her just so. She was a pretty woman. Her hair was that new flippy style before it got all messed up. Her nails were done. I didn't see a mark on her. No blood, either."

"I'm sure the autopsy will tell us something," Matt replied. He gave a distracted wave of acknowledgement to the officer who directed them ahead of the few waiting cars, and pulled onto the highway. "There's no apparent evidence of an accident. And it's not like she got sick or something and died out there on her own. There were no clothes at all around the body - that's pretty odd. I'm not aware of any missing person reports in the last few days, are you?"

"No. None at all."

Back at the station, Nick and Matt sat down to do their paperwork. The case unsettled Nick and he grew anxious for his shift to end so he could get home to Kay and the kids. Nights like this made him wonder if Kay and his parents were right when they urged him to give up law enforcement. They worried too much about him, but he was tougher than most guys. During his stint in the Marines he'd proved he could do anything he set his mind to. He'd never regretted joining the troopers, but seeing the woman like that on the highway was really getting to him. Maybe it was time to think about a different job. Or, maybe he was just tired.

The chip of diamond on the dead woman's finger told him some other husband wouldn't get a chance to hold his wife again after last night. Nick wondered who was searching for his missing wife right now, brushed a weary hand across his head, rubbed his fists into his eyes, and checked the clock before bending to his reports.

Chapter 3

PRESTON MILLS WAS tired. Apartment hunting was far from his favorite thing to do and rents in Anchorage were higher than he'd expected. He gave a weary sigh, loosened his suddenly constricting tie, and tried to wriggle the ache from his lower back. It was as if the long drive from Boston, being alone in a strange city far from home, and the feeling of being out of place, all were hitting him at this moment. He had to find somewhere to live soon, get a place to unpack, settle in, and relax after all those days on the road.

His eyes had looked droopy, shadowed and deeper blue than usual in the bathroom mirror at the motel this morning. He ran his fingers through the hair his mother loved to describe as chestnut, and tried to smash down the East Coast spiky style that labeled him an outsider here in Alaska. He hoped he looked presentable enough to convince a landlord that he was a good risk as a potential tenant.

Maybe this apartment would be better than the dozen or so he'd looked at during the past few days. It sounded unusual and the ad said it had a view. The directions were tangled, with unusual street names like

Kasillov and Saldana. The roads had twisted and turned back on themselves until he didn't even know which direction he was heading anymore, only that he was going farther and farther up the steep, winding mountain roads of the neighborhood known as the Hillside on the southern edge of Anchorage. Finally, there it was, Stoneridge Drive. The directions said to take the first driveway up to the left. Preston pulled up to the end of the long curving driveway and turned off his Jeep.

A petite woman, light curls framing her face, hurried out the enameled red double doors on the side of the house. "Mr. Mills?" she inquired.

Preston got out of the car. "Yes, I'm Preston Mills. I called about the apartment his morning." Even at five ten, he felt tall next to her. Most of the young women in his life so far had been sleek and long limbed, nearly matching him in height, but he had to tip his head down to meet Karen's eyes. He brushed his tie down flat and stuck out his hand. Hers felt tiny in his, but her grip was solid.

"Pleased to meet you. I'm Karen," she said. "The apartment's this way."

He followed her around to the front where a separate entry door nestled beneath a gray painted wood deck that ran the length of the house. While Karen fiddled with the lock, Preston turned and looked over his shoulder at the sprawling homes separated by mature trees and thick brush that spilled down the mountainside below. Stately, white-tipped mountains ringed the distant, miniature city and a long, glimmering body of water stretched along its western edge. Preston could just make out the airport where a barely visible plane the size of a mosquito advanced upward into a spreading red-gold sunset.

"It's an amazing view," he commented.

"Yes," she replied. "It changes every day. Sometimes the clouds are actually below us. It's really beautiful. And it's so quiet and private way up here." She pushed the door open and turned to study him. "Where did you say you were from?"

"Boston" Preston gave her a grin. "I've always dreamed of living in Alaska, so when I got a job offer, I took it and hit the road." He drew a deep breath of sharp air that carried a hint of ocean. "This is a whole different world for me. I've been a city boy all my life."

"You're a lawyer, did you say when you called?"

"Yes. I start downtown with the Public Defender's office Monday. I drove from Boston by myself. I've only been in town for three days."

"So you don't know anybody at all?" she asked.

"No. But I'm kind of a loner, anyway, so that doesn't bother me."

Fifteen minutes later, key in hand, his spirits rose as he pulled away. He'd found the perfect place. Karen and her husband, empty nesters who didn't need such a big house, had divided their lower level into an apartment just right for a single person. The rooms were small and very clean. There wasn't much storage, but that was fine since Preston didn't have much other than the books, clothing, and personal items that had fit in his car for the long drive. Karen assured him he could have a dog, since the yard was five untamed acres and they had two chocolate Labs of their own. Navigating the driveway might be a challenge in winter, but the view and privacy more than made up for any shortcomings and, anyway, the Jeep had four-wheel drive.

What a relief it would be to get out of that motel and settle into the apartment this weekend before he had to report to work Monday morning. Starting a life of his own here far from the expectations of those back home lifted his spirits like nothing else had ever done. He quashed a flutter of trepidation at being completely on his own for the first time in his life. But this is what he'd wanted. To be independent. To stop trying to please everyone else. He drew a deep breath, feeling uncharacteristically liberated, unafraid and confident. This had felt right from the very first mile out of Boston. He shook his head to clear the image of his mother's worried eyes and his father's disapproving frown as they'd diminished in the rear view mirror. Now after making the nine day drive across the U.S., Canada, and eastern Alaska, he was ready to start the job, had an ideal apartment and was finally on his own for the first time in his life. The whole thing was being treated by his parents simply as a temporary step off the path of the life they'd envisioned for him. Well, he'd show them he wasn't their puppet.

LATER, HIS THOUGHTS turned to his job while he unpacked his meager wardrobe, boxes of law books, a few bags of groceries, a bean bag chair, his small TV, and the sleeping bag and air mattress he'd use for a bed. It wouldn't be an easy job he'd start tomorrow. Everybody cautioned him that defending clients who weren't paying their own legal bills was a tough way to start a career. But the Public Defender's office was the only job offer he'd received. At least it was a start on life here. Maybe he'd make some contacts in the legal world and be able to move on to a better job with a private firm within a year or two.

Settled in his simple little home that smelled of Pine Sol, with a glowing red sun slipping behind the tips of the distant shadowy mountains, a stab of unsettling loneliness took him by surprise. The apartment felt cold, empty. It would be a while until he could get a real bed and more furniture, and the refrigerator and cupboards would take more than a few trips to the grocery store to fill. He popped a frozen pizza into the oven and mindlessly watched the news. For the first time he could remember, he wished he had someone to share his life. Discontented, at odds, not yet comfortable in these new surroundings, he hit his air mattress early, fretting and unaccustomed to this place. The enormous full moon that blazed into his bedroom windows made it hard to sleep. He lingered on the edge of sleep, listening to the light click of Karen's dogs' footsteps overhead, wondering what his first case would be like.

Chapter 4

AT THE END of a frost-covered dirt driveway bordered by spindly evergreens, Gary climbed out of his truck, kneading at the stiffness in his hips and back. Daisy ran to greet him and wound around his legs, woofing and snuffing her usual canine greeting.

Gary pushed open the cabin door, chugged down mouthfuls of milk straight from the carton, stuffed a leftover doughnut into his mouth, and stumbled toward the bedroom. "Man, what a night," he muttered to Daisy. He fell onto the bed still in his clothes and wrapped his arms around Daisy when she leapt up and snuggled in beside him.

He awakened a few hours later to foul dog breath and Daisy's tongue slurping his lips. "Agghhh! Get away!" he snarled even before being fully awake, and shoved her away. Wiping his mouth in disgust, he opened his eyes. "Oh, you gotta go out, do ya?"

He rolled off the mattress and got to his feet. At that moment, memories of last night hit him and he spoke aloud. "God! That dead woman! No wonder I feel like crap. I was up all night. Now I gotta go into Wasilla and give a statement to them troopers. Damn!"

Daisy pushed herself against his leg in understanding, then ran to the door and gave a sharp bark of impatience. Gary shuffled through the kitchen and opened the door. Daisy dashed out and squatted on the first patch of flat snow she found while Gary watched her, wrapping his arms tight across his chest against the glacial wind that blew through the screen. He scowled. Saturdays were his time to get things done around the house. Shoulda put the storm door on a month ago. And there was a week's worth of laundry piled in the bedroom, most of it caked with job site dirt. Maybe it wouldn't be so bad to have to go into town since the refrigerator was empty, too. He could go to the laundromat, stock up on groceries, and drop his paycheck at the bank. Maybe even get that cell phone Cindy'd been pestering him about. Needed beer, too, and dog food. Might as well head into town right away, and stop at the troopers' station on the way in. Wonder if they'd found out who the naked lady was and what in hell she was doing out there all alone like that.

NICK AND MATT arranged three chairs around a gray metal table in the interview room. They'd been on duty for thirteen hours already, but fatality cases required that they stay until the initial reports and interviews were completed. Last night's image of the dead woman in the moonlight would haunt their dreams when they finally made it home - that was certain.

Nick had called Kay a half hour ago just to hear her soft hello. He'd loved the mellow sound of her voice from the first moment she spoke to him ten years ago. His heart warmed as she gave him ordinary news of the day and told him her special spaghetti sauce was simmering, just waiting for him, no matter what time he got home.

"Think he'll be here pretty soon?" Matt called across the room.

"I have no idea," Nick replied. "We did tell him he had to come in and give a statement first thing today, but he's the kind of guy who'll show up when he feels like it. I'm starting to wonder what he was doing out there so late and what he'd been up to 'til then."

"Yeah. I've been wondering the same thing. I know that road is his way home, so he had a reason to be driving there, but I can't figure out why he was the only one who spotted her. He didn't act like somebody who just discovered a naked body." Matt agreed.

"It doesn't feel right to me, either. He could be our man," Nick said.

Matt shrugged. "Well, we'll see how he acts when he gets in here. Should we Mirandize him?"

"For sure."

A few minutes later, an announcement summoned them to the front desk where Gary waited, leaning against the counter. He made hasty eye contact with Nick, followed by a forced half grin that displayed a glimpse of crooked, stained lower front teeth. When Nick stuck out his hand, Gary shook it with a quick, callused grip.

"Mr. LaVassar, please follow me," Nick said.

Gary nodded and followed him back to the windowless room where yellow lined legal pads and a small tape recorder sat ready on the table. Nick motioned Gary to the seat opposite the door. Gary's murky, deep blue eyes shifted around the room and then back to the officers. He took off his baseball cap, put it back over his thick, matted hair, then laced his fingers together on the table top as if they needed to be quieted.

Matt turned from fiddling with the tape recorder. "We'll start by recording your statement. That makes it easier for us to get it all down and keep it accurate." He pushed the start button without waiting for an answer. "Case number 1390. November 4th, 2015, Wasilla, Alaska. Present are Alaska State Troopers, Nick Kerrans and Matt Radantz, and witness, Gary LaVassar."

He turned to Gary, "I'm going to read you your Miranda rights. When I'm done, you have to answer out loud that you've heard them. You can't just nod. You have the right to remain silent, everything you say..."

Gary leaped from his chair. It banged against the block wall behind him and toppled over. "Wait! Whadda ya mean? Read me my rights? I'm just here to tell you what I saw. What the hell is this?" His eyes blazed. He glared at the troopers and pulled himself into a defensive stance, legs wide apart, arms cocked on his hips. "Whadda ya mean? My rights?"

Nick stood, too, and offered reassurance, "Hey, wait a minute, man. Settle down. This is standard procedure. Everybody we talk to in a fatality case gets rights read. It's no big deal." He sat back down and motioned to Gary to sit down, too.

Gary took several deep breaths, then stooped to pick up his chair. He righted it and slid uneasily back into his seat, face now flushed, eyebrows drawn together, lips tight. Tiny beads of sweat appeared on his upper lip. He massaged his beard with a shaky hand.

A sudden flashback of his cell at the Anchorage jail caught him by surprise. His stomach lurched when he remembered the long year he'd spent in jail after that last driving under the influence thing. How he'd hated being caged. Despised the smells of other people that saturated the prison, and the bland food that was never hot. Resented having to be in the shower alongside other men. Hated having no control over the TV and having to wear those baggy yellow jumpsuits. He grimaced at the memories, and remembered the agony of worrying about Daisy and Cindy all those long months. He fought panic as his thoughts raced, remembering how he nearly went crazy all those endless, boring days. He had to stay cool now. Hadn't done anything. They'd have to let him go as soon as he told 'em what he saw last night. They had no reason to hold him. His hands begin to shake. He gripped them tight together and dropped them into his lap so the tremors wouldn't be noticeable, scooted his chair up close to the table, and took a deep, steadying breath.

When Matt finished speaking, Gary answered. "Okay. Yeah, I know my rights. Let's get this over with. I got groceries and other stuff to get and a dog at home gettin' hungrier by the minute. I know ya prob'ly already looked me up in them computers. I been in the can twice. You seen that, right?"

When Nick nodded, Gary went on, "Been over three years since I got off probation. Been clean ever since. No trouble at all."

Nick shot a quick, meaningful glance at Matt. Their subject's unease was apparent. He was starting to sweat, talking too fast, and obsessively stroking his beard.

"We checked you out," Matt replied. "It seems you've stayed out of trouble since that last DUI. And the assault was over ten years ago. So let's just get your statement, OK?"

Gary climbed back into his truck twenty minutes later, relieved, and headed for his errands. On the way back home, an unsettling spasm pulled at his gut when he noticed scraps of yellow tape fluttering from the trees as he passed the site of last night's activity. Spotting the indentation in the gravel where the body had lain, he shuddered and gunned the engine, flying past the scene. Needed a beer real bad.

NICK AND MATT played the tape back a second time and compared their written notes before pushing back their chairs.

"Well, we can check it out with Hannah at the Buck Shot," Matt said. "LaVassar said he stops there all the time, so Hannah will know him. That's his only alibi. It shouldn't be too hard to confirm,"

"Okay, why don't you take that?" Nick replied. "I'll check with the coroner's office to see if they've pinpointed a time of death. That'll help us determine if LaVassar could've been involved. If it was during a time he was at work or confirmed at the bar, then he's off the hook. Something about him just hits me wrong, though. Let's get to it first thing tomorrow. I'm heading home to get some sleep."

Nick's cell phone buzzed. He swiped it and read the screen. "Coroner. Maybe we have an ID. Hold on." Minutes later he turned to Matt. "Got it. Jennifer Williams. She was a kindergarten teacher at Valley Elementary. Her husband's a dentist in town. He's made a positive ID already."

"A kindergarten teacher? It won't take long for this to get the public stirred up," Matt replied. "We better get out first thing tomorrow and talk to her husband and neighbors. And her coworkers." After a pause, he added, "It'll be big news. A kindergarten teacher, huh? We're in for some pressure on this one."

Chapter 5

PRESTON WOKE EARLY on Monday morning, made coffee for the first time in his new kitchen, and slapped eight pieces of thin salami between slices of whole wheat bread. He liked his sandwiches dry, not only because he couldn't stand the taste of mayonnaise or butter, but if he had to carry his lunch in his briefcase longer than he expected, there wouldn't be any mess. Better to have a lunch along. He didn't know what his work days would be like. Maybe there'd be long lawyerly lunches in fancy restaurants with colleagues. Maybe everyone would work like crazy and eat at their desks. There'd probably be a break room with a refrigerator and microwave.

He grabbed a bottle of water and headed out the door into the intense glow of a rose-colored dawn. He stood outside the door for a moment, drinking in the sight of the spectacular metallic light reflecting off the surrounding snowy mountain slopes. This is what he'd imagined Alaska would be like.

Enchanted, he walked to his Jeep and used his only credit card to scrape an oval of ice from the windshield. He slid in, hunkering into his jacket against the chill of the car seat, and turned the defroster button as high as it would go. He grew enthused, eager, and confident to start this first day of a new life, finally on his own. When the windshield wipers had cleared enough space for him to see, he started down the icy, sloping driveway.

Three blocks later, a large dark animal bolted from the brush bordering the road. Preston gasped and pumped the brakes just in time for the oblivious beast to cross in front of him. The huge, ungainly animal high-stepped on spindly legs to the other side of the road, lowered the wide rack of antlers that looked out of proportion to his head, and began to munch on the crumpled leaves of a row of saplings. The animal's dark rump stuck out halfway across the oncoming lane.

Preston's breathing returned to normal. He'd almost hit a moose. On his first week in Alaska, no less. He watched in fascination as the tangle of dark, matted hair danced beneath its chin in rhythm to the chewing. It seemed impossible that such frail looking, skinny legs could support a bulky animal like that. Clumsy looking hooves, almost as big as loaves of bread, anchored the legs. Its body was much thicker than a horse's and its shoulders would have touched the roof of Preston's car had it been any closer. But he couldn't just sit and stare any longer or he'd be late for his first day of work. He put the Jeep into gear and drove carefully around the moose, which continued to ignore him.

THE PUBLIC DEFENDER'S office in downtown Anchorage, bigger and more crowded than Preston had expected, hummed with intensity. Paths worn in drab commercial carpeting led from the central cluster of secretary desks to individual attorney's offices along the window walls of the octagonal space. Copy and fax machines, crammed into scattered areas, hummed beneath fluorescent lighting that gave the area a stark, almost too bright look.

Preston mouthed his name to a red-haired receptionist at the main desk, and she poked a pencil toward an empty desk toward the back before returning her attention to the constantly buzzing phone lines. Preston wound his way past oak veneer bookcases bulging with three-ring binders and legal books. He passed two small conference rooms, each with an oak laminate table that would seat eight on the standard wood and fabric chairs pulled up around them. Beige and black file cabinets crowded against each other along walls wherever space allowed. The contrast to his father's luxuriously furnished office back East stunned Preston.

He made his way to a bulky, standard metal desk that had seen better days. It held only a phone, computer keyboard and monitor, basic office supplies, and new Anchorage and Mat-Su Valley phone books. Dust wafted to his nostrils when he opened the top drawer and he sneezed.

"Mills, someone'll be around to see you shortly," the receptionist called over to him as she hung up one line and punched another.

Preston set his briefcase down and walked back to her desk. "Restroom?"

She motioned down the hall while still speaking into her mouthpiece. Preston hurried to the men's room, tore a few paper towels from the dispenser, moistened them at the sink, and headed back to wipe out his desk.

While he was crouched cleaning out the back of the lowest drawer, a loud slap of paper above his head startled him. He jerked upright to meet the eyes of a fiftyish man in a rumpled navy suit. The word 'gnome' popped into Preston's head at once. The man was short and heavyset, with a pock-marked complexion that roughened his round face. His ears were too large for his head, his neck almost nonexistent. Hunched shoulders sank into a squat body. A pelt of graying, tightly waved hair covered his head and fell so far down onto his forehead that it almost met his matching bushy eyebrows. Despite his remarkable appearance, he exuded power.

"Mills? Preston Mills?" the man asked in a voice so deep it was almost a growl. Without waiting for an answer, he continued, "Frank Gallion. Public Defender. Welcome aboard. Here are your cases. As soon as you can, come into my office."

He flopped a pile of manila folders and a business card on Preston's still damp desktop and motioned to the far corner of the room where a large private office was visible behind glass walls. Frank turned his back and strode away before Preston could respond.

Preston stooped to finish wiping out the last drawer, tossed the filthy towel into his wastebasket, wiped his hands along his pant legs and reached for the top folder on the pile. That one looked like a charge of child endangerment. Next was a shoplifting case. He glanced through the labels on the rest, and dropped them back on the desk. With another nervous brush of his hands over the front of his shirt, tie, and trousers, he headed for Frank's office. Several people looked out from their open office doors as he passed, gave brief smiles and bent back to the paperwork before them. Desks were piled high. Stacks of folders spilled across the floor next to many of them. Phones buzzed.

Preston neared Frank's office and the man inside waved from behind the glass wall. He pointed a beefy finger at a cracked brown leather chair set close to the front of his desk, finished the call he was on, banged the receiver down and rose, extending a wide fat hand that gripped Preston's with near crushing strength.

"Hello, Mills," he said. "Sit."

Preston dropped into the chair, massaging his hand as unobtrusively as possible.

"Frank. Call me Frank." The words set Preston a little at ease. "Glad to have you join us. First days, well, first weeks, hell, even first months, are pretty tough around here." He spoke abruptly, as if only the most necessary words were allowed to rumble from his throat. "Most of us work too hard. Put in too many hours to get to know each other right away. Best is when you work with somebody on a case. Then the partnerships kind of develop on their own. You'll be swamped, maybe have twenty five cases on your desk at the same time." He settled back into the bulky black leather chair that nearly swallowed him, and looked at Preston.

"I'm glad to be here," Preston responded. An awkward pause followed, during which Preston wondered desperately if he should remind Frank that his abilities so far in his career were based only the past year spent slaving over the research and document preparation needed to support corporate and civil cases in his father's huge law firm in Boston. He was distracted by a flicker of curiosity at the pattern of subtle flying ducks on Frank's dark green tie and wondered if he was a hunter.

Frank spoke. "So. Won't ask you how you like Alaska. Know you haven't been here long enough. Ready to get to work?"

"I'm ready." Preston surprised himself with the quick and definite reply. Empowered by a glimmer of acceptance in Frank's eyes, Preston rose.

When he turned to go out the door, Frank added, "Hey, Mills. Welcome aboard. It's gonna be tough. I don't know how you work yet. Be sure to keep me in the loop on everything. No matter how small. Questions?"

"No. Not yet," Preston replied. He returned to his desk and set about organizing, now highly motivated.

Chapter 6

NICK AND MATT were preparing for a meeting with the victim's husband, Dr. Dan Williams, that same morning. Nick was eager to get the meeting over with and call it a day. He still couldn't get over that young wife, laying there all alone on the road in the cold and darkness, exposed to the raw wind. The tightness in his throat wouldn't go away and he had to fight persistent thoughts of how he'd feel if it had been Kay.

The case had dominated his thoughts and he hadn't slept well last night because of it. Although the kids had been tucked in early and Kay fell asleep nestled snugly against his chest as usual, he hadn't been able to fall asleep. The image of the woman's half frozen, naked body all alone there on the roadside floated through his mind like an elusive ghost every time he closed his eyes.

As the night had dragged on, he'd thrashed in the dark, mashed the pillows this way and that, and pried Kay carefully away from him, trying not to disturb her. He worried about how such a thing could happen here in Wasilla and went over again and again what they'd learned so far about the Williams woman. Hers was a young family, no history with the law, no problems that had ever brought them to the attention of law enforcement, no reports of difficulties with neighbors or family or friends. Nothing came up in the computer for either Jennifer or Dan Williams. They appeared to be normal law-abiding citizens who came to Wasilla five years ago. The dentist worked out of a small office building along the frontage road of the freeway into Anchorage and the victim had taught at the elementary school for the past four years.

Nick could think of no reason at all for Jennifer Williams to end up on the shoulder of the Knik-Goose Bay Road, abandoned, nude and half-frozen, on a November night. Baffled and frustrated, he felt certain that her husband wouldn't be the only one demanding answers very soon. So far, they'd uncovered no clues or answers at all. Nick puzzled it over and over, wondering who would do this. What possible reason could there be for this to happen to a kindergarten teacher with no history of enemies or problems? As far as he could tell, she was just a nice young wife and mother.

It made no sense and Nick couldn't turn his mind off. He had to find a hint of a reason. Anything at all. During his miserable night, he'd crushed his wife too tightly against him, causing her to mumble in her sleep. In vain, he'd sought comfort by burying his face in her soft, fragrant hair. He'd dragged himself out of bed when the alarm finally went off and headed for the station, groggy and out of sorts.

Nick listened while Matt reviewed the facts of the case to date. Jennifer's husband had reported her missing early Saturday morning and made an immediate identification of the body, which had arrived at the morgue while he was still at the station asking about filing a missing persons report. Dr. Dan Williams assured authorities he'd been at home all night with their young son. He said his wife had gone out after dinner to their neighbor's house for some kind of kitchenware party. Williams said he fell asleep in bed watching the ten o'clock news, confident that Jennifer would slip in beside him before long. He'd been shocked to find her side of the bed empty in the morning.

Matt shoved a pile of papers to the edge of his desk and read out loud from the top page. "The coroner did a quick looksee right away, but there was nothing obvious, not a mark on her. He found no indication of a sexual assault so he suspects it was an unidentified medical condition or poison of some kind. He hasn't been able to make a final pathological diagnosis about the cause of death yet. And the lack of clothing – he doesn't have any idea how that fits in to anything." With a shake of his head, he added, "Williams will be here any minute, probably steaming. There's a lot of talk out there. People are scared. She was just a normal person, one of them. We better have something to report." He frowned. "The media will be on it big time in the next day or two, for sure."

The victim's memorial service would be on the week-end and the people of Wasilla had been expressing their worries about the murder on talk radio, in grocery stores, at meetings, and on the phone to each other. Some had even called the FBI with demands for action. There was fear in the air, along with the inevitable call for law enforcement to get someone convicted right away. Nick wasn't positive that the someone responsible was Gary LaVassar, but it would be imperative to have someone in custody pretty soon. Things always settled down as soon as a suspect was arrested.

"Okay, Matt," he began. "We're gonna have to tell Dr. Williams something when he gets here. What else do we have?"

The intercom interrupted them with an announcement that a Dr. Williams was at the front desk. In a moment, Dan Williams was escorted in, red-eyed and grief stricken. Tall, serious, with thinning brown hair. pressed gray slacks, and an expensive-looking black sweater over a white shirt and silver striped tie, he appeared to be a respectable, upper-middle-class guy. The deep creases between his eyes and his stern demeanor made it clear this would not be a cordial meeting.

"What've you found out?" he demanded after introductions had been made. He leaned back in his chair, arms crossed across his chest, long legs stretched in front of him awkwardly, as if the chair was too small. His eyelids were rimmed with red behind the trendy gold-rimmed glasses he jammed back up onto his nose as soon as he settled into the chair. His lips pinched together like he was having trouble maintaining control of his mouth. Hostility and grief chased each other across his features.

Nick knew he'd feel the same way if it had been Kay laying alone out there on the highway like that. Maybe even more crazed, enraged, more demanding of answers, more overcome with grief.

He looked the man straight in the eye. "Dr. Williams. We're the primary troopers on the case." At Williams' curt nod, he went on, "The coroner so far has been unable to identify signs of trauma or injury. We don't have much more than that at this point."

Williams dipped his head again in acknowledgement, his face tightening with anguish. Nick waited a minute, unsure what to say next.

Williams finally broke the awkward silence, "The autopsy. We didn't want to let them cut her up. Her parents and me. We didn't want that. We wanted to let her rest in peace...but they had to...they said..." He dropped his face into his hands and his shoulders began to shake.

Nick and Matt read each other's glance, instincts telling them he wasn't the type to murder his wife. His reactions were too real. Obviously he was devastated. Although the husband always had to be considered a person of interest in such a case, Nick deduced that it wasn't likely he was the perpetrator. Williams was as agitated and upset as anyone would be under the circumstances.

After a few minutes, Williams gathered himself, pushed his glasses back into place, swatted away the wetness on his reddened cheeks and looked up.

"Sorry." He took a deep breath and let it out slowly. 'I still can't believe this is happening." He gave a long sigh and shrugged his shoulders. "So what exactly have you found out? What can I do to help?"

"We're treating it as a homicide for now," Nick explained. "It wasn't likely due to natural causes – the clothes missing..." he stammered, embarrassed. He'd seen this man's wife naked. "We're working on finding the clothing, but nothing's turned up at the scene yet. They're still searching the area and we're taking dogs in again today. But there's nothing so far. She didn't have any medical conditions that could have caused this?"

Williams rose from the chair, agitated, his face flushed. "Of course not. She was young and healthy, nothing wrong with her. Someone did this to her. She didn't have any clothes on, for God's sake. What about that guy? The one who found her? I heard he was brought in."

"Hey," Matt spoke up. "We've interviewed him. We can't give out our findings yet. Not even to you. It could compromise the investigation. The guy is only a person of interest. Not a suspect. Sit back down, man."

Dan Williams sank back into his chair with a sigh of resignation. "Okay. Okay."

Nick added, "Give him a break. He found the...Jennifer. He stayed with her until we got there. As far as we know, he was just passing by and did the right thing. We have no grounds to pick him up or hold him or charge him. His alibi so far holds up. We're looking elsewhere right now."

"Do you recall what Jennifer was wearing the last time you saw her, when she left for the party?" Matt asked.

Williams looked to Matt, then Nick, a glimmer of hope flashing across his face. "Sure. She had on her favorite blue sweater and jeans. I think she had on her Kamloops boots, too, since it was pretty cold that night. She loves...she loved...those boots." He dropped his head for a moment, swiped again at his cheeks again and looked up. "Did that guy you brought in have any female clothes in his possession?"

The husband's desperate attempt to pin things on Gary LaVassar irritated Nick. Relatives and friends and the public invariably demanded immediate answers and a scapegoat after something like this happened in their community. But he'd seen the impact of rash action on innocent suspects before.

Nick swallowed his annoyance. "We're working hard on this. The best thing you can do right now to help is answer our questions. Every bit of information you can give us about Jennifer will help."

Williams answered their remaining questions with apparent sincerity for the next half hour. But after he left, the troopers had little more to go on than they had before he arrived.

"So, do you think he's satisfied with what we've told him?" Matt asked.

"Well, it's the only thing we can tell the poor guy," Nick replied. "We have to give him some hope, at least. Anyway, I bet we'll have something before long. Somebody has to know what happened. Somebody had to see something." He wagged his head in frustration. "There's gotta be a clue out there. Someone's bound to show up with a hunch or a tip about something unusual that night. That kitchenware party she went to was only three houses down from hers. And that's a nice new neighborhood. How could this happen when she only had such a short way to walk home?" Matt glanced down at his report. "And the neighbors saw nothing? Heard nothing? Her friend who had the party does daycare for the Williams kid, too. So the women were real close. Everyone seems so normal. And all of 'em are totally shocked."

Nick turned to answer the buzz of the phone. He listened intently, hung up and turned blazing eyes to Matt. "Hannah just reported that LaVassar was gone from the Buck Shot for a while that night around nine o'clock. She says she thinks the victim was there earlier that night, too. She watches that place and everybody in it like a hawk, you know. So this is reliable information." He stood. "LaVassar didn't tell us that. I wonder why. Maybe he has something to hide, huh? It looks like he lied. Let's get the paperwork going to charge him. We can pick him up at the job site in the morning."

Chapter 7

GARY DROVE STRAIGHT home at quitting time Monday in need of a hot supper, a wrestle with Daisy, a few cold beers, and sleep. He'd hardly slept at all since finding the body and it had taken its toll. He microwaved a chicken pot pie and ate it in his recliner while watching *America's Most Wanted* until he began to doze off. When he pulled back the quilt on his bed, Daisy jumped up to join him as usual. She nestled against his side, burrowed her nose halfway beneath the pillow and began the light snore that was almost a purr. That sound and the solid warmth of her snuggling against him was comforting, especially on cold nights like this when the fire was bound to go low toward morning.

"Hope them troopers got somethin' to go on by now," he murmured to Daisy just before sleep claimed him. "That'll let me off the hook. This ain't my mess, but I can't help bein' sorta worried. Ya never can tell with them guys."

THE NEXT MORNING when Gary stopped for gas and coffee at the Shell station on the way to work, he sensed an odd tension in the air. Shirley made only furtive eye contact and didn't banter with him like she usually did from behind the counter. The guy behind him in line turned away self-consciously when Gary stuffed his billfold back into his pocket and started out the door. There was an unfamiliar and uneasy feeling to it all that puzzled him.

He had it figured out by the time he'd driven a few miles down the highway. People thought he was involved in the murder. He floored the accelerator and cursed aloud, "Dammit. I didn't do nothin'. I'm just the sucker who found the body."

Things were the same on the job site when he got to work. Guys who'd always greeted him cheerfully now slunk away when they saw him coming. "So that's how it's gonna be," he grumbled as he walked to his grader. "Sure wish I woulda gone right on by that night. Never shoulda stopped. Hell, anyway, now I know who my friends are."

He was so absorbed in moving dirt an hour later that he didn't notice the troopers' car pull in.

AT THE SAME time, Preston was studying the cases Frank had dropped on his desk. His phone lit up.

"Frank wants to see you," the receptionist announced. "Right now."

Preston hopped up, breath coming fast, and headed for the corner office.

Frank looked up when Preston knocked and waved him in. "We got a new case. Big one. Just got it a few minutes ago. Possible murder Friday night up in

Wasilla. A kindergarten teacher." He shoved a folder toward Preston.

Preston rose and leaned forward to reach it while Frank continued. "Troopers up in Wasilla arrested a suspect a few hours ago. Guy says he can't afford an attorney." He looked over and punched at the blinking line on his phone until it stopped. "This folder's all we have so far. It'll be a tough case, but Larry Jenkins, that's who shoulda taken it, had to fly to the Lower Forty Eight over the weekend. Cleveland. His mother's terminal. Cancer. Sudden."

He shrugged. "A murder case is big, so I have to be in on it. I can't assign a case this important to anyone else, and anyway, they're all swamped. So you'll have to do the initial grunt work for me - document prep, keep up with the schedule - until Jenkins gets back. It should be only a week or so. I know you have experience drafting documents, maybe not like these, but...well, you're getting trial by fire."

Frank didn't mince words. Preston liked that in a person. He'd never been much for small talk himself. It annoyed him to have to waste time with such false pleasantries as how are you, how is the family, golf game going okay? He hated that phoniness. Nobody really listened to what the other one said. Nobody really cared. He suspected he might grow to like Frank.

Preston clutched the folder to his chest, and began backing out of the room, thoughts racing. A murder case? Didn't Frank know how inexperienced he was? A flash of determination followed when he realized he'd just been given the opportunity to dig into a major case right off the bat.

As soon as he sat down at his desk, his attention was drawn to a commotion at the reception counter. A young woman's agitated voice rose above the hum of the room. "Well, who do I see then? Who's handling it?"

Preston noticed first the lush mop of light brown curls that tumbled over the young woman's shoulders and halfway down her back. She was petite, and her voice sounded spunky. The receptionist turned and pointed her pencil directly toward him. At that, the young woman spun away from the counter and glanced his way. Preston gulped and swung around to look behind him, hoping she was heading for someone else.

But she marched straight to his desk. "Do you know who's handling that case about the body found up by Wasilla this weekend?"

Her voice was pitched lower now, smoother. She was cute. Bright caramel-colored eyes flashed above the freckles that lightly sprinkled her cheeks. Pert nose. Straight dark brows. Preston had trouble concentrating when he noticed the high bow of her full upper lip. It looked so kissable. Shocked at these inappropriate thoughts, he stuck out his hand, mind racing. Williams. That must be the murder case Frank had just given him.

"Yes, Frank Gallion, the Public Defender will be handling the case himself. I'm Preston Mills, his associate. I'll be starting the paperwork."

Placing a small, firm hand in his, she shook his and said, "I'm Cindy LaVassar. Gary LaVassar is my Dad. He's the one who found the body." Her voice cracked. "I need to find out about this murder charge. The troopers questioned him Saturday. Now they've arrested him. Early this morning. Right after he got to work." She sucked in a ragged breath. "He didn't do anything except find the body."

Her eyes watered and her face began to flush. She lowered her eyes and took several deep breaths. Preston glanced up at the receptionist who was watching with interest. She recognized the question in Preston's eyes and pointed toward the first door to the left across from her desk.

"Ah, let's go to a conference room," Preston breathed.

He had no idea what to say to her, and felt unnerved by her presence. He couldn't keep his eyes off the way her jeans hugged a tight, perfectly shaped bottom as she walked down the hallway before him. He shook his head to clear it, surprised at himself. This wasn't like him at all.

He settled Cindy into a chair at the conference table, took a deep, steadying breath and asked, "Would you like something, Miss LaVassar? Coffee? A soft drink? Water?" He hoped she hadn't been able to detect the slight stammer in his voice as he reined in his improper thoughts.

"Yes, a Coke, please," she answered.

She was polite. Had good manners. He fled the room. The receptionist directed him to the break room. He grabbed a can of Coke from the refrigerator and headed back to the conference room, mind racing. He shouldn't be turned on like this by someone involved with a case. What was wrong with him? He couldn't believe how quickly he'd become entranced by this woman and hoped he could act normal. By the time he settled into a chair across from her, his heart was thudding so hard he wondered if she could see it through his shirt.

"Here," he said, snapping the tab back and sliding the Coke to her.

Cindy tipped the can to her lips, then set it back down and turned serious eyes to him. "Thank you. My dad didn't do it," she said, her voice brittle. "The troopers stopped this morning at his job site right after he got to work. They took him into the job trailer in front of everybody and asked him more questions. Then they arrested him!" She swallowed hard. "He thought he was done with them last weekend after he gave his statement."

She paused to take a deep breath and another sip of Coke. A drop clung to her lip. Preston wondered how it would feel to lick it off. He gave a slight shake of his head, disgusted with himself, and focused on what she was saying.

"Everybody around Wasilla's heard about the woman's body Dad found along the highway Saturday night," she went on. "He called me on the new cell phone he got Sunday and told me about it. But he said he'd been interviewed and everything went fine. Now he's been arrested." Her voice rose with anxiety. "It looks like he needs a lawyer. But he doesn't have money for one. They told me he qualified for a public defender and I should come to this office right away." She paused. "That's you, right?"

"Well, yes."

She swiped at the tears that had begun to slip down her cheeks and interrupted, "My dad could never do something like that! He's a good man. I went right to the police station after he called me this morning, but they wouldn't let me see him. The guy at the desk said he was still being processed. When I told 'em he didn't have any money for a lawyer, they told me to come right down here. What do I have to do? I have to help him!" Cindy's face had grown splotched with red. "What do I have to do?"

Preston's felt an overpowering need nearly consuming him; he had to make this right for her. What was wrong with him? He didn't even know her. He dug his fingernails into his palms to bring himself to reality, took a deep breath, and then another. 'Well, my boss has the case. I'll go ask him if he can meet with you right now." Preston rose and turned toward the door.

"I have to help my dad!" Cindy cried. Her white knuckles gripped the Coke can until it dented in.

"Just stay here a minute. I'll be right back." He bolted for Frank's office.

Frank waved him in, shoved back from his keyboard and barked, "What?"

After Preston explained, he muttered, "Jesus, a murder case and Jenkins gone. We're drowning in

44

cases." He rose and pounded his desk. "If the suspect's been arrested for murder it's a felony charge and he'll need to attend a first appearance hearing tomorrow - they'll set conditions and bail at that time. The courtroom'll be packed with reporters. Damn, I hate that. The next day, the suspect'll have to appear again for an arraignment. I already have two hearings and a trial this week. I can't fit that all in and I sure can't meet with the daughter right now." He stabbed at a button on the blinking phone. "Barb, send Bergstrom in."

An intense, dark-haired young woman in red-rimmed glasses hurried in a minute later, eyes expectant. "Yes, Frank?"

"Clare Bergstrom. Preston Mills." Frank introduced them without looking at either of them.

Preston tried to fade into the background while Clare and Frank held an urgent discussion on who could handle the new case if Jenkins didn't get back soon.

Finally, Frank threw his hands in the air. "Dammit. We're swamped. Why can't they ever give us enough staff?" He dropped into his chair and waved the woman out the door. "I'll figure it out. Thanks, Clare."

Preston stepped forward. Frank turned to him, eyebrows lifting in surprise as if he'd forgotten that Preston was in the room.

"I can help with it, Sir. I'll put in as many hours as you need," Preston said, trying to tamp down the eagerness in his voice. He faltered. "Well, anyway, I'll do everything you ask...I know I can do it..." He dropped his gaze from Franks' surprised stare.

Frank hesitated, glanced down at the piles of paperwork on his desk, shook his head in annoyance at the buzz of the phone and shrugged. "Oh, what the hell. Yeah, go for it, Mills. It's my case and I guess an eager associate might be valuable, at least until Jenkins gets back. He's handled our felonies for years. But you'll be on very thin ice. Screw up once and you're off. And I have to know every damn thing. Every detail. You're looking at a lot of hours. You sure about this?"

At Preston's nod, he waved dismissively. "Keep me informed. I have to know everything as soon as you do. Get discovery requests done as soon as the court signs an order appointing our office as his lawyer. That'll probably happen tomorrow. Find the three ring binders called 'standard pretrial motions' to start your research into the motions we need to file. They're probably in the wood bookcase right along the wall outside my door. And let me know every detail of what you're doing. And get all the paperwork in on time. Got it?"

"Yes, Sir."

"Get the hell outa here," Frank said with the hint of a smile. "And go tell that daughter what the procedure will be."

Chapter 8

PRESTON RUSHED BACK to the conference room and explained to Cindy that Gary would need to appear before a magistrate tomorrow to officially sign the appointment order. Then he'd have to appear again the next day to be arraigned and have bail and conditions set. Preston, meanwhile, would be working on discovery requests, information gathering, and beginning to plan pretrial motions.

Hope replaced the despair on Cindy's face, quickly followed by a determined statement. "Well, then. Let's get it done. Let's do whatever we have to do." She pushed back her chair.

Preston's thoughts raged. *She's so cute, and so eager to help her dad. We could be a team on this.* He blinked hard, surprised at himself. "Let me review the charging documents and make a few calls. We just got a file this morning. Do you have somewhere to wait, something to do for an hour or so?"

"No, I left work as soon as I heard. I work way up in Wasilla, at a dog yard. I'm a handler and my boss is out of town so the responsibility for the care of the dog team is all mine." She hesitated and gave an anxious look toward the door. "I should get back. Take my cell number, and Dad's, too. He just got it Sunday so I hope he knows how to answer it. You could call us and let us know what's happening, okay?"

Her voice left no room for argument. *She was stubborn, decisive, tough. Perfect.* He scribbled down the phone numbers she read off to him. He watched her walk out, shook off the heat that resulted, entered the numbers into his phone, then scrambled to his desk. He searched out the troopers' phone number in Wasilla and poked the only line that wasn't blinking.

A few minutes later, his heart pounded, dreading the call he had to make. He dialed Cindy's cell number knowing she'd still be on the highway, but she needed to know what the troopers had just told him. When she answered and began asking why he was calling so soon, Preston interjected a quiet, "Miss LaVassar, please pull over, I have news about your Dad."

The line went silent until she murmured, "OK, I'm parked on the shoulder. What?"

"They do have grounds for arrest." He explained the bartender's report about Gary's absence from the bar earlier on the night the body was found and the victim's presence there, too, wincing at the sound of her gasp.

"Oh no! That means they think he did it." Her voice broke with the beginnings of a sob she couldn't quite stifle.

"I'm sorry," Preston said. "I left a message on your Dad's cell phone for him to call me but I doubt they've let him have his phone in the processing and intake area. The Department of Corrections has a phone system in all its facilities that allows them to monitor prisoners' calls. Cell phones aren't allowed at all. The troopers must have just picked him up and had him booked, and they might not have told him exactly what the charges are yet. I'll need to see him right away." He took a deep breath. "Your dad's absence from the bar could be very damaging evidence. He should have mentioned it when he was interviewed. He looks like he lied, so now his alibi is shot."

The worry in Cindy's voice made him wince again. "Okay, I'll check in at work and then go right over to the Mat-Su Pretrial Facility and wait for you to get there," she said. "I'll be in a green Subaru in the parking lot as close to the door as I can park. I'm sure Dad has an explanation for this, though."

After quick goodbyes, Preston located the documents he needed and hustled to his car. He was barely out of Anchorage, maneuvering through blowing snow on the Glenn Highway, when his cell phone bleated. He steered to the shoulder and swiped at his phone. A recording advised him the call was being made from an inmate in a correctional facility before a man's agitated voice blurted through the receiver. "This the lawyer Mills? What the hell's goin' on? Somebody said I left the bar that night? Who said that?"

"Mr. LaVassar?"

"Yup. Gary LaVassar. They just brought me a message my daughter left at the desk here. It had your phone number. Says you're my lawyer. I asked for my call. Somethin' about me being gone from the Buck Shot Saturday night. What the hell's goin' on?"

"I'm on my way out from Anchorage to see you right now," Preston answered. "I need to meet with you. I should be there in about forty-five minutes. Until then, don't say anything to anyone. Not a word. You don't have to answer any questions. Got it?"

"Yeah. I got it. Should my daughter be here, too, when we meet?" Gary asked. Worry etched his voice.

"She already knows about it. She'll be there." Preston felt a flutter in his chest at the thought of seeing Cindy again. He said goodbye to Gary and tried to force his mind back to the details of the shoplifting case that had been on the top of the pile on his desk. What a waste of time that would be. He wanted to concentrate on Gary's case. Make it all better for Cindy. Impress Frank. Why did he have to spend his time and effort on the cases he'd glanced through? It looked like they'd be just hassles, with lots of paperwork. A murder charge mattered. A stolen laptop didn't. A marijuana pipe in a car didn't. A mother repeatedly charged for not sending her kids to school every day was nothing compared to this. Maybe he should have held out for a private practice firm where he could concentrate on cases that mattered.

Chapter 9

GARY HUNG UP the old-fashioned black wall phone and followed the guard back to his cell. He agonized after the guard left. Feel real bad. More for Cindy than for myself. This could blow up big and affect her, too. And I'll probably lose my job if I can't show up for work.

In the dimly lit block-walled cell, Gary bent forward on the edge of the bunk's thin mattress that reeked of other people and dropped his head into his hands. *This is a goddamn nightmare. It ain't right I was picked up and slammed in jail like this. They better let me out soon. Damn soon.* He shook his head and muttered, "They read me my rights again. That means I'm a suspect."

He worried about Daisy, concerned that he might not make it home to feed her by nightfall, and fell back onto the bunk in despair. He could count on Cindy to go out to the cabin and feed Daisy and give her a little affection, but the old dog was used to sleeping with him. *How would she do all night alone? She was old and she needed him. It'll be too cold for her if I'm not there to keep the fire going.* He hated to have to ask Cindy to do stuff for him. She'd only been at her job six months now. She couldn't afford to screw it up it by taking extra time off. She'd lose pay, too, for all the hours she'd have to spend helping him out of this mess.

And there was his job. Everybody on the job site had stopped working to watch him being led away in handcuffs. Gary couldn't blame the boss if he hired somebody else to run the grader. After all, there was a project deadline and the work had to get done before it turned even colder and they wouldn't be able to get through the frozen ground.

Sick inside with growing helplessness and frustration, he thrashed around on the lumpy mattress, unable to get comfortable. He regretted more every minute stopping that night and cursed the full moon that had lit up the body like that. Finally, he threw himself out of the bunk, pacing and fretting. *That lawyer sounded so young. He couldn't have much experience.* Gary's jumbled thoughts nearly overwhelmed him.

WHILE GARY WORRIED, Preston pulled into the parking lot of the Mat-Su Pretrial Facility and spotted Cindy already waiting. She hopped out the second he drew up beside her, and gave him a quick wave of greeting. Neither spoke. Preston slid a sideways glance at her grim face as they walked toward the station door. She looked so worried, so vulnerable, so in need of someone like him to stand beside her. A slight tremor rippled through his legs at simply being this close to her as he hurried to open the heavy glass entry door for her.

They checked in at the front counter and within minutes a guard ushered them into a tiny room with pale green block walls. The room was badly in need of fresh air. Preston gulped, nearly suffocated by the stench of old coffee and stale cigarettes and other odors he couldn't identify. It was another of his quirks, this need for fresh air. He couldn't understand how people who lived in closed up apartments and houses didn't need to open their windows at least a little bit every day to get the dead air out.

Cindy sat down, shoulders hunched, arms crossed tightly across her stomach. Preston slid into a chair next to her, willing himself to appear professional. He straightened his tie, pulled at his sleeves, and kept his eyes from Cindy's face, afraid his thoughts would show.

Finally, Gary was escorted into the room by a uniformed officer. Cindy jumped up and rushed to her father's arms as soon as the officer was out of the way. The guard stepped forward to stop the contact, but at Cindy's blazing look, he retreated with a sheepish warning, "Step away, ma'am. Rules. No contact allowed."

"Daddy! Oh, Daddy. Oh..." Cindy wailed, ignoring the guard as she fell into her father's arms.

Gary patted her back ineffectively. "It's okay, Honey." His eyes betrayed agitation and anxiety he couldn't hide. He turned, awkward in the wide legs of his ill-fitting yellow jumpsuit, looked over at the glaring guard, and gave Cindy a gentle push away before directing his attention to Preston. "You my lawyer?"

"Yes. I'm Preston Mills with the Public Defender's office. The PD, Frank Gallion, will be handling your defense. I'm his associate," Preston answered. "I need to interview you and start some paperwork so we can get you out of here."

The confidence in his voice surprised him. He'd had only one semester of criminal procedure and two semesters of criminal law. He shouldn't feel this confident, but he did. Maybe it was because Cindy needed him.

Cindy stepped completely away from her father and turned to face Preston.

Before she could say anything, Gary spoke, "I didn't do it. I'm just the one who found her, the...body. I was on my way home that night." He wove a hand through his hair. "I can't believe I'm in here. You gotta get me out."

He spoke with such intensity and sincerity that Preston immediately believed him. Better watch out, he told himself. They warned law students about this very thing. How criminals were masters at playing with the truth. You had to defend your clients, whether you believed them or not, but everyone knew of the many cases in which attorneys had been completely buffaloed by skillful liars.

In the silence that followed Gary's words, Preston studied his client. Sixty or so, judging by the gray streaks in his beard and eyebrows, the wrinkles on his face, and the white-flecked dark hair. Working class.

He'd probably seen the inside of more than a few bars. An ordinary fellow who needed some serious grooming. A little heavy in the belly. Bail probably wouldn't be easy for a guy like this to come up with. He hoped Cindy wouldn't be the one who had to post it. But it was likely she'd have to.

Preston spoke, "You were picked up because both the bartender and someone else say they remembered you leaving the bar Friday night for a while. Maybe a half hour to an hour right around nine o'clock. Did you go somewhere, maybe go get something to eat? The bartender says she recognized the victim's picture in the paper and that woman was at the bar that night, too. Why didn't you tell the troopers about that when they interviewed you Saturday?"

Gary's face twisted in puzzlement. He squinted through a long silence. His voice was deadly quiet when he finally spoke, "Now I remember. Damn. I forgot all about it. I went out to my truck, yeah, right around eight thirty, nine."

His mouth tightened and discomfort spread across his features. He avoided Cindy's questioning look. "Yeah, I sat in my truck and had a smoke and took a few swigs of Jack from a bottle I keep in the tool box in the back. Sometimes I do that to kind of bump up the beers so I don't have to hand so much money over the bar."

He paused and lowered his eyes to the floor, embarrassed. Preston remained silent, taken aback that someone needed so much of a buzz that he had to supplement his beers with straight whiskey. Cindy's face reddened while she listened. She kept her eyes downcast to the hands in her lap

Before Preston could think what to reply, Gary continued, "I'm in big trouble, ain't I? I forgot all about going outside for a bump of Jack's. I do it all the time. Cheaper than payin' inside. And I do remember seeing her, the one... she was with her friends. They didn't look like they belonged there. Guess I kinda forgot to tell about that, too."

When Preston didn't say anything right away, Gary asked, "What's gonna happen now?" He pawed at his beard.

"Did anybody see you while you were sitting out in your truck?" Preston asked, hoping his voice wouldn't betray the heat that coursed through him at being so close to Cindy. "Did you talk to anybody? Were there cars coming and going in the parking lot? People around you?"

Gary hesitated, "Naw. I always park on the far edge of the lot so I can just sit there in the dark and let the booze warm my innards for a while before I go back in. I don't remember seeing nobody. Most of the reg'lars stay put inside, not much comin' and goin'. Specially on a cold night like that." He turned worried eyes to Preston. "I'm in deep shit, ain't I?

Preston nodded.

"Can I get out on bail?" Gary asked.

"We can try to arrange it. But this is a felony charge. You have to make a first appearance before a magistrate within twenty-four hours of arrest. You'll be advised of your rights and the nature of the charge.

Bail or release conditions will be set and my boss will be appointed as your public defender. But the prosecutor has forty eight hours to demonstrate whether you might pose a danger to the community or if you might be likely to take off. If bail's granted and you can put it up, you'll be released immediately. Conditions will be set and the next step is an arraignment where you're formally advised of the charges and will be asked to plead guilty or not guilty."

He listened to Gary talk for the next ten minutes.

Cindy hung on her father's every word, her eyes scrunched with worry. She turned an agonized face to Preston when he finished. "What happens next? What do we have to do?"

Gary turned from Preston, and with a look of determination swiveled his chair toward Cindy. "Hey, Honey, this is my battle. You got your own life now. You gotta concentrate on your own stuff. I'll get through this. But, Daisy, can you...?" His voice wavered despite his best efforts to sound confident.

"Daddy. I'm in this with you. We'll beat it together," she protested. "Of course I'll go out and take care of Daisy. Don't worry."

It was hard to see father and daughter part when they finished, knowing Gary would most likely have to remain in custody for at least a few more days. As the officer began to escort Gary away, Cindy crumbled, and Preston instinctively reached out for her. She fell against him, burrowing her face into his chest.

Preston held her protectively, overcome by powerful emotion. This woman fit into his arms perfectly. She smelled of something lightly floral. When her soft, full chest heaved against his, intense warmth spread through his body. He bent away as subtly as he could.

When she began to pull away, Preston was reluctant to release her. "Come on. I'll take you for something to eat. It's almost noon. Is there a place near here where we can grab a bite?"

"I have to get back to work," Cindy replied. "There's snow coming, the weather forecast says."

Preston saw the hesitation in her eyes that belied her words. "I know, but you need to eat. And we have to talk. I need to know more about your Dad. Every speck of information I can get will help me defend him." His words were mostly a ploy to convince her to go to lunch with him. But he did need more information and he badly wanted more time with this woman. He ended with a firm, "You're coming with me."

She dipped her head in agreement and soon they were sitting in a high-backed wooden booth in the cafe on the ground floor of Wasilla's oldest hotel. While they waited for their bowls of clam chowder, Preston was mortified to feel himself respond when Cindy licked a drip of melting butter from the end of her breadstick. Sweat broke out across his forehead. He wiped it away by pretending to brush his hair aside.

"Just start," he managed, fighting the quaver in his voice. "Tell me as much as you can about your father.

Everything I learn will help me build this case for his innocence."

"So you believe us," Cindy asked.

"Yes. I believe you. Now tell me all you can."

By the time their bowls were empty, Preston knew that Cindy and her Dad had lived a hardscrabble life in Gary's log cabin five miles outside Wasilla. He gained scant knowledge of Gary's previous brushes with the law, but realized Cindy had probably been protected from the details since she was only eight when her father went to prison for assault after a drunken brawl. She'd had to learn self- reliance when her mother abandoned them shortly after Cindy turned thirteen.

"Another man," Cindy explained, giving a wan smile. "A commercial fisherman from Cordova she met through a friend. We didn't know anything about it until she left. She never wrote or anything. Just left and that was it."

Preston swallowed hard, not knowing what to say. He listened while Cindy explained how she'd studied diligently in high school for her good grades, worked as a waitress to put herself through veterinary technician school at the University of Alaska in Anchorage, and valued her job at the dog yard for a veteran musher who mushed the Iditarod every year. She'd been sixteen when her father had to spend a year in jail for driving under the influence, forcing her to take care of Daisy and keep the wood heat going in the cabin during cold weather. Now she was renting her first apartment in Wasilla and very proud to be on her own.

They finished their meal and Preston walked her to her car with a promise to call her with an update as soon as he had more information. He drove off in a daze, heart thrumming, Cindy's face and voice and story filling his thoughts, not even aware of the mist of snow beginning to coast lightly from a graying sky.

Chapter 10

By the time Cindy had spread fresh straw for all twenty dogs at the Lazy Dog Kennel, Preston was reading the reports from the troopers. He was taken aback at the animosity of the lawmen when it became obvious that they wanted only to pin this case on someone as fast as possible and be done with it. The prosecution was arguing that Gary was the only thread to whoever had left the body alongside the highway. They believed he'd had lied about his alibi and that was enough to focus on him as their major suspect.

The troopers trusted what the bartender told them. Hannah, husky, nearly six-feet tall, a frizzled dishwater-blond ponytail hanging nearly to her waist, had worked at the Buck Shot Saloon for fifteen years. She knew everybody and everything, and was well known to Wasilla law enforcement as a trustworthy source of information. She presided over the bar and its crowd of misfits and regulars who seemed drawn to the dark, smoky interior and each other's company.

"Did you see the latest sign Hannah had on the menu board?" Nick grinned. "'Kitchen's open and the cook is cranky, drunk, and ready to quit'? And she has that yellow caution tape all over the wall by the entrance and a sign telling people to enter only if they dare. I never know what we'll find when we go in there."

Matt chuckled and ran a hand through his springy black curls, "Yup". He began explaining as much to himself as to Nick. "Well, I'm sure we had grounds to pick LaVassar up after his alibi fell through. He was at the scene, he's no stranger to the law, he and the victim were both at the bar that night. He failed to mention that to us. Why, if he didn't have anything to hide?"

He paused and glanced at Nick for confirmation. "But I have to admit, the way her body was placed like that, it kind of looked like somebody cared, so we better look at another possible suspect. There was a problem with the mother of one of the victim's kindergarten students. The school principal told me about it when I interviewed him. I think we just need to eliminate that woman, though. And work on trying to find motive or more of a connection between LaVassar and the victim. We need to check out his background, in other states, too."

"I agree," Nick added. "We need to find out more about that woman from the school and if she had an actual altercation with Jennifer Williams. But I don't think there'll be much to it. We had just cause to bring LaVassar in," he said. He shook his head. "I really don't think there'll be anything significant about the woman at school. Besides, LaVassar was right there at the scene, and he has a record. And then the call from the bartender just blew his alibi. Why didn't he tell us he left the bar for a while when we talked to him or that he'd seen the victim earlier that night?"

At Matt's shrug, Nick went on. "O'Brien told us to nail the guy. Get it over with. He never cares if the suspect is guilty or not. He just wants the prosecution over with, to be able to pin the blame on somebody so he can chalk up another win. He'll be pressuring us."

PRESTON BENT OVER his desk and muttered to himself as he studied the troopers' report. "Maybe he did just forget to tell the troopers about going out to his truck. He said he does it all the time to knock back a few swigs from a bottle he keeps in his toolbox. He noticed Jennifer and her friends at the bar, so what? It's a small town. I don't think LaVassar's the one. What about this woman at the school? I have to get her name and whatever they have on her."

He grew anxious to investigate this woman himself. It was very possible that another woman had done the crime, especially with the way the body had been placed so carefully. There was no evidence of sexual assault and no apparent injuries. Even if it was a stretch to consider a student's mother as the murderer of her child's teacher, it looked like Gary's only chance right now was to find another suspect.

Preston fumed. The prosecutor, O'Brien, obviously was determined to pin it on the guy who found the body. They had a suspect who was at the scene, had a hole in his alibi and had lied to them, and that had been enough for the prosecuting team to issue the warrant. They apparently didn't care what they were doing to the guy if he was innocent. Preston rustled in his chair. It was time to get an investigator to help on this. This was a high profile case and if anyone could get an investigator right on it, it would be Frank.

Preston pushed back his chair, frustrated, angry, and pondering the resistance from the troopers. Shouldn't they all be working together to find the murderer? They acted like they just wanted to put somebody away so it looked like they were doing their job. It was obvious they didn't give a damn about Gary.

Preston's spirits had sunk while he read the bartender's recollection that Gary had left the bar for a while the night of the murder. The bartender had known and liked Gary for many years, so she'd hesitated to bring it to the attention of authorities when she finally remembered it. But when another Buck Shot regular mentioned his own memory of Gary's absence that night and they recognized Jennifer's picture in the paper, they realized they better report it.

To his relief, Preston got a message from Barb telling him his afternoon meeting with Frank had been postponed. He spent the last few hours of the day hunched over his desk, poring over files similar to the LaVassar case, ignoring the other files on his desk. He had a mission. He didn't notice the office noise gradually diminish as others left for the day, and was thankful nobody approached him while he absorbed every detail of the case.

It was almost six o'clock when he looked up at the nearly empty space around him, tossed Gary's file in his briefcase atop an uneaten sandwich, and headed for his car. He hardly noticed the bluish-tinged mountains surrounding Anchorage and wasn't aware of winter in the air until his ears grew cold. He looked up, feeling for the first time, the drifting snowflakes that melted against his skin. So much snow already this early in November. This was the Alaska he'd dreamed of.

Chapter 11

THE NEXT DAY wasn't an easy one for Preston. It was after noon by the time he worked through most of the paperwork for the pile of cases he'd been handed. He'd spent another hour last night poring over Gary's case at home, making sure he prepared the pretrial motion exactly right, and now felt sure about the course of action he should take.

He munched a chicken salad sandwich from his briefcase while at his desk, not even tasting it, unsettled by his phone call home last night. He'd realized that he owed his parents the obligatory weekly call when he got home from work, certain they'd be hovering not far from the phone, waiting for it to ring. It was his first call home since he'd started his job and moved into the apartment. It hadn't gone well.

At his mother's bright "Helloooo?" he'd felt an unexpected twinge of homesickness. His mother routinely drew out the last syllable of her greeting. Always courteous, she believed that this would allow the caller time to prepare the first sentence of a conversation. Her greeting had sounded good to

Preston, familiar and comforting. When she heard his voice, she'd called out, "Gordon, come in here. It's Preston!"

Next came the boom of his father's voice "Well, Son. We're on speakerphone here. How are things going?"

While Preston explained about his apartment and what had happened so far on his new job, they listened, commenting at the appropriate times, just as Preston expected.

When he paused, his father asked, "So, then, it's going well? Are you still planning to stay awhile?" His voice held the note of disapproval Preston had become so accustomed to.

"Yes, Dad, I'm fine," Preston replied. "So far I have just routine cases, except I get to help the PD on a murder case until the lead attorney gets back. I'm in the review process on all the other cases I've been handed."

"Oh? A murder case? Don't they know...?" His voice faded into silence, leaving the words unspoken. "Well, your mother misses you. Don't you, Muriel?"

"Yes, Preston. We surely do miss you. Oh, I ran into Victoria at Nordstroms yesterday. She asked about you. Can you believe she's leaving before Christmas for training with some philanthropic organization and then plans to teach in a third world country? She'll be gone for a whole year." She gave a brittle laugh. "It's as if the two of you decided to become the rebels. We're all just shocked at her!"

His father broke in. "We always thought you two would end up together, you know, and now look."

At the scolding tone, Preston had a vision of his father's face the morning he'd left for Alaska. Preston had been standing by his loaded car, hugging his mother, trying to ignore her brave smile and tear-streaked cheeks. He'd glanced at his father where betrayal and disappointment were evident from the frown and knit eyebrows his father made no effort to hide. Reproach had burned through the air between them.

His father's words came back. "Are you sure, Son? Are you absolutely sure you want to drive all that way by yourself? Alaska is so far away. Let's talk about this some more. We can make a new plan, one that'll..."

Preston had jerked away in annoyance, and his father's voice trailed off into resignation. They'd been over Preston's decision to move away too many times.

When Preston had noticed the help wanted ad in the law journal a few months before, an unexpected urge for independence had possessed him. He suddenly realized how smothered he'd been feeling. He'd been overcome with uncharacteristic defiance and the need to escape from the orderly, upper middle class lifestyle his parents expected him to live. He understood, finally, that the restlessness he'd been feeling after graduation was a longing to experience another way of life, to break away from the life planned for him and experiment with a different world.

His father's words now brought back all the guilt, the feeling of letting them down, the betrayal that had smoldered in his father's eyes for all those final months. He remembered that last day, as his parents became smaller in the rear view mirror, how his father's arm had slid across his mother's shoulders, drawing her to his side. It had been almost impossible to swallow around the lump in Preston's throat as he gunned the accelerator away from his parents, away from life as he knew it.

Preston felt unable to form a reply now, not only from the wrench in his gut at his father's voice, but at the news about Victoria. His father asking if Preston planned to "stay awhile" was just a sneaky way to get in another dig and remind Preston that he was expected to get this Alaska phase over with, come home, and resume the life that had been planned for him. And the news about Victoria surprised and rattled Preston. He thought it was over between them.

"How about the Red Socks?" his father asked. "The Yankees learned a lesson this year, didn't they?" His voice held a false heartiness, a ploy meant to draw Preston's attention back to Boston, back to what he'd left behind.

Preston swallowed his irritation. Filled with discomfort, he finally managed a goodbye. "Yeah, Dad. Yeah. I gotta go. Bye, Mom. I'll call again next week." He hung up, stomach burning.

PRESTON WAITED ALL afternoon the next day for word on Gary's bail, but heard nothing. He'd learned from his review of other cases that the prosecution would undoubtedly make a motion that personal recognizance or execution of an unsecured appearance bond were not warranted in a felony charge like this. As the hours went by, he feared that was what was happening. What he'd read so far about the prosecutor sounded like O'Brien was a stubborn and difficult opponent who never compromised.

To keep up with his other cases, Preston researched some of Judge Nelson's recent rulings, trying to get a feel for this judge. When he saw Nelson was a stickler for detail and proper procedure, he became worried and wished he had more experience with cases such as these, as well as with the system here. He prepared the first appearance papers for Gary, dropped them on Frank's desk in his empty office, then turned again to his other cases.

A fifty-year-old woman back in court for the third time for shoplifting. It might be difficult to get her off. A repeat offender on possession of marijuana who insisted that the passenger in the back seat of the car she was driving had tossed the pipe into her lap just as the officer stopped them. It looked like she would have an attitude, based on the long list of previous similar charges and her denials of everything each time. Her defense this time was that the officer had no right to stop them, even if he thought he saw the passenger drawing on a small pipe and the car had been filled with smoke. Then there was a woman who'd been refusing to send her four children to school because she felt the bus ride was too long and they had to stand out alongside the road in the dark every morning for too long. She'd been cited for the same thing several times before, but was stubbornly refusing to cooperate.

A mother repeatedly charged for not sending her kids to school was nothing compared to a murder case. Preston knew this one would need some research and wondered if they put parents in jail in Alaska for such a thing. Again he wondered if he should have held out for a private practice firm rather than have to deal with these frustrating clients.

The list went on. Petty stuff, mostly, with far from ideal clients. Preston made an effort to prepare more of the papers for these cases and reviewed the court docket that was posted in his computer. He had to have two of these ready to go for preliminary hearings by Friday and decided to contact them for interviews first thing tomorrow. But his heart was with Gary's case, and with Cindy.

It was after six when he trudged across wet sidewalks and into the grey slush of the parking lot. This time he noticed the snow-covered mountains surrounding the Anchorage Bowl gleaming against a sky tinged with the brilliant rose of sunset. A gust of damp, salty-smelling ocean air filled his nostrils. He pushed his chin deep into his open collar and gave an involuntary shiver as the wind snaked down his back. He needed to buy a hat. He'd have to figure out how to handle the constant darkness with the worst of winter approaching. He'd read that in June when it never got dark at all people mowed their lawns, fished, and played golf and softball as late as midnight because it actually stayed light all night. He couldn't wait to experience that.

He wolfed down an Arby's fish sandwich as he drove up the winding, slick mountain road in the darkness, anxious to reach the sanctuary of his new little home.

The apartment felt more like home that night. He made a packet of microwave popcorn, settled into his bean bag chair and began reading the Alaska Journal newspaper he'd picked up on his way out of Arby's. There was a report about the well-being of the zoo's only elephant that had been sent to live in a more natural climate with others of her kind. And a feature story about women in Barrow sewing hides for whaling boats. There were stories about dog sledding, upcoming snow machine races, halibut catch limits, a crab boat captain, and a big colored picture of a moose munching frozen flowers from a planter on someone's porch. The obituaries fascinated him since they appeared to be written by the families and included expansive and flattering detail about each of the deceased. The blatant liberal slant of the editorial page made him shake his head. He decided to call tomorrow and subscribe to this absorbing slice of Alaskan life.

When he went to bed at ten o'clock, the moon lit his room so brightly that he had to tape a towel across the window.

Chapter 12

NICK PULLED THE bedroom drapes shut to block out what the local news described as a "dazzling harvest moon". He settled into bed, relieved to feel exhaustion finally claiming him after being awake most of the past few nights. He draped an arm around Kay and sighed with contentment when she snuggled closer to him in her sleep. He fell asleep with his nose buried in her shoulder, comforted by her smell and the smoothness of her skin.

But morning found him grouchy and unsettled. Vivid visions of the naked woman lying alone on the gravel shoulder of the road had haunted him again all night, dominating his subconscious. He nudged Kay from his side and slipped from bed, fighting his ornery mood. *Might as well shower and go down to the kitchen. Make the kids some pancakes. Go over Natalie's spelling words with her while she eats breakfast, too.*

But even the pounding hot shower that always refreshed him did little to improve his disposition. He still couldn't quite pin down what had bothered him during the interviews with Jennifer Williams' coworkers at the school the day before. Something hadn't made sense but he couldn't figure out exactly what it was.

He padded back into the bedroom, a towel wrapped around his waist. Kay greeted him with a sleepy "Good morning", flung aside the sheet, and stretched. She slept in the nude, and now tucked her tumbled blond hair back behind her ears as she sat up. Nick admired the slim legs she swung over the edge of the bed and let his eyes rove to her breasts. Suddenly overcome, he strode to the bed, guided her back down into her pillows without a word, and to his surprise, almost wept while making love. He couldn't imagine losing her. Couldn't bear the thought of an empty bed or nights without her cuddled in beside him. Jennifer Williams' husband had to wake up every morning now to an empty bed. He was sure he'd be able to kill, without a second thought, anyone who dared harm Kay.

Nick rolled aside from Kay and covered his face with an arm.

"Hey," Kay asked, her voice soft with love. When he didn't respond, she continued, "Is it that murder case? The frozen woman on the highway?" The words demonstrated her uncanny knack for sensing when he was upset. She usually had a good idea of what it was about before she spoke.

"Yeah. I can't figure out what's been bothering me. I just don't know exactly what it is." Nick rose, stepped into his favorite grey sweatpants and slid a tee shirt over his head.

"You mean something about the suspect you have in jail?" Kay asked.

Nick started to explain as he pulled on his socks, but before he could say any more the bedroom banged open and Andy charged in, Spiderman pajamas proclaiming his current hero. Natalie was on his heels, her fluffy blond mane flying behind her.

"Dad! He opened the bathroom door when I was in there!" she wailed.

"No, I didn't! I didn't know anybody was in there! Maybe she should lock it so people know there's somebody in there!"

"I don't have to! It was shut! He should know!"

Nick grabbed his little daughter in a bear hug. Her muffled protests were half-hearted. "Dad. Daaaad! Let go!" she cried in mock indignation, trying to wiggle from his embrace.

Andy watched uncertainly, his eyes testing Nick's for signs of playfulness.

"Hey, son. Do we have to build you your own bathroom out in the tree house?"

"Yeah! That would be great!" Andy shouted, hopping with glee, sure now that his father was in a playful mood.

"Go get dressed for school, both of you," Kay commanded from beneath her sheet. "And speaking of knocking, what about knocking before you come into our bedroom? Remember, you're always supposed to, right?"

Both muttered their agreement before scampering out the door.

"Hey, Baby," Kay suggested. "Let's go for a ride after the kids get on the bus. Maybe head down to Eagle River and check out those wood burning stoves that were on special in the paper."

Nick smiled. Their best talks always happened in the car, no interruptions, just time together to talk about whatever came to mind. They'd always liked going for rides. It was a legend among all who knew them that he'd actually proposed to her in the car on the Seward Highway on the way back from a halibut fishing trip out of Homer.

Nick grinned at the recollection. Kay had been self-reliant, a good sport and perfect companion on that trip, even baited her own hooks and helped him clean the slimy, bloody salmon right there on the boat. That trip was when he realized she was the one for him. He'd pondered it during the first few hours of the drive, and then asked her outright a little past the Whittier cutoff. Even though they both smelled like fish, her nose was sunburned and her hair stuffed beneath a baseball cap, it felt like the right time so he'd just blurted it out, "Let's get married." He remembered Kay turning to him with a grin and answering "Sure" without hesitation. He'd never regretted asking her.

His mood was substantially improved by the time the kids set their syrup-covered plates in the dishwasher, rounded up lunches, hats, mittens, boots and backpacks and bounded out to meet the bus. A ride to Eagle River was a good idea.

While the level meadows of state game refuge's hay flats flew by alongside the Glenn Highway, Nick explained his puzzling feeling about the confrontation between the murder victim and a student's mother. "We have LaVassar, the one who found the body, in custody," he began. "He could be the one. But there was a kindergarten mother who had a big blow-up with the victim a few days before the murder. I need to eliminate her before I can really feel sure LaVassar did it."

"Start from the beginning," Kay replied.

"Well, the principal mentioned a kindergarten mother who had a problem with Jennifer Williams not placing her daughter in the highest pre-reading class. I guess the mother went bonkers while meeting with Jennifer Williams, and then went and made a big scene in the principal's office when she didn't get her way. You know that kind of parent – the sun rises and sets on her child, life revolves around that perfect little creature she created."

"Well, what makes you think that's important?"

Nick turned to her, "Because it's the only thing, the only damn thing that's even a remote possibility other than LaVassar. There's not another hint of trouble in the victim's life that raises any kind of a red flag. Nothing at all. Her life was perfectly clean. She was a typical wife and mother. No trouble, ever. That upset mother of her student is the only thing we've heard that isn't just absolutely normal about Jennifer William's life. I guess I'm kind of bothered because LaVassar doesn't have any motive. And this woman might have. At least in her own mind."

"So that's why you've been moody?"

Nick sighed. "Yeah, I keep thinking how I'd feel and what I'd do if anything like that ever happened to you. I can't get the image of Jennifer Williams' body out of my mind. She was out there alone, naked, freezing in the dark."

Kay unfastened her seat belt, slid over, put her arms around his shoulders, and nestled her head into his neck.

He leaned toward her, kissed the top of her head and went on. "Everybody else at the school had only praise for Jennifer Williams. She was well liked, good at her job. So this irate mother's behavior was abnormal, irrational, really weird."

"Yeah, you better take a good look at her," Kay said. "Maybe she did it. Wasn't the body laid out real nicely? Kind of like a woman would?" She pulled back a bit. "And I've never known you to put someone away when you had doubts. You have doubts about this LaVassar's guilt, don't you?"

"Yes, I do. But we need to have somebody in custody. The prosecutor's determined to nail this guy and get it over with because the public's up in arms and they're scared. They've been demanding an arrest since day one. So we made one."

"Well you have to make sure you're right, don't you?"

Suddenly, he couldn't wait to get back to work. The nagging guilt about putting LaVassar behind bars lessened a little when he realized that he should run this irate mother thing by Matt and they should focus on it. He sure as hell didn't want to be the one blamed for putting the wrong person in jail. He looked forward to getting into the office to pull that Ritter woman's report from the file. And he owed that public defender, Mills, her contact information, too. But O'Brien had told him to hold off until Mills demanded it, and even then delay as long as possible. He couldn't wait to check the Ritter woman out and make sure she wasn't the one. Then he could feel easier about LaVassar.

Chapter 13

WHEN PRESTON DROVE out of the driveway Wednesday morning, the same moose had its rump stuck out halfway across the road. It again appeared oblivious to passing vehicles while it chomped the frosty, dense alders along the ditch. Preston had no time to watch it today and hardly slowed as he passed it by. His face heated at the memory of last night's dream in which Cindy had been prominent. He tore his mind from the picture of her petite body, the intensity of her warm brown eyes, and the cascading soft curls she seemed unable to tame.

By the time Preston walked into the office, he had himself under control. The receptionist held out her hand when he passed. "Hey, I'm Barb," she greeted him. "Sorry I didn't make you more welcome before this. It gets too crazy around here sometimes to even say 'Hi.'"

Preston set his briefcase on the floor and shook her hand.

Barb smiled, "I'll introduce you around. How're you doing? I'm supposed to be available if you need anything. But I'm here for all of you, so realistically you can't count on a whole lot." She spread her hands and shrugged. "But I try."

While she answered a call, Preston waited, deciding he liked her. Her smile was genuine, her words sincere, her handshake quick and solid. It was apparent she knew what she was talking about. Barb was a tall, spare woman, with one of those complicated silver wedding bands surrounding a minuscule diamond on her left hand. Her red hair bloomed from her head in the wild spikes that he'd noticed other women wearing lately. Crinkles at the edges of her eyes told him she wasn't exactly young anymore and the tiny vertical lines on her upper lip hinted of cigarettes.

She gave her earpiece a quick tweak and resumed where she'd left off. "So I hear you met Frank already. And he's put you on that murder case out in Wasilla with him. What a way to start! Here's a message from him. He wants you in his office this morning at ten sharp."

It was surprising how much she knew. He'd only been here a week and Barb had knowledge of all of the important things that had happened in that short time.

"Hey, there's Mark," Barb called. "Mark, c'mere a minute."

A man who appeared to be Preston's age hustled over in response to Barb's call. He stuck out his hand and gripped Preston's. "Hey, welcome. Welcome to the madhouse of the Anchorage Public Defenders' office."

He grinned, displaying perfect white teeth. Clear, friendly blue eyes sparkled at Preston from beneath a lock of sandy hair hanging over one side of his forehead. His neatly trimmed red-tinged beard gave him an air of authority he probably nurtured due to his youthful appearance. He wore the standard uniform of the young lawyer – belted tan Dockers, a light blue shirt with one button open at the neck, a loosely knit yellow tie. Preston smiled when he noticed that Mark wore water-stained leather hiking boots with thick red laces in place of traditional loafers. Mark appeared handsome, cheerful, with an aura of self-assurance and confidence.

"Good to meet you," Preston replied.

"Do you have time for a drink after work tomorrow?" Mark asked. "A kind of a get to know each other thing? We wind down every Friday over at the Seafood Restaurant and Bar. Want to join us?"

"Sure," Preston said.

"Okay. I'll stop by your desk at the end of the day. The free appetizers from five until seven are out of this world. Clam strips, coconut shrimp, barbequed ribs, smoked salmon, deep fried halibut. The hot chicken wings are killer good, too. But they make you so thirsty you need lots of really cold beer." He grinned. "Try the Alaskan Amber. It's unique. You can get a good steak dinner and salad bar there, too. So, see you tomorrow, then? I'll introduce you to the gang." He waved and hustled off.

Barb shooed Preston away from her counter. "I have to get busy now. I'll bring a few others around during the day to introduce you when I can. Mark's a good guy. His dad just retired from the bench here. Anyway, off with you. Good luck on the murder case.

Everybody says it's gonna be a big one." She punched a flashing light on her phone and adjusted her ear piece.

Preston hurried to his desk and spread out his files, concerned about making sure he'd done everything exactly right on the bail request for Gary. At the thought, Cindy's face filled his mind. He blushed when he remembered what he'd done with her in last night's dream. He forced himself to concentrate on what lay on the desk before him.

He was still buried in it when Frank walked by, snatched the file and muttered in passing. "Anything I should know that's not in here?"

Preston shook his head, taken aback, and Frank strode off into his office.

Minutes later, his phone buzzed. "Preston, Frank wants to see you right now," Barb announced. Preston's stomach rolled. That fish burger hadn't set well with him last night. He rarely ate such food and today he remembered why when his stomach began gurgling as soon as he woke up. He rose and walked to Frank's door.

Frank barked, "So do they really have anything with this alibi problem? And the victim being at the bar, too? What about the coroner - any progress on cause of death? There anything to this school mother theory?"

Preston grimaced, wishing he had more information. He'd documented everything to date in the folder Frank held but he didn't have anything new to report.

A flash of disapproval crossed Frank's face. "You know this is a high profile case. I've delayed responding to requests for interviews from two of the local TV stations, and the Journal's rehashing every bit of it every day. Editorials are pouring in. One reporter told me this is being picked up nationally. They've dubbed it "Wasilla's Frozen Lady" or some damn thing like that. Prosecutor's talking to all of them, making his case through the media. Bastard. We'll have to talk pretty soon, too, explain what we're doing." He shrugged. "Tomorrow it'll have been a week since it happened."

"Right, I understand, Sir. I've talked extensively with Mr. LaVassar. At this point, I believe he's just the poor guy who found the body. They had to arrest somebody and he's the unfortunate one. I don't..."

"I know I dumped a bunch of cases on you," Frank interrupted. "They have to be taken care of, but this has to be your priority. Leave me the file and I'll go over it this weekend. Go ahead with the bail request. It's been over forty-eight hours now so they'll have to grant something today or explain why not." He gave a snort. "If there's any problem, let me know. You should have the reply by day's end. If they demand an appearance bond or a third party custodian, put it in motion. There could be a lot of conditions for our client. Make sure he's aware of them all." He flipped a few pages of the file on his desk. "Did they provide contact information for the school mother?"

When Preston shook his head, Frank grimaced, "Well, get it. They have to give it to us. O'Brien's stalling, the bastard. Go ahead and draft official discovery requests to serve on O'Brien. You and I will meet again Monday morning at ten. I'll need a statement for the media by then. Are you sure the suspect's told you everything? You positive?"

"Yes, sir," Preston managed. Frank waved him out.

Disappointed that he didn't have better answers for Frank, Preston decided to take all his files home for the weekend. Frank wouldn't be the only one working. And maybe it would be wise to spend some more time with Gary. Make sure there wasn't anything else Gary had forgotten or needed to tell him. He'd call Cindy to ask her to join the meeting, too. Heat rose in his face at the thought.

PRESTON WAS ALREADY seated at the defense table in the courtroom by twelve-thirty to be sure he wouldn't be late for the two cases he had on the afternoon docket. But, to his relief, neither defendant showed up, the judge issued bench warrants, and he hurried back to the office.

Mark stopped by Preston's desk on his way out for the day. "Hey, we heard you're on that murder case with Frank. That'll keep you busy." He raised his eyebrows. "You still planning on going to the Seafood with us?"

"Sure," Preston replied, flattered that Mark had remembered to invite him along.

Preston had never been good at socializing and felt a familiar flash of uneasiness at the invitation. He wasn't much for small talk, and would be further hampered now because he didn't know any of his coworkers. But he better go and try to fit in. Maybe it would be fun. Anyway, he'd been surprised to feel a bit lonely lately. A juicy steak and baked potato actually sounded pretty good.

After being unable to reach any of his clients he had to represent in court in the next week, Preston received Gary's release order from the court. The judge had been generous, freeing Gary on his own recognizance. Preston faxed the documents right away and followed up with a call making sure Gary would be released by the end of the day. Then he reviewed his other cases, wondering how these people could have no phone numbers and how he was supposed to reach them. He'd ask Barb first thing in the morning. She'd know. She knew everything.

Preston pulled into a discount store on the way home to pick up a wastebasket, dish and laundry soap, a blackout bedroom shade, silverware, and a few other things he needed at the apartment. He chuckled aloud at the sign posted on the entry door *"Remove Ice Cleats Before Entering Store"*. Only in Alaska. He looked down at his polished, tasseled loafers. It might be smart to get a pair of boots, kind of like Mark's.

While loading his purchases into the back of his Jeep, he noticed a group of people with their faces upturned to the tall, leafless trees bordering one side of the parking lot. He followed their gaze to four huge bald eagles perched at the very top of the branches. With their white heads shining in the waning sunlight and their wings tucked snugly to their sides, the magnificent birds balanced on the high branches with ease, surveying their surroundings. Preston stood mesmerized, sharing the wonder, feeling patriotic, feeling Alaskan for the first time.

He stopped at the furniture warehouse store he'd noticed along the highway and ordered a bed, dresser, sofa, end tables, lamps, and a kitchen table and chairs. He left the store, eager to start making his mountainside abode a real home, and imagining showing it to Cindy.

Karen was returning from a walk, her Labs scampering around her, as he pulled into the drive. While the dogs sniffed him thoroughly, bumping against his ankles and whapping him with friendly tails, Karen agreed to let the furniture delivery men into his apartment the next day.

Chapter 14

FRIDAY TURNED OUT to be one of the most frustrating and challenging days of Preston's life. As of nine, neither client he had to represent in court had been back in touch with him and the cases were due to be called in another hour. He'd had to prepare as best he could without actually talking to them since neither one had a way for him to reach them He hadn't heard from Gary or Cindy, either, so he assumed things had gone fine with the release and they were both back at home.

He settled himself in the courtroom and when his first case on the docket was called, a woman answered to her name from the row of benches in the back. He turned to see her scooting up into the seat behind him. She whispered, "You my lawyer?"

Preston couldn't help recoiling from the strong whiff of cigarette smoke. He nodded, and turned his attention back to the proceedings. He gave a no show response when his second case was called, and then turned to the woman. "Go outside," he mouthed to her.

Outside the courtroom door, Preston asked, "Are you Lillian Edwards? The one with the marijuana pipe in the car?"

She bobbed long, straggly gray curls. Preston recognized hard living in the ragged, dirty nails, the hair badly in need of a trim, and the rough complexion. Mask-like black eyeliner defined her upper and lower lids. A prominent stomach pushed against the faded yellow tee shirt dotted with faint food stains. Even though it was so cold, she wore only scruffy black flip flops on her bare feet. Her toenails were dirty. She smelled. Preston tried not to pull back in revulsion.

"We can ask for a delay," he told her. "Then I can go over things with you before we have to appear again. But we need to get right back in there."

She tipped her chin in acceptance and they hurried back in. The docket was just beginning to be read for the second and final time when they slipped back into their seats. When the Edwards name was called, Preston asked for and received a postponement date for a week away. His other case had to be defaulted because the defendant still had not appeared. Preston could only shrug at the judge's disapproving frown. He turned to the seating area and motioned Lillian to follow him out.

"We need to go over your case. When are you available? Is there some way to contact you?"

Lillian stared at him without answering.

Preston waited.

Finally, she said, "Well, I'm here now." Her tone was pouty, with a touch of belligerence.

Preston had planned to return to the courtroom to observe how this judge worked. He needed to familiarize himself with the system, especially for Gary's case, but it looked like he better grab this chance right now to talk to Lillian while he could. "Sure, now is fine. We can meet in the conference room here. It's just two floors down." He turned to go.

"Got a smoke?" Lillian called out as she began to follow him.

Preston shook his head, trying to hide his aversion, and walked faster. He could hear Lillian flapping along behind him, sounding ever more winded by the pace as she huffed along. They rode the elevator in silence, her odor wafting through the small space. Preston tried not to breathe.

Lillian asked for a Mountain Dew and a snack as soon as he settled her in the conference room. She grumbled that it had been a tough morning having to get to court so early and she hadn't had time for breakfast. Preston hid his disgust. *What was so hard about getting someplace by nine in the morning? Especially when she obviously hadn't put much effort into dressing appropriately, and she must have known about this appearance for days ahead of time.*

He apologized for the lack of refreshments, gingerly sat down across from her, and began questioning her. He marveled at her answers as Lillian refused to take any responsibility for her situation. She blamed the officer who had stopped them, claiming there'd been no reason for him to pull her over just because the car looked smoky inside.

"Well, yes there is a possible reason, Preston explained. "If he saw smoke in the car, and it turned out to be marijuana, the driver could possibly be implicated as an operator under the influence, and he'd have grounds to stop her."

Lillian tossed her head. "Well, it's his word against mine about seeing a pipe in the car before he pulled me over. And he never asked if he could search the car, just started looking. I never gave permission." She narrowed her eyes. "I want you to get me off. I can't keep coming to court. I gotta take a taxi and it costs, ya know. He had no right to stop me."

Preston suspected she might be right. She was possibly savvier about this kind of thing than he was. "I'll look into it. How do I reach you? Are you sure you can be here next Friday?"

"Damn straight. This ain't goin' on my record. Ya know what ya gotta do. Get me off. That's your job and I expect ya to do it." She stood. "I gotta go. Need a smoke. I don't have no phone. I'll call ya if I can. Got a card?" She snatched the card from Preston's hand and tucked it in her crackled, black vinyl purse. "See ya next week."

PRESTON ACCOMPANIED MARK to the bar and restaurant after work where their coworkers straggled in and joined them around a large table made of polished driftwood. The first round of beer was soon in front of them and the appetizers were just as plentiful and tasty as Mark had described. Huge, tasty coconut shrimp, thick chunks of steaming, spicy reindeer sausage, and the crispiest onion rings Preston had ever tasted didn't last long before the hungry group. The Alaskan Amber beer in tall frosty mugs that Mark recommended tasted smooth and robust, a surprisingly refreshing change to an Easterner more accustomed to wine and cocktails.

Preston tried to keep the names straight – John, Craig, Don, Ann, George, Rick, Kelly. He enjoyed the lawyer talk more then he'd expected and picked up a few tips about the legal world in Anchorage that might make his job easier. It actually felt good to be part of the group. Hanging out with coworkers was kind of fun and he felt a buzz not only from the beer but from the camaraderie.

HE ARRIVED BACK at his apartment a little after ten o'clock, relaxed, still full from the steak dinner, and feeling more comfortable about his work than he had just a week ago. He paused with his key in the apartment door, his attention drawn by the view far below where the lights of Anchorage sparkled like gold, red, blue, and green jewels. Tiny planes with barely visible flashing lights rose from the airport, vanishing into the darkness. To the south, the long, narrow waters of Cook Inlet reflected a dim, phosphorescent blush of burnished copper light. Shadowy mountains on the horizon brooded against the night sky. He'd never seen stars as bright as the ones above – the sky fairly glittered with thousands of brilliant points of light. Maybe it looked this way because there was such a lack of artificial light so high up on this mountainside to compete with the stars. Awed and delighted, Preston wondered when he'd get to see the northern lights. He needed to find out about that aurora thing. Maybe stay up later in order to see them. He pushed through the door and tossed his jacket on his new sofa.

Preston unpacked his purchases, aware that it was time to call home again. But he hadn't figured out how to overcome the troubling reluctance to mention a growing attraction to a woman in Alaska. Cindy was attractive, appealing, smart, self-reliant, tough, and very sexy, but those qualities weren't what people back East thought were important in a woman. Cool, polite Victoria was. But Victoria and young women like her had always been judged on their appearance, grooming, social standing, and their affiliation with others of their kind. If they possessed any of the qualities Preston admired in Cindy, Preston had never seen it. The women in his life back East had no concept of hardship and would never need to be self-sufficient. It seemed they merely slid through life, while Cindy actually lived it.

Victoria had shown surprising spunk at the end, a trait Preston never expected in her. A tug on his heart surprised him at the thought. She'd been his closest friend for seven years. She'd never given him trouble. His parents had treated her like a daughter-in-law. The betrayal on her face when he told her he was moving to Alaska flashed before his eyes, followed by an intense pang of guilt.

He reached for his cell phone, then dropped his hand. It was too late to make the call back home. He didn't know what to say, anyway. He couldn't take his father's barely veiled disapproval right now. Then there was the guilt he felt whenever his mother tried to sound supportive. He could tell she wasn't being sincere. And he certainly wasn't going to call Victoria. He slammed the new wastebasket into place under the kitchen sink.

Before going to bed, Preston studied his reflection in the bathroom mirror and pondered the idea of growing a beard. Most Alaskan men had facial hair of some kind. He'd never had a beard, never even considered it before now. The long ponytails he saw on men here repulsed him and many beards were unkempt and bushy, but quite a few men looked masculine, even handsome, with trimmed facial hair. He'd think about a beard. He ran a hand through his styled hair and decided to let it grow out a little. *Nobody wears it like this here. It needs to look a little more casual. Maybe like Mark's. Maybe Cindy would like it longer, more like guys wore it around here.*

At that thought, he picked up his phone. Cindy answered on the first ring and he felt relieved that she was home on a Friday night.

When she repeated her "Hello," Preston realized he hadn't said anything yet. "Miss LaVassar?"

"Yes? This is Cindy."

"Cindy, it's Preston Mills, the attorney. Sorry to call so late. But I'd like to meet with you and your Dad again as soon as possible. I was wondering if you had any time tomorrow? Anytime would be... if you..." Preston heard himself babbling.

"Sure. In the morning, about nine o'clock? Maybe at the cafe in the hotel again? Would that work?"

Preston held the receiver against his chest after agreeing and hanging up, her voice fresh in his ear. He'd get to see her tomorrow. He tipped his chair back from the kitchen table and stretched his arms above his head. Tomorrow would be a good day to start growing a beard.

Chapter 15

PRESTON WOKE EARLY, restless and eager to begin this day. He was on the Glenn Highway shortly after eight, heading northeast out of Anchorage toward the neighboring communities of Wasilla and Palmer. A lemony sun crept over the mountain peaks ahead of him, chasing away the still dark morning. White-carpeted tundra dotted with humps of brush stretched away from both sides of the highway to the mountain ranges beyond. He shifted the Jeep into four-wheel drive after he hit a patch of slick pavement and skidded sideways, his heart pounding.

He tried to shake off the guilt and uneasiness he'd been unable to get rid of since deciding not to call his parents again yet last night. The tone of his father's voice would be critical and chastising as usual. Preston's stomach knotted at the thought. His mother's news about Victoria on the last call had unnerved him. He and Victoria had been the go-to dates for each other all through college. They'd slept together in his fraternity house bedroom and later at his law school apartment where Victoria would undress, place her neatly folded clothing on a chair, smooth her already smooth blond hair, then slide into bed, immediately closing her pale blue, perfectly made up eyes. Her body, slim and firm from tennis, swimming and good nutrition, lay willingly and passively beneath him until he finished. She was always gone in the morning when he awoke. They never talked about that part of their relationship and Preston was sure he was missing many of the wild and passionate things he heard other guys brag about.

Victoria was one of the reasons he'd decided to strike out on his own and move so far from home. Life with her would consist of years of such nights, and would surely include the big formal wedding, a brick house with white trim in a suburb not far from his parents. They'd have two good-looking, pleasant children who played tennis and went to summer camp. His life would be just as planned by his parents, boring, dull, stagnant, monotonous, stifling. He shuddered at the thought. His parents considered "the Alaska thing" to be just a phase, an unusual and defiant step along the way in his life. They'd campaigned hard to change his mind, and their final disapproval and disappointment had made his last month at home unbearably awkward.

When he'd told Victoria he was leaving for Alaska, she'd shown the most emotion he'd ever seen from her. It had been apparent from her hopeful face that she expected the news to include a proposal. She'd expected to be part of an adventuresome and unique way start to their lives, a cause for the envy and admiration of their social circle. But her initial, excited demeanor had withered before his eyes when he made no mention of taking her along. While he explained the details without using "us", her face had gone pale, then crimson. She'd pressed her lips into a thin hard line and whirled away without a word, refusing his calls since that day. He hadn't really felt the loss then, just unexpected relief. Now she was showing surprising gumption by joining some organization going to help build schools in a third world country. Maybe he'd been wrong about her. Maybe they'd both slipped into what was expected of them all those years. He missed her for the first time.

He was jolted back to the present when a gust of blowing snow forced the Jeep to career sideways again. Preston corrected the slide, then pulled the visor down against the rising sun and drove on, pushing his parents and Victoria from his mind.

BY THE TIME he got to the café, he'd remembered that his first task Monday morning would be to check the roster of the Anchorage jail. He'd been astounded to learn from his coworkers that about half of their clients were incarcerated at any one time, usually for parole violations or offenses unrelated to the pending cases that had just been assigned.

He spotted Gary and Cindy right away and realized they must have arrived early. They appeared deep in conversation and didn't notice him until he stood next to the booth, slightly toward Cindy's side. She smiled up at Preston, scooted over, and patted the empty space on the bench next to her. He breathed in a hint of flowers while he settled in. The dark blue fleece sweatshirt with Lazy Dog Kennels embroidered in red beneath a picture of a sled dog's friendly face told him she must be going to work after this.

Gary fidgeted in his seat across from them, looking haggard, worried, his complexion grayish. His greeting was gruff. "Hey, Mills. Thanks for the quick work on bail. It sure felt good to get out. How're we doin'?"

"Mr. LaVassar, don't even blink anywhere near a law officer. You can't afford even a jaywalking ticket," Preston answered, voice stern. He reminded Gary of all the conditions of bail and advised him to let him know the instant he remembered anything else about that night.

Cindy bobbed her head in acknowledgement while the waitress plopped steaming omelets bursting with mushrooms, reindeer sausage and cheese onto the table in front of them. Thick slices of crusty sourdough toast perched along the edges of the plates.

"We ordered the same as us for you, okay?" Cindy asked. "I have to get to work so we couldn't wait to order."

He thanked them and was glad to see Cindy and Gary dig in and eat heartily. He picked up his fork and joined them, enjoying the warmth of their company in sharing a meal. This is what it would be like if they were family. When Cindy wiped her mouth with a napkin and then flicked her tongue over her lips, he had to tear his eyes away. He noticed Gary watching him and looked down in embarrassment. He reached for his knife to spread strawberry jam on his toast, face flaming.

When they finished, Preston motioned for the check. Gary made a half-hearted protest, but Preston insisted, "On me. Cost of doing business. I'll write it off." He didn't know if that was the truth, but Cindy and Gary appeared to buy the explanation.

Too soon, Cindy slid out of the booth and headed for the cafe door. He watched her walk away, fighting the certainty that a relationship with a client's daughter fell into the category of unacceptable professional conduct.

He turned to find Gary's speculative eyes on him and spoke quickly. "Okay. Let's go over everything again. Tell me about that night at the bar. Everything. Starting from the moment you got there. Who else was there, who did you talk to?"

Gary began recounting the details of that night, then stopped and his face reddened. "And I did see that woman. The dead one. She was there with her friends for just a little while. Maybe around seven."

"How could you have forgotten to tell us that?" Preston asked.

Gary shrunk back slightly and slid his gaze to the side. "I plain forgot. I remember recognizing it was her when I found the body, but I just didn't think about it again." He looked back at Preston, chagrined. "Sorry. Guess I got kind of bamboozled with it all happening so fast. All them questions from the troopers, and then how everybody looked at me. It was kinda hard to think straight. And then I had to be in a cell again." He hung his head in embarrassment and turned his head to the wall. "Wish I'd never stopped that night, that's for sure."

"Okay, that's all," he said to Gary. "Is there anything else you should tell me? Anything at all?"

Gary hung his head. "Nope."

Chapter 16

PRESTON HURRIED FOR the Monday morning hearing before Judge Webster. What a nuisance to have to try to help losers who came in and out of the court system so frequently that their files were a foot thick. The defendant this morning had been impossible to reach so Preston had no idea who would slide into the seat beside him, or if anybody would show up at all. He knew only that the man was thirty five, with a rap sheet of burglary and assault eighteen items along. Today it would be only necessary to enter a plea, but Preston planned to ask for a delay so he could at least meet briefly with his client. He was surprised to find the client waiting for him in the courtroom.

"Public defender?" a scruffy man asked as soon as Preston entered. At Preston's nod, he announced, "Jeff Griffin here," and jumped up to walk beside him.

Judge Webber had a reputation for toughness that Preston discovered was justified. The judge glared his disapproval of the request for a delay before granting Preston a revised spot on the docket and lectured the defendant for failure to keep his lawyer informed of his whereabouts. Griffin appeared so unfazed by the proceedings that Preston suspected this wasn't the first time he'd showed up without first bothering to consult with a court-appointed attorney.

They moved from the courtroom to a conference room and eyed each other. Across from Preston sat a skinny, unkempt man with a deeply pitted face and a loosely wrapped, skinny tail of tangled hair that apparently hadn't seen a barber's shears, much less a comb, in a long time. He glowered at Preston, waiting in obstinate silence for his attorney to say the first word.

This guy is a mess. Doesn't he own a comb? He smells, stinks actually. And he won't talk. Just sits there and stares at me. Look at his shoes – they're so worn out that they are flopping off his toes. His shirt obviously hasn't been washed in weeks.

Squashing his thoughts, Preston began, "Well, for starters, how can I get ahold of you? We have to be able to communicate if I'm going to defend you on the shoplifting charge. Where...?"

The man cut him off. "Don't have a phone number. I live in the camps in the parks. Maybe you can leave a message for me at the St. Ignatius Center. They got a bulletin board. I ain't got a permanent address, so sometimes I stay there if I hafta, like when it's cold or raining." His stained teeth hung crookedly from bright red gums and Preston couldn't help reflexively shoving his chair back away a bit from the sour breath that filled the space between them. The man reeked of stale alcohol, tobacco, and God knew what else.

Ten minutes later, Preston gulped deep breaths of fresh air outside the entrance to the courthouse and began the walk back to his office building, the wet sidewalks soaking through the soles of his loafers. His client shuffled away in the opposite direction. Although Preston had stressed how important it was to reappear before the judge again this afternoon at one, he felt there was only a fifty-fifty chance, at best, that Griffin would show up. How was he supposed to defend someone who apparently didn't care about being sent to jail? Mark and the others from the office had told him about the many repeat offenders who actually welcomed occasional jail time as a chance for regular meals and a warm place to sleep. It looked like Griffin might be one of them. Preston took a quick glance at his watch and hurried his steps so he wouldn't be late to see Frank at ten about Gary's case.

Frank was troubled by Gary's initial failure to mention the victim's presence at the bar. "It's the prosecutor's job to prove that as fact. Let's not stir things up. Let 'em make the next move. Goddamn, what was the guy thinking? Not to tell anyone that?"

"LaVassar said he forgot all about it because he's so stressed by his involvement in this whole mess. I kind of believe him." Preston answered.

Frank shook his head in disgust, then agreed to assign an investigator to the case right away since the school mother looked like a possible suspect. He appeared pleased that Gary's bail had been granted, but warned that Gary had to be very careful with everything he did or said.

Preston settled back at his desk, but a call an hour later crushed him. When the troopers informed him of the news of Gary's arrest for DUI a short time before, Preston slumped into his chair. *Not this. Gary would face jail time for sure now. It's unbelievable what he'd just done. Drinking and then getting behind the wheel. He should have known those troopers would be watching him. How could someone drink, in the morning no less, and then get behind the wheel? With a prior drunk driving conviction? What had he been thinking? He'd been told he had to stay away from alcohol as a condition of his release. He'd be going to jail and this this time it wouldn't be so easy to get him out. He'd miss a lot of time from work. Maybe lose his job. And Cindy. She'd probably have to move back up to Gary's cabin, facing long winter drives in the dark twice a day, heating with wood and taking care of Gary's dog. Life was going to be way tougher for her from this moment on.*

Preston turned back to his desk and pushed the numbers for Cindy's cell phone, dreading what he had to tell her.

Chapter 17

PRESTON COULD TELL that his call devastated Cindy by the way her voice faded to almost nothing. But caring for the huskies couldn't be crammed into much less than the eight hours she usually spent, so she told him she'd hustle through the chores without a lunch break in order to make it to the jail before visiting hours ended.

Preston was waiting in the lobby when she rushed in. He ushered her into a small conference room after a brief greeting. Gary was soon escorted into the room, clad once more in a baggy yellow jumpsuit, and Cindy rushed into his arms.

The guard stepped forward and protested, "No contact, Miss. The rules." When she turned fierce, blazing eyes to him, he backed to the corner of the room and, trying to maintain some semblance of control, admonished her, "Make it quick."

"What happened today?" Cindy asked, pulling away from her father.

"I screwed up. I stopped at the job site, but the boss said he had somebody else scheduled on the grader already today so I didn't have to show up until tomorrow. Had a few beers after breakfast. Kind of celebrating being out, ya know. I stopped in at that bar across from the visitor's center. Knew they opened early. Guess the beer tasted too good. I never shoulda done it." He bowed his head. "This is bad. I'm sorry, Honey."

Preston spoke. "I learned you'll be taken into the Pre-Trial Facility in Anchorage tomorrow. You're on the morning court docket. But my boss said not to get your hopes up because not much is likely to happen. It never does when conditions of release are broken so fast. A DUI is serious. Especially a repeat one. My boss said you'd probably have to put up five hundred thousand, if you can even get bail at all. The prosecutor's known for trying to make release impossible by requesting high bail and he has a lot of public pressure on this case. It doesn't look good."

Cindy folded back into her chair while Preston explained, and Gary's face grew shadowed with deep creases of fatigue and worry. "How would we get five hundred thousand? The deed to the cabin?" he asked. He pulled back, anger and frustration chasing across his features and turned to Cindy. "You'll have to take off work tomorrow."

Cindy pulled herself up straight and raised her chin. "Dad, it's okay. I can get up early and get some of my work done so I can head for Anchorage in time. I'll make it. I can finish with the dogs afterward. I need to be there. We have to try to get you out."

Gary dropped his head into his hands and his shoulders began heaving. His voice was muffled.

"Dammit, Cindy. I'm sorry for dragging you into my mess. I can't believe this is happening. I just saw that woman along the road and couldn't let her lay there all alone in the night. And then them beers tasted so good this morning." His voice broke.

Cindy rushed to hug his shoulders from behind. She threw a challenging look at the guard who stepped forward as if to hold her back from more contact with the prisoner. The guard retreated sheepishly, shaking his head.

Cindy dropped her arms around her father's shoulders and nuzzled next to his ear. "It's going to be okay, Daddy."

Gary pulled himself together, rose, and pushed her away to arm's length. "Okay, you go now. You have lotsa stuff to do and Daisy's gonna be waiting at home tonight. I'll see you in the courtroom in the morning. Bring along the deed to the cabin – we'll probly need it to guarantee bail. It's in that gray metal box under my bed. Go on now."

He gave her a firm push away and stepped toward the guard.

WHILE HIS DAUGHTER finished her work at the kennel and drove to the cabin, Gary lay in his cell, eyes wide, mind spinning, hoping he'd get bail again. He was very worried.

Preston was worried, too. *Those troopers. They're everywhere. It's hard to believe Gary got picked up first thing. I made it very clear to Gary that he couldn't risk even the slightest infraction of the law. And then the fool went and did it, right away. After he'd omitted two pieces of crucial and possibly incriminating information from his initial interview with the prosecution. This case was getting tougher every day.*

Chapter 18

PRESTON ARRIVED IN court Tuesday just as Gary was escorted in and positioned in the front row, handcuffed and chained to three other men, all in matching prison jumpsuits, their toes poking through clear plastic sandals. Gary looked back over his shoulder and sought Preston's eyes. His face reflected embarrassment, anxiety, and fatigue, and Preston's heart went out to him despite his anger at Gary's foolishness. He gave Gary a slight nod of acknowledgement and what he hoped was reassurance.

Preston turned to his statement, reviewing it before court convened.

To his surprise, Frank slid into the seat next to him and slapped the file before them on the table. "This is gonna be tough. I thought I better be here."

Both turned to a commotion at the prosecutor's table. A beefy man, face florid and scowling over double chins, black suit crumpled against his thick body, flung his bulk into a chair, swung to look their way, and gave a curt nod. He turned back, ran a hand over his few strands of hair, and bent to whisper to the man beside him.

Preston gave Frank a questioning look. "O'Brien?"

"Yes."

A sudden whiff of a familiar floral fragrance caught Preston's attention and he turned to see Cindy settle onto the bench directly behind him. She gave a quick wave to her father, before turning anxious eyes to Preston.

"Hi," she whispered, leaning forward and laying a hand on his shoulder.

"Hi," Preston answered through a constricted throat. He moved his hand atop hers in reassurance. A navy blue belted dress accented her waist, and her slim legs were encased in pantyhose and heels. She had tamed her curls into a low ponytail at the nape of her neck, giving her a mature look. Old-fashioned pearl earrings glowed, matching the strand at her neck. Her hand warmed beneath his.

Cindy leaned forward further. "Dad looks okay, don't you think?"

Preston gulped. At this angle, two slight mounds of silky skin threatened to spill from the neckline of her dress. He badly wanted her to lean in, to see more of that soft flesh, touch it, feel its weight it in his hands. *God. What am I thinking?* Preston jerked himself back to reality. He swallowed, hoping his voice would come out normal. "Yes. We're ready. Do you have the deed?"

"Right here." She patted her purse.

Suddenly, Preston realized that Frank had turned to Cindy, too. He lifted his hand from hers, feeling his cheeks burn. He made the introductions, then met Frank's eyes and recognized the warning there.

Frank nodded to Cindy, then shook his head at Preston in a disapproving manner. "See me in my office before you leave today." He turned forward, shoulders stiff.

The judge asked only a few questions, for which Preston was well prepared. But to their disappointment, a sharp and decisive rap of the gavel remanded Gary back to jail without possibility of bail. The judge gave them a glance and a slight shrug as if to say, 'Sorry, can't do it'. Gary turned to them with a look of despair before being led away. Frank rose and strode out without a word.

Preston turned to Cindy. "It looks like the judge had to uphold the law. Especially on a high profile case like this. The DA's demand for a half million dollar bail is typical because he knows defendants can't come up with it. And they accused your dad of being a danger to the community due to his former DUI."

Cindy dipped her head in acknowledgement while he went on. "We'll need to see your Dad a lot in the next month or so. You'll only hurt his case if you say a word to anybody – it could come back to us in the wrong way or be misquoted

Her face paled with alarm. "Okay," she murmured.

"Don't worry."

Cindy clutched her purse to her chest. Her face was drawn and colorless, her eyes too bright. "I have to get back to work," she answered in a flat, small voice. Preston dragged his eyes from her face.

"I'll call you with any news. We're working hard on this," Preston promised.

They rode the elevator down together and as he held the carved wooden exit door open for her. She walked away, back straight, high-heeled steps hurried. He started for his office, but couldn't help turning after a few steps to watch her. At the same moment, Cindy turned back, too. They shared a long look.

So she felt something, too. He paused and drew the frigid air deep into his lungs, buoyed by the look, yet feeling terrible for Cindy. She'd been impressive throughout, composed, competent, right in there helping her father with everything. He wanted to make things okay for her. Do anything he could to help her. She was determined. And so damned cute. He sucked in another breath of frigid air.

He remembered Frank's words of warning and strode toward his office building. It was relief to see an empty office in the far corner when he got back to his desk. The meeting with Frank could be put off, at least for a while. A flash of anxiety followed. What did Frank want? Had he noticed Cindy's familiarity and the overlapping hands?

Preston spent the next few hours becoming up to speed on his other files while trying to fight his disappointment about Gary's bail. But he had to admit that the judge had done what was necessary and appropriate under the circumstances.

PRESTON WAS RIGHT about Jeff Griffin's failure to show up for the one o'clock hearing. With visible annoyance and a scowl, the judge issued a warrant for failure to appear and Preston was free to go back to his desk. He was deep into reviewing precedent setting cases similar to Gary's when Frank caught his eye and summoned him by waving him in from across the room, Preston stepped into his boss' office, trying to project confidence.

"Whatcha got, Mills? This DUI fiasco is gonna hurt. O'Brien's gotta be lovin' this. What do we have? " Frank asked, his voice brusque while he pawed at the piles of papers on his desktop. He shoved the LaVassar file toward Preston. "There's a real hue and cry for information out there. I can't put the press off any more. The prosecutor's been blabbing steadily. Has 'em convinced LaVassar's their guy. I have to talk to the media today before they get wind of this DUI thing and really blow it up. Repeat offender and all that. I have to have my answers ready. I need something to tell them."

Preston felt a trickle of sweat slide between his shoulder blades. "I still don't believe LaVassar did it. I'm getting the school mother's contact information from the troopers this afternoon. I need to find out more about this other suspect. It sounds like the woman had quite an altercation with the victim a few days before the murder. I think we should put the investigator on it and interview her tomorrow."

"You get on it right now." Frank pounded his desk. "You call those troopers and make them provide you with everything. They can't withhold evidence or information. O'Brien's just being obstinate. That's always his strategy. I need solid information. Get it." He glanced with annoyance at the beeping light on his phone. "And, Mills. What the hell was that I noticed with you and the girl? You have something going on with the defendant's daughter?" He glared at Preston.

Preston sucked in a breath. "Well, not really. Well, maybe a little... "

Frank frowned. "Put the brakes on it right now. We don't need the complication. It's inappropriate to get involved with a client. You know that. Save it for after the trial. Understand?" He motioned Preston away. "Get back to me on the other suspect. I need more for the media."

Preston backed out of the office, his shirt now clinging to his back. "Yes, Sir. I understand. I'll have more information for you as soon as I can." Frank's only answer was a flick of his hand.

Preston hurried back to his desk and sank into his chair. He'd been ordered to do more on Gary's case. He'd been scolded about Cindy and told not to see her. Well, he'd work harder on the case. He knew he could impress Frank, especially if that school student's mother turned out to be a legitimate lead. But to eliminate Cindy from his life wouldn't be possible. She needed him to help her get through all this. She was alone, trying to help her father. He kicked at the leg of his desk in despair. Frank wasn't going to overlook disobedience on a matter like this. He dropped his head into his hands. Best thing to do was get this case over with as soon as possible.

Chapter 19

PRESTON DIALED THE troopers, bolstered by new resolve. "Hey, Kerrans, Preston Mills here from the PD's office. I didn't get the kindergarten mother's information on the LaVassar case yet. My boss just reamed me for more information on her. Where is it?"

"It's in the reports."

Preston spoke into the silence that followed. "C'mon man. Don't make me request those documents again, and then wait for them."

Nick gave a loud, aggrieved sigh. "Okay. Okay. Her name's Elizabeth Ritter. She lives over in Palmer. I'll scan over her contact info." He snorted. "She claimed she didn't remember anything about making a fuss at the school about her kid and was downright uncooperative. It's your job to bring her in as another suspect if you expect to clear LaVassar. Right now, we have our man. He lied to us. He doesn't have an alibi." He hung up.

IT WAS ONLY his second week in Alaska and already Preston felt an immense amount of pressure. Things hadn't been this intense back East, not even during

117

finals. He pictured Cindy working at the kennel. Her boss was scheduled to get back tonight and she'd probably work late to get it all perfect for him. Preston didn't know how to force himself to get over his attraction to her. His mind told him one thing, his emotions another. But he better obey Frank. The stab of a headache coursed through him and he reached up to knead the base of his neck.

He shook it off, hustled out to his car, and scraped the snow from the windshield with his new plastic scraper. Within minutes of leaving the city limits, the splendor of the jagged peaks and ridges of the Chugach Mountain Range beyond the flats along the highway tugged at Preston's consciousness. Meadows of snowy tundra spread from the freeway toward dark, dense spruce forests that climbed the massive mountains' shadowed lower slopes. The mountains nestled into pale, grey winter skies, their rugged tops frosted with snow as pristine and white as powdered sugar. A tinge of pink, described by locals as alpenglow, hung in a vague, misty fog along the horizon. The imposing size of the mountains amazed him. This vast and rugged beauty captured his soul in a way he'd never imagined. How could he feel this way so intensely after such a short time in Alaska? It was almost like he'd finally found a place where he felt he belonged.

He rubbed his throbbing temples. He had no idea how to get Cindy out of his mind. There was something potent and intoxicating between them. He toyed with the idea of defying Frank's orders. Cindy's face filled his mind at the thought. Her shapeliness when she walked ahead of him to the conference room that first day. The mass of sexy curls that tumbled down the middle of her back leading to the dip of her waist and the curve of her hips. He drew a desperate breath to keep his mind on the road. Frank's face flashed before him. And the curt words, "Cool it with her. Understand?"

A sudden burst of heavy, blowing snow whirled across the road. His Jeep shook as the wind picked up, and by the time he reached the sign for Wasilla, it took all his concentration to hold the steering wheel steady. This must be the start of the blizzard that had been predicted on last night's news. Cindy was probably out in this shrieking storm, getting the dogs settled in before the weather hit.

Unable to get Cindy out of his thoughts, he pulled off to a frontage road near the new hospital construction site and called her. "It's Preston Mills. Got time for a quick lunch?"

"Oh, Hi," her voice told him she was pleased to hear from him. "No, sorry, not really. Bob gets back tonight, and a blizzard's due. It's starting to snow here already. I have to bed down all the dogs with extra straw and make sure they have water before it freezes overnight."

"We'll make it fast. There's news on the case."

"Oh, well, okay then, I guess. Same place?"

"Uh huh. See you there."

Sure, there was news about another possible suspect, but he dreaded what else he had to explain to her. He had to stop seeing her outside of formal meetings on the case, try to stop thinking about her, stop letting something develop between them. He couldn't compromise Gary's case. Couldn't disregard Frank's order.

Cindy showed up right on time, but seemed distracted by her need to get back to work, as well as her deep concern for her father. Although she was happy to hear about another suspect, she only picked at the meatloaf and mashed potatoes that was the day's special. Preston grew uneasy, unable to bring up the subject of cooling the budding relationship they were both aware of but hadn't actually acknowledged to each other. Conversation faltered. Wind-blown snow driving against the windows blotted out everything outside the café.

Finally Cindy managed a quiet "Thanks, Preston, for all you're doing for Dad. For trying so hard for us and for keeping in touch so well." She slid an arm into her jacket. "I better get back to work before this weather gets worse."

"But, Cindy, there's…"

"And thanks for lunch," Cindy murmured while rising. "I…" Her voice broke and it was apparent how hard it was to hold in the anxiety about her dad. She tried to hide her pinched face by turning away.

Preston heard a muffled whimper, shoved aside his plate and rose from his seat. He rushed to her and folded his arms around her, oblivious to the curious glances from others at adjoining tables. "Hey, I'm here for you. You're not alone."

Cindy sagged against him and began to tremble. Faint, mewling sobs she tried to stifle escaped as she burrowed into his jacket. Overcome by an overpowering need to protect this woman, he held her tightly against him. He'd been right when he imagined holding her again. She was so soft. A sense of protectiveness consumed him.

Finally, Cindy pulled away, brushed at her face, shrugged into her jacket, threw back her shoulders and walked out without a backward glance. Preston dropped his empty arms. He watched her walk to her car, head bent into the blowing snow, looking so small, so alone.

He breathed in, hoping for a lingering hint of her scent. He was sure now that she felt the same as he did. He could tell by the way she'd snuggled against him without reserve. The hell with Frank. He slapped a twenty on the table. He'd fix this for Cindy and be there for her. He'd get her father off the charges. And he'd have her in his arms again, too. Soon. He kicked through the drifting snow to his car feeling charged, determined, smitten, and defiant. He wouldn't be giving her up.

Chapter 20

PRESTON MADE THE call to the investigator who agreed to do the Ritter interview right away. It was time to keep this case moving, finish it up, get Gary out. Acting bold and decisive like this was just what Preston had been looking for by leaving the established world back East. Maybe this was what it felt like to be an Alaskan.

As he pulled away from the curb, his father's words came to mind. "Remember, Son, the Mills family has integrity and a reputation to uphold. We do the right thing and obey the rules." How many times had he heard that? Before rugby games and debates. Before every one of the dates he'd had in high school. As the final lecture before his parents drove away after settling him in at the fraternity house his freshman year. Preston felt an exhilarating freedom now. He wouldn't be ending it with Cindy. He'd figure out a way to be very discreet, but he had to be with her. And he'd call his parents when he felt ready, not on their schedule anymore. It was his life now and he liked having control of it. He ignored the surge of anxiety these thoughts brought, welcoming a newfound determination.

THE NEXT AFTERNOON, he listened to the investigator's account of his visit to Elizabeth Ritter. Mike slid a folder across Preston's desk and brushed a hand over his curly black hair. "It's all in here."

He seemed eager to tell what happened. "Well, there was fierce yapping on the other side of a real fancy carved wooden front door when I knocked. I could hear music inside so I knew somebody was home. But I had to knock hard twice and stand there for quite a long time while I waited for an answer. It was a nice place. There was a barn-type garage with a huge raspberry patch beside it and a corral in the rear toward the woods. I was wondering if that yapping dog would ever settle down when the door got jerked open by a tall brunette in a red velvet tracksuit. She was breathing hard like she'd been working out. She stooped down and gathered a fluffy little white dog into her arms and then looked at me, kind of hostile-like. Her hair was cut in that spiky short style, kind of like the pixies in fairy tale books. But she was no pixie."

Mike grimaced. "There was no hello. She just said, 'Well?' kind of curt and rude. I told her I was from the Public Defender's office in Anchorage and needed talk to her about the Williams case. She told me she already talked to the trooper and had nothing else to say and said she knew she didn't have to be interviewed again."

Mike threw up his hands. "She complained that nobody told her someone else would be coming out. And she demanded to know why we didn't have the courtesy to call. So I apologized for not calling ahead. I told her we've been chasing every detail of this case for the past week and I just slipped up by not calling ahead."

He went on to tell Preston how there was no reaction to his apology. Instead, Elizabeth continued staring at him while patting the dog's belly.

"I told her I'm the one who has to write up a report on her for the public defender department and I do it for all involved parties." He looked at Preston sheepishly. "It was a long way out there from Anchorage, and this broad was just plain rude. So I told her the trooper didn't give us enough information to file the report. There were just some basic things we needed and she could come into Anchorage and talk to us or it at the office or finish up right there with just a few more details."

Mike explained how he'd felt rebuffed and a bit angry by then. He'd brazenly returned her stare, hoping she couldn't detect his half-truth, and took a bold step forward partway through the door.

"I've dealt with her kind before. You can't let them be in charge," Mike said.

"How'd she take that?"

"Well, that little dog growled at me, and Ritter fluffed its ears and calmed it down. Then she took a step back into the entry, kind of reluctant, and demanded to see my credentials. She told me it better be quick because she already told the trooper she didn't really know that Williams woman. She said Mrs.Williams was her daughter Courtney's teacher, but the school year was just starting, and she'd only met her once, at the parent teacher conference in October."

Mike said he'd waited, surprised that she'd actually given in and went on. "She finally stepped aside, acting even more unwilling, and led the way into an exceptionally neat living room that looked like the picture of a model home in a magazine. Not a thing was out of place. There were fresh vacuum tracks on the carpet. There wasn't a newspaper, an empty glass, or a TV guide anywhere. The plant leaves shone like they'd just been polished and pillows that matched the rug were a perfectly spaced row along the back of a white sofa. I wondered if anyone ever sat on that sofa, or actually even lived in that house," Mike said with a shrug.

He told how Elizabeth pointed him to the sofa and took a seat on the edge of the matching loveseat across from him. She continued to hold the dog, which squirmed until she gave its collar a quick jerk and it settled down again. When it struggled she gave its collar another hard jerk and it dropped back into her arms.

"She really controlled the animal. She probably controlled everything in her life just like that." Mike leaned against the corner of Preston's desk and went on. "I noticed a slight twitch in the skin just below her left eye. A nervous tic. She was the type to have one. I wondered if it was because I was here or if it was always there. I asked her if my information was correct that her only contact with the victim was at a conference in her child's classroom a few weeks before the murder. She answered with only a quick nod, no words. Then she said she told the trooper all this and didn't want to go over it all again with me."

Mike's face reddened. "I knew she was lying since the trooper's report said she'd refused to talk to him at all. This woman wasn't gonna intimidate me. So I decided to make her tell me every detail. I told her I knew the basic facts. That I needed to fill in some details and then I'd be on my way. I asked her to first get to the part about her dissatisfaction with Ms. Williams' placement of her child in a reading group she didn't agree with."

Mike grinned. "One thing I've learned is to allow long pauses so clients and interviewees get uncomfortable and blurt out things they might not say otherwise. So I waited. I'd make her tell me everything. And she did."

Mike continued, "She told me her daughter, Courtney, was gifted. Her face started turning red and she squirmed back into the cushions when I didn't say anything. Then she went on telling me that the teacher needed to realize Courtney's abilities, that Courtney belonged in the top reading group, not the second tier."

"I just kept making notes without saying a word," Mike smiled, a gleam of mischief in his eyes. "And she went on that Courtney was already way ahead of all of her classmates in everything. Ritter didn't accept Mrs. Williams' opinion to the contrary. So when the teacher wouldn't listen to her at the conference, she just went to the principal. She told me you have to go to the top to get things done the way you want. Her face got redder and redder while she was talking and the twitch below her eye was fluttering like crazy."

Mike's smile grew almost gleeful as he went on. "I asked her if she and Mrs. Williams had words there in the classroom during the conference. Her voice was pretty shrill by now. She said they'd talked a little and as soon as it became clear that Courtney wasn't going to get moved up, Ritter decided to go over the teacher's head. She was pretty defensive and challenging toward me by then. Hostile, actually."

"So she did go to the principal then?" Preston asked.

"Yes, Mike answered. "She told me she went in the next day. The principal listened to her and said all he could do was look into it and talk with the teacher. He told her Mrs. Williams would have the final say. But she was certain she convinced him that Courtney should be moved up and that's how it was left."

"So she denied any hard feelings or conflict between herself and the victim?" Preston inquired.

"Yeah, she said there were none whatsoever."

Preston remembered that Dan Williams recalled how upset Jennifer had been after coming home from conferences that day. Jennifer had told him how a nasty mother kind of freaked out, insulted her, challenged her evaluation of a student, and stormed out of a conference shouting about going higher up. Jennifer had felt bad that her ability as a teacher was being questioned, and had been rather despondent about the incident, according to Dr. Williams.

Preston was hearing a much different version right now. It was apparent who was lying. Elizabeth Ritter was definitely becoming more than a person of interest.

"I asked her where she was that Friday night," Mike added. "And if there was anything else she wanted to tell me. Boy, did that set her off! She got up and pointed me to the door without another word."

Mike recalled how Elizabeth had stepped back into the house far enough that a handshake would be impossible, and ignored his goodbye. The door slammed behind him, followed by the loud and definite click of a deadbolt.

PRESTON DROVE HOME that afternoon with a pale sun flickering weakly through the heavy snowfall that obscured the surrounding mountain ranges. The roads were already covered with drifting snow that hadn't been there just hours before. Cars crawled ahead and beside him through the thickening of snow. Only barely visible pricks of headlights identified traffic in the oncoming lanes that were filled with a steady stream of commuters heading home trying to beat the storm.

It was a relief to finally make it up the driveway to his apartment. The steep roads had been slicker than any he'd ever driven on before, and his wheels skidded twice on curves, almost throwing him into the ditch. He warmed at the sight of his place, and realized it felt like home. He imagined Cindy waiting there for him.

Chapter 21

GARY PACED HIS cell. The bunk was too hard. The thin mattress was lumpy, the pilled blanket stiff and scratchy. The pillow that God knows how many other guys had used reeked. He couldn't stay in that bunk anymore even though the night was only half gone. Weak moonlight barely managed to penetrate the darkness of the chilly block cell. The night held faint sounds of too many people in too small a space. He longed for his own bed and the silence of his yard. Wished for the sound of Daisy's soft snores and her warmth snuggled against his side.

He remembered the brilliance of the luminous moon only weeks ago. How he wished that night had been this dark. Then he wouldn't have noticed the body. He'd have just driven on by. He'd be at home right now with Daisy, maybe on the couch if they'd fallen asleep watching a late show after a few beers. A beer sounded so good right now. And he was hungry. *That crap they served for dinner wasn't even real food. How could they call that slimy gray glop gravy? And they might as well mash up some cooked cardboard and call it potatoes. Damn it. And poor Cindy. Godammit anyway.*

He stomped back and forth from the bars to the window wall, fuming, muttering. "Wish to hell I'd never stopped for those beers that morning. What in God's name was I thinking? Wasn't, I guess. Now look. My life is screwed up. I can't afford this trouble. My little girl. She's had it so rough so far in life. Just when she was gettin' ahead. Now I went and did this! Damn! I wanna go home. I miss my dog. I just wanna be home."

He stood and stretched. Somebody else was on his grader at the job site by now for sure. They'd have to wind down the earthwork pretty soon because the ground had to be near frozen under the permafrost by now. When he got out, he'd have to go on unemployment. But maybe he could find something else for the winter.

NICK WAS HAVING trouble sleeping that night, too, the murder case constantly on his mind. He cuddled in closer to Kay's fragrant warmth and marveled at how she could just lay her head on the pillow like that and be sound asleep within seconds. Her days were busy and tiring, what with the kids and the house and all, but he'd had never been able to understand how she could just abandon thoughts and cares and fall asleep like she did.

The murder case intruded on his thoughts again. *Was the Ritter woman guilty? If she was, how'd she do it? It's hard to believe a young mother has been murdered in Wasilla. That kind of stuff just doesn't happen here. Especially if another woman was responsible. Maybe*

131

Elizabeth Ritter actually did it. It's already apparent she's kind of a bitch. Maybe she was so protective of her child that she took care of what she perceived to be an obstacle to a perfect life for her kid. Maybe she used poison. Yeah, that actually is possible.

He'd check with the coroner tomorrow to see what kinds of poisons were available, the kind that leave no obvious trace. He just didn't feel right yet about pinning it on LaVassar. There was no motive. Only a random connection between him and the victim. Nobody remembered them even looking at each other at the bar. And it was feasible that a guy like that would sit out in his truck and swig a few to save money.

He mashed the pillow another time and burrowed his head, frustrated, desperate for the blackness of sleep to overcome him. Outside his bedroom window, a colorless, nearly transparent half-moon, with scraps of clouds scudding across its face, moved slowly across the black canopy of the Alaska night.

PRESTON WAS UP late that night, too, hunched over the LaVassar file where it lay spread out on his coffee table. After examining every detail over and over he finally he stumbled off to bed. He didn't need to pull the curtain shut tonight. Outside, the inky black of the winter night was broken only by twinkles of faint light from the sleeping city below and the anemic glow of a colorless half-moon shadowed by clouds.

He ran his hands through his hair before settling into the pillow, surprised at how shaggy and long his hair felt after just such a short time. The bristles from his beard made it hard to get comfortable, but he didn't care. It was time to become more Alaskan. Maybe he'd look rugged and Cindy would like it.

What would his parents think about how he looked, though? Better call them tomorrow and tell them he was growing a beard, and at least mention Cindy. They'd be worried since it had been almost two weeks now since the last call. They seemed far away for the first time in his life and he liked the feeling. There was a mild curiosity about Victoria, but it drifted away, replaced by Cindy's face. His mind turned to thoughts of Cindy and he imagined kissing her very carefully so his beard wouldn't be scratchy against her tender face. And holding her close while they drowsed together in the warmth of each other's arms after making love. Comforted and soothed by these thoughts, he finally drifted off.

Chapter 22

THE ANNOUNCEMENT OF Gary's re-arrest became breaking news that interrupted TV programs and made the front page headline in the Journal. People called in to talk shows, pouring out their relief that a suspect was off the streets. Outrage against Gary dominated their opinions. It was the hottest topic of conversation at workplaces, restaurants, bars, and in homes.

Preston felt thankful about Frank's decision to lay low and not react, and to keep the possibility of another suspect quiet for now. Doing it this way wouldn't alert Elizabeth Ritter to their suspicions. Then, when they got Gary off, O'Brien would look like a fool.

Relieved for the moment that things were progressing, Preston turned back to his other cases. A call to the mother who'd been refusing to send her kids to school because the bus ride was too long took one case off his desk when she informed him in a sheepish tone that a neighbor had agreed to give the kids a ride every morning while dropping off her own daughter. Since the kids now didn't have to get up so early and stand out in the bitter cold and darkness for the bus, the mother had decided to cooperate with the school. One down.

Sure enough, Jeff Griffin had been picked up for failure to appear in court and was apparently quite happy to be incarcerated. The woman shoplifter hadn't returned any of Preston's three calls even though he left a detailed message on her machine each time. Her case was scheduled for this afternoon. Preston could only guess if she would be there. How bizarre that these people just didn't seem to care. They faced warrants, jail time, and fines for failure to appear, but they didn't bother to show up or even return calls from their attorney.

The skanky woman with the marijuana in the car was a different story. Her case was scheduled to come up tomorrow and she still planned to fight the charge. She'd called Preston twice, luckily catching him at his desk both times. She insisted that he should be able to get her off and stated emphatically that it was what she expected. Preston spent the morning studying marijuana laws and similar cases in Alaska and decided she was probably right. Not only was it legal to possess small amounts of the substance for personal use, but it appeared that the officer had no legal grounds to stop her and search her car the way he did.

Preston finished the case's pretrial motions and turned it in to Barb at the front desk for filing with the court. He also turned in what little he had on the shoplifting case, feeling annoyed and inadequate. It wouldn't be professional to appear before the same judge with another no show client so soon after last week. He better go see Gary and then try to find the shoplifter's address.

When escorted into the tiny conference room, Gary's face had deep lines Preston hadn't noticed before. His eyes were red-rimmed and the rumpled jumpsuit he wore was at least one size too big. How humiliating it must feel for a man like him to be wearing those plastic sandals. Preston sympathized as he rose to shake Gary's hand. But Gary didn't notice the gesture and dropped into the chair across the gray metal table.

"Hey, Mills," he said, voice low and gruff.

"Mr. LaVassar." Preston replied. "How're you doing?"

Gary shook his head. "I can't stand it in here. Can I get out? Do they need more bail?" His voice was flat with hopelessness, his face creased with worry and fatigue.

"It's not likely we can get you out. Don't get your hopes up." Preston felt helpless and ineffective.

Gary sighed in understanding. "Thought so. You seen Cindy? She ain't been here."

Preston nodded. "Yes, for a few minutes. She's pretty worried, but doing okay. I'll let her know you asked about her." Good, a reason to call her. "I'll be going to Wasilla later today. I can see her if you want. Then tomorrow I'll let you know how she is, okay? I'll be seeing you pretty much every day from now on."

Gary dropped his chin, dejected. "Yup. Thanks. Anything happening I need to know?"

Preston debated telling Gary about the Ritter woman, and decided against it. It might get his hopes up for nothing. He had to know more before he told Gary about another possible suspect. "There's hope. That's all I can say for right now," Preston said.

Gary grimaced, gave a flick of his hand in acknowledgement, clambered to his feet and didn't look back when the guard led him away.

PRESTON RETURNED TO his desk in the bustling office but couldn't concentrate. He dialed Cindy. "Hi, it's Preston."

Cindy's voice, unusually subdued, replied, "Yeah. I know. Did you see Dad? What's happening?"

"I just left him. He's okay, but not happy. I'm coming out there later. Maybe around five. Are you available to meet?"

"Sure. Same place?"

"Yup. See you there."

Preston's heart leaped as he hung up. He'd get to have dinner with her. Sit next to her. Watch her eat. He'd tell her about the second suspect. She needed the hope. She'd be able to keep it to herself and handle whatever transpired, he was sure. He couldn't wait to give her something to hold on to about her Dad's case. Feeling like a naughty boy, he remembered Frank's instructions not to let anything develop with someone involved in the case, but felt wanton and uncharacteristic disregard for Frank's words. He'd never really been a troublemaker or challenged authority. He'd hold Cindy in his arms again tonight and the hell with Frank.

He shoved stacks of folders into a rough pile on his desk and headed toward the shoplifter's address in west Anchorage. Her apartment complex was surrounded by such a crowded, muddled parking lot that Preston had a hard time finding unit K14. He finally found it at the top of three flights of exterior stairs with wooden railings and a rough plywood roof, all painted an ugly dark brown. There was no answer to his repeated knocks, so he tucked his card into the door just above the lock and turned to go.

As he looked down at the woods bordering the back of the building he was surprised to see a young moose dozing only ten feet from the bottom of the stairway. Preston was sure it hadn't been there when he arrived or he would have noticed such a large animal so close to the steps. He stood, awed. He hadn't heard a thing while he was up there. The moose must have just drifted in and lay down in the snowbank while he was knocking. He shook his head, wondering how a wild animal could wander in so silently and then relax in a congested area like this crowded complex.

He descended the stairway with quiet steps and tiptoed past the moose. All four legs were curled against its stomach and its head was tucked into a little mound of snow along its shoulder. It slept just like a puppy. Preston could see every coarse brown hair, the stomach rising and falling with every breath, even the veins in its eyelids. He detected a whiff of animal smell and wondered how many people had ever been close enough to a moose to smell it.

Chapter 23

PRESTON DROVE TOWARD Wasilla on the newly plowed roads, gaze drawn to the crackled, bare branches of the skinny tamarack trees that climbed toward bands of snow-flocked black spruce on the higher slopes of the Chugach mountain range. He marveled once again at the large gold highway signs informing drivers of the number of moose killed along the highway so far this year. How could it be in the hundreds? How could so many moose be hit on a freeway? He remembered his coworkers' tales of moose collisions that had totaled cars and even resulted in drivers' deaths. Alaska was truly the last frontier, a remarkable place. Preston stroked his new whiskers, his almost beard, and mussed his hand through his hair.

His phone vibrated in his pocket. He pulled it out and glanced at the screen. Area code 857. Boston. His parents were probably ready to scold him about his lack of contact. He jammed the phone back into his pocket, defiant. Right now wasn't the time to deal with them. But the anxiety that he'd been trying to stifle caused a lump to form in his stomach. It would be a difficult conversation. How could words explain how he felt about Alaska, and about a new woman in his life? So soon? They'd be disapproving, judgmental, upset. Maybe they'd even fly up as soon as they hung up the phone, determined to pull their only child back from what they'd perceive as the brink of disaster. He pounded the steering wheel.

His breathing accelerated at the thought of being with Cindy. The dashboard clock already read five. He feared Cindy might already be at the café. He'd be late. He pulled off at the next wide shoulder, rustled his phone out and dialed. "I'm on the road. I'll be a little late. I was caught getting out of Anchorage in rush hour - there was a backup by Merrill Field."

"Okay. I have plenty to do 'til then," Cindy answered.

When Preston hung up, he realized they hadn't needed to identify themselves. They knew each other's voices, a sure sign of a deepening relationship. He disregarded a flash of Frank's scowl and growled instructions. He fought off the thought of the words he knew he'd hear from his parents. He pressed the accelerator, eager to get to Cindy.

He spotted Cindy's hopeful face as soon as he entered the café, and slid into the booth beside her with unaccustomed boldness. Never had he felt such possessiveness. This recklessness was unlike him and he scooted over close enough to touch Cindy's thigh with his. She didn't move away. Impulsively, he leaned in and touched his lips to hers in greeting. Her lips were soft and warm, and met his firmly. She tasted good, minty and fresh.

He leaned back and smiled into her eyes. "Good to see you," he murmured.

"You, too", Cindy answered.

With the touching of their lips and those words, he recognized a new level to the relationship. Preston glanced at the closed menus that lay on the table, fighting sudden shyness. "Know what you want?" he asked.

When Cindy's face flushed, he grew embarrassed, too.

"From the menu… I mean," he stammered. Both burst into self-conscious laughs.

"Yes, I do," Cindy said, flashing daring eyes.

"I'll have the same," Preston played along.

Before long they were digging into salads while they waited for the spaghetti special. Preston filled Cindy in on every detail since they'd last been together. Her eyes grew wide with hope when he described Elizabeth Ritter's involvement. By the time they'd finished the meal, Cindy knew everything he did about the case. Preston wondered if sharing all the information was a breach of confidentiality, but he felt certain Cindy could keep it confidential.

"Hey, this is privileged information. It can't go anywhere, okay?"

"I understand," Cindy replied. Her sincerity evident. He trusted her completely.

While the waitress cleared away the plates, Preston stalled for time. "Did your boss get back? Did that all go okay?"

"Yup. He got back right on time. He was happy with the dog yard. He said I can take tomorrow off. I need to move some of my stuff up to Dad's cabin. It looks like I'll need to stay up there for a while."

Preston's heart quickened. "I'll help you. How about right now? Can we do it tonight instead of tomorrow since I'm already here?"

A flicker of surprise flashed across Cindy's face. "Well, I guess so. Are you sure? It might be late by the time we load up and then drive all the way up there and finish."

Preston had never felt more sure of anything. "Yes. I want to help. Let's go."

Chapter 24

WITH RISING EXCITEMENT, he carried armfuls of Cindy's clothing and belongings down the apartment steps to her car. His heart fluttered when he thought about getting to see where she'd be sleeping tonight. They put a few remaining boxes into the back seat of his car and pulled onto the Parks Highway. He followed Cindy's taillights with growing anticipation. He'd get to see where she grew up.

Cindy turned off the highway onto a narrow dirt driveway between skinny birch trees, their crackled branches a black maze against the darkening sky. There was the cabin, pretty much as he'd imagined. Unfinished gray siding showed the effects of years of exposure to the elements, a wooden front porch held a green plastic lawn chair, its seat filled with a mat of dead leaves. Small windows with chipped, flaking trim that had once been painted white bordered the aluminum front door and its torn screen. The yard, left to its natural state, displayed a patch of dirt where Gary obviously parked his truck. A dusting of snow covered the trampled path leading from there to the cabin door.

Daisy came bounding from beneath the porch when they pulled up and frolicked at Cindy's feet, twirling and nudging as close to her as he could get. Cindy patted her and crooned, "Hi, there, good girl. How's my Daisy?" The dog wiggled in delight, then took off to the edge of the woods, returning with a stick in her mouth. Cindy took it and tossed it across the yard. Daisy flew after it and bounded back for more.

They hauled Cindy's belongings into the cabin and it didn't take her long to tuck her things into the closet alongside her father's clothing in the lone small bedroom. She unpacked a few more things onto the unpainted wooden shelves along one wall, and turned to Preston, "Well, this is it. This is where I grew up."

Preston's heart went out to her. The place was so small. Where had she slept when she lived here? That sofa? He looked around, trying to hide his dismay. There was only one bedroom with a raggedy striped blanket for a door. Instead of cabinets, the kitchen had open wooden shelves holding a red plastic coffee can, a small green and white cardboard box labeled "lard" with torn waxed paper hanging out the open end, several cans of soup, two more of baked beans, and a mismatched assortment of plates, glasses and cups. Deep reddish rust stains blossomed beneath the faucet of the once white porcelain sink and black plumbing pipes hung in the opening beneath it. Salt and pepper containers sat next to a well-used cast iron frying pan on the small white stove shoved tight against a hulking refrigerator with "Philco" in tarnished chrome letters above the broken handle. A half loaf of bread sat atop the refrigerator along with several boxes of cereal and a crumpled doughnut box.

Preston turned to Cindy to find her watching him, waiting for his reaction. He was overcome with a fierce and astonishing desire for her. That she had survived this kind of a life and turned out to be so capable and lovable endeared her to him.

He took a few quick steps, reached out and drew her into his arms. "I like this place. It's so rustic and quaint. It's cool to see where you grew up." A second later, he realized she was crying. "Hey..."

"It's just, it's just..." Cindy began, and sucked in a wavering breath. "I feel like I should be ashamed of Dad's place. On the way here, I started to worry about what you'd think. But, but you said you like it. I..." she stammered through tears.

Preston pulled back and wiped away her tears. Feelings he had never felt before washed over him. With surprising strength, he lifted her into his arms and strode toward the bedroom. She clung to him, not resisting. When he bent to lay her on the bed, she reached up and drew him to her as if she didn't want to let go. He tumbled onto the bed beside her, stunned at his own actions, even more amazed at her response.

Their clothes had been kicked into a pile on the floor within minutes. Crazed with desire, Preston let his hands roam her hips, cup her satiny, plump breasts and the dip of her waist. He nibbled her earlobes, kissed her eyelids and nuzzled deep into her neck like he'd dreamed of doing. Cindy responded with quiet moans of pleasure while her hands gripped his back and pulled him tighter against her. He grew drunk with desire and her scent.

Suddenly, through his passion, he was jolted by a vision of Frank's face. And the words, "Cool it with her. Understand?" At the same time, Preston realized how vulnerable Cindy was right now. She was dealing with her Dad's problems, had been ashamed of what Preston would think of the cabin, and was juggling work and an apartment on her own.

Preston halted, rose up on his arms and thrust himself off to the side, throwing his arm over his eyes, breathing hard. He couldn't do this. Couldn't jeopardize Gary's case. Couldn't defy Frank. Couldn't take advantage of Cindy. He rolled off the bed and reached for his clothes.

"Preston?" Her words were tentative.

"I...I can't..." he stammered. Not able to look at her, he rose, grabbed his shirt and stuffed his arms into it. Cindy lay quietly while he finished dressing, the sheet pulled to her neck. He couldn't meet her eyes. Rolling away from her was the hardest thing he'd ever done.

He felt shaky and weak while he tied his boots. "I'm sorry," he managed, choking back the words he really wanted to say. He started through the doorway to get his jacket from the other room, hardly able to breathe.

"It's okay," Cindy said, her soft voice following him. Clutching the sheet around her shoulders, she followed him through the bedroom doorway. When Preston dared glance at her, she dropped her gaze to the floor, the rosy flush fading from her face while a pinched whiteness began at her eyes and quickly crept up her entire face.

"I have to go," Preston croaked, sick inside.

"I know." Cindy met his eyes. "It's a long drive back to Anchorage. It'll take least an hour. Maybe more. The Glenn Highway in from the valley is terrible after dark." Her words came too fast. She twisted the corners of the sheet she clutched in her hands and stared back down at the floor.

Will you...can we...tomorrow... ?" Preston stammered, overcome by shame, guilt, and embarrassment. He should tell her why, but words wouldn't come. "Tomorrow?" he finally managed.

Cindy's voice held a hint of coolness he'd never heard. Her chin rose. "I have the day off. I need to stay here and settle in tonight. But I do plan to drive in and see Dad tomorrow."

"So you'll be in town?" Preston asked. Good. He could see her. Maybe he'd figure out by then what words he could use to explain. "Will you call me when you're on your way? My court case is at one o'clock so I should be free by mid-afternoon. Can we meet at the jail and talk to your dad together? " He felt breathless with the need to be sure he could see her again as soon as possible. He'd be able to tell her then why this had happened.

Cindy replied. "I'll be at the jail by three. And thank you very much for helping me bring my things out here." Her voice now held a touch of formality, almost as if she was talking to a stranger.

"You're welcome. See you later," he said and forced himself to walk out to his car.

The crisp, piercing air held the raw aroma of woods, mountains, and earth. He engaged the Jeep's four wheel drive and backed out through a new, wind-driven berm of snow that nearly reached the top of his tires. He felt protective and powerful as he drove back and forth through the drift so Cindy would have an easier time of getting through it with her car.

Large flakes of snow had begun to drift lazily onto the windshield, making the wipers necessary by the time he reached the freeway. He drove back toward Anchorage through the cottony darkness, missing her terribly, feeling empty without her.

His pulse quickened at the memory of Cindy's warm breasts pressed into his chest and how her body fit so perfectly with his. He swallowed hard to calm himself and shook his head. The familiar feel of the steering wheel in his hands helped bring him back to reality and he had to concentrate as vehicles sped around him in the darkness, splashing dirty slush high behind their rear wheels. The radio was on, but it was impossible to focus on what the voices were saying. All he could think about was how it felt to lay with Cindy naked beneath him. He worried how he'd be able to explain why this had happened like it did. It was his fault.

His bed felt cold and empty when he finally reached his apartment. His sleep was fitful.

Chapter 25

"HEY MILLS." THE words startled him as he stepped off the elevator.

"Hey, Mark. Hey. How's it going?" he answered, jolted to reality by his colleague.

"Busy." Mark replied. "Are you coming to the bar with us again tomorrow night?"

"Sure," Preston answered without thinking.

"How's the murder case going? I heard your client's locked up, isn't he?"

"Yeah. It's been tough going. I'm pretty sure the wrong man's being held. We had him out on bail and he blew it. It's been kind of consuming me. Then there's all my other cases, so I'm keeping busy, too, to say the least," Preston answered. "How about you?"

"I have a tough one, too. A child in need case. It's pretty nasty. The mother has no resources at all and the ex-husband's a hostile son of a bitch. I have a bunch of other routine ones, too. The usual too many." He glanced toward his desk. "Hey, I better go. My phone's blinking. See you tomorrow night?"

"Sure."

Preston spent the morning doing paperwork, forcing his mind off last night. He dreaded facing Frank this morning and fought growing resentment at having to restrict his feelings for the woman who'd so completely captivated him. The woman who needed him, who set him on fire.

He appeared before the magistrate to defend the shoplifting charge against a weary young woman who showed up at the last minute in her black and white waitress uniform. Preston had talked to her only once by phone since she told him she worked two jobs and couldn't afford to take time off work to meet with him. With a paralyzed husband in a wheelchair and two young children at home, the woman barely scraped by in life. Her misdemeanor had been the theft of a bottle of children's vitamins from the midtown Walmart. She'd been unable to provide any motive or excuse other than saying she just didn't have the extra eighteen dollars and needed to get her kids their vitamins. Preston knew the store had a reputation for prosecuting even the smallest shoplifting incidents. He foolishly considered telling the woman to steal from somewhere else next time. At the thought, he marveled at the recklessness that had taken a weird hold on him since being in Alaska.

That state of mind still had a hold on him while he argued the woman's misdemeanor defense before the judge. Preston surprised himself with an impassioned speech about the challenges faced by families who have to struggle through extraordinary hardship. To his delight, the judge empathized and let the woman off with only a stern warning.

The woman turned to Preston when they reached the corridor outside the courtroom. "Thank you. Thank you so much! I couldn't have handled a fine or more time away from work and the kids and John. You did good!" She gave him an impulsive, awkward hug and turned to walk away.

"Wait," Preston said. "Here." He dug out his wallet and thrust a fifty dollar bill at her. "Buy the vitamins. And some for yourself, too."

The woman's face reddened. "Oh, no. I couldn't," she protested weakly, never taking her eyes off the bill in Preston's hand.

"I insist. Take it," Preston ordered.

She grabbed it and with a grateful, embarrassed smile hurried away down the sidewalk, apron ties dancing behind her. Preston turned to walk back to the office, his heart light.

He pulled his phone from his pocket when it chimed, not bothering to look at the incoming number. "Preston Mills here," he answered.

"Preston?" The velvety, refined, familiar voice stopped him in his tracks. Victoria. He managed to take a few steps across the sidewalk and lean against a building, breath caught in his throat.

"Victoria," he managed. "Ahh… I'm surprised to hear from you."

"I saw your mother at the club yesterday. She said you might like a call from me before I leave. She told you I'm going overseas?" Her words were hurried, as if rehearsed, layered with a hint of hesitation and caution he'd never heard in her voice before.

Memories flooded. His knees grew weak. Beautiful, blond, cool Victoria. A pang of homesickness shot through him. A voice from home. Visions of her in his bed. Coordinated sweaters and skirts, formal dresses in pastel colors, her long, lean legs and clean, citrusy scent. The wide, oak-lined avenues of their neighborhoods.

"Preston?" she asked into the silence. "Are you there?"

"Yes. I'm here. Mom did say something about you going abroad. Uganda is it?"

Another awkward, too long silence. Cindy's face intruded. His warm and real Cindy. Her long tumbled curls against the pillow, the ways his hands fit perfectly around her hips, the way she'd panted beneath him. How much she needed him, how much she gave back to him, how much he had to explain to her.

He stood up straight and raised his chin. "It's nice to hear from you. Good luck with your trip. I admire that. It should be quite an adventure." Preston felt distanced from her, from that world. After last night, he had no doubt that his heart belonged completely to Cindy and Alaska. Victoria was a part of the past.

He could hear the hurt and curiosity in her response. "Preston, are you all right? Your parents asked me to call. They haven't heard from you." She waited. Expectant. Willing him from afar to explain, to be more courteous, to revive a spark of what they'd had.

"Can I call you back?" Preston asked, shaken. "I'm right in the middle of something. I'll get back to you within the next few days, okay?"

"Well, all right, then," she answered, her voice again hesitant. "We do need to talk some more."

Preston clicked his phone shut and strode toward the office. He felt a flicker of trepidation when he realized Victoria would undoubtedly report the conversation to his parents and they'd probably call, expecting an explanation. And he'd agreed to call her back. He shook off the thoughts and opened the door to his building.

Chapter 26

GARY COULDN'T HIDE his resentment at having to wake to the clamor of his fellow inmates even before weak morning light managed to penetrate the prison corridors. It was so damn hard to get to sleep at night and every morning the din started before dawn. His cellmate bumped clumsily down from the top bunk and tried to start a conversation.

"Shut the hell up. Leave me alone," Gary grumbled, despising this place. He hated smelling everybody's farts and hearing them cough and spit and belch and holler and bang on their bars. He'd go crazy if he didn't get some peace and quiet. He hated the smells and the unceasing noise and being crammed in a cage like an animal. Now he had to stand in line to get some cold pancakes and warm milk in a little carton like a school kid. He longed for a mushroom and reindeer omelet from the café and a good strong hot cup of coffee in a real mug.

With a sigh of despair, Gary pulled his jumpsuit on, jammed his feet into the plastic shoes and stood waiting for his cell door to be opened for the chow line. He worried. What if they convicted him? It was a murder rap. He could be stuck here the rest of his life. And what in hell was that lawyer doing? Did he even care? He was so young. Gary fumed. *He just wants to ball my daughter I saw how he looks at her. I gotta get outa here. I gotta get home. Daisy's missing me, wondering where I am. This ain't right. I shouldn't be here. I'm gonna ask to make a call to that lawyer today. What's that guy doin' for me, anyway?*

Enraged, miserable, he shook the bars in frustration and waited to be fed, feeling like an animal. He bent his head, swallowed back the tightness in his throat and pinched his cheeks to block tears that threatened to slide down his cheeks.

"Let me outta here. Let me go home. Please, God, let me go home," he muttered.

NICK ARRIVED HOME just in time for dinner, still troubled by the case. Seldom had he been so affected by one as he was by this Williams murder. Jennifer Williams' husband wasn't having a family meal like this tonight. Dan Williams would have to put his son to bed and face quiet hours alone in the house, maybe do a load of laundry, clean up dishes in the kitchen sink, toss the pizza boxes, pick up toys and socks. Then he'd have to force himself to go to the cold empty bed where his wife used to lay next to him. Nick shuddered a little at the thought. Kay met his eyes. He gave her a small, secret grin of love. She smiled her acknowledgement.

Sleepless while the light of a bright half-moon spread its glow across the silvery mountaintops, Nick rolled out of bed and stepped to the window. Not long ago, on a night just like this, Jennifer Williams had been found. It had been too long now without real progress. Tomorrow he'd spend all day on the case. It was time to move it along.

NICK WAITED WITH Andy and Natalie at the bus stop until they boarded the bus in the morning, then hurried to his car for the drive to the station. He hustled through the lobby with only a brief nod for the receptionist, anxious to get to his desk.

"Matt," he barked across the room while tossing his coat on a chair. "What do we have on the Williams case?"

Matt looked up from his desk. "Ah, nothing much new." He turned puzzled eyes to Nick. "Something happen? What's up?"

"Nothing's up. That's the problem. Nothing's happened. That poor sucker LaVassar is sitting in a cell, maybe for something he didn't do. I'm having doubts. If he was just a good Samaritan, he's paying a damn heavy price." Nick flopped the LaVassar file open across his desk. "We have to focus on this. Somebody out there knows something. We can't just let it lay. What about the coroner? He should have something by now."

"Yeah," Matt pushed aside the paper he'd been working on. "Here's what I have. A report came in from the coroner yesterday. There was nothing unusual he could identify in her system. He did find part of a smudged bloody fingerprint next to her lip.

They're trying to match it right now. They're looking at LaVassar's fingerprint records as we speak."

"No shit? A fingerprint?" Nick asked.

Matt nodded. "Yeah."

"Did you hear if that public defender, Mills, is it, actually had an investigator go see the Ritter woman?"

"I don't know." Matt scowled. "I'm not calling him begging for information. We'll get it through channels. His client's a fool. Driving under the influence the very day he got out. Lying to us. Now a possible fingerprint. He got turned down for bail, I see."

"I feel kinda bad for the guy," Nick answered. "But there's nothing we can do until we get something else. Should we try to find out more about that Ritter woman?"

Matt grunted. "I don't think she's the one. But we do need a formal meeting with her just to get it on record. Should I set it up?"

"Sure," Nick answered. "And Dr. Williams. What about him? We haven't heard a word from him. Not a word since he was here that day after the funeral. What's up with him?"

Silence followed his words, while both realized how strange that was. Following a murder, the victim's next of kin invariably called daily, held media interviews, and often went on rampages for information and progress. Why wasn't Dan Williams in contact? Did he simply believe LaVassar was the murderer? Why hadn't there been the usual agonized demands for information from the victim's family? Williams' silence was disturbing. Nick's uneasiness about LaVassar's guilt went up another notch.

"I don't think Williams is a suspect," Matt said. "He's devastated. Seems really broken up. Just a regular guy. I thought we discounted him right away."

"Well, we better take a good look at him," Nick stated, his voice firm. "Cover our asses. I need to find out why there's been no contact from him. That's not normal. You think he's back at work?"

"Maybe," Matt answered. "His office is just south of town. It's out past the lake on the highway. Big sign, Williams, D.D.S. There's a red and white State Farm logo on the same building, too."

Feeling more uneasy than ever after the conversation, Nick decided to make another trip out to the scene. Maybe the wind had blown hard enough to turn something up. Maybe a clue would come to him if he just sat out there and thought. Maybe they should talk to LaVassar again, too. He couldn't put a man away on a murder rap unless he was sure.

"I'm gonna check out the scene one more time." He picked up his jacket. "We better get a call in to Elizabeth Ritter, too. Let her know she has to come in and talk to us. Let the boss in on this, too."

Nick drove his cruiser toward Knik Goose Bay Road. He had to stomp the brakes when a mother moose with twin yearling calves trailing behind stepped out from the ditch to the right. They high-stepped in single file across in front of him and he imagined telling the kids about it at supper. He continued, driving more cautiously now. Moose were always on the move this time of year, coming down from the higher mountain meadows to yard up.

He slowed, expecting the crime scene to be easy to spot if the yellow tape was still hanging from the trees. Just then a shred of yellow caught his eye.

He pulled onto the shoulder, opened the car door, and drew in deep, refreshing breaths of glacial air. *I bet LaVassar really misses this. He lives right up here and now he's sitting in a cell in Anchorage. If he didn't do it, this is a helluva bad deal for him. I bet he wishes he'd never stopped that night.*

Nick stepped from the car and tramped down through the ditch into the surrounding woods. He walked slowly, kicking leaves, scuffing dirt, head bent, searching for the slightest thing that looked out of place. He knew the search crew with dogs had spent at least a day doing just this. But you never knew.

He took a quick glance at the deserted highway, then stepped behind a huge cottonwood tree to relieve himself. While zipping up, he tipped his head skyward and was puzzled to see what looked like a bundle tied to the tree trunk about ten feet above his head. *What the hell is that?*

He grabbed a fallen spruce branch from the ground and poked at the bundle. At his prodding, something white slipped a few inches out. He dropped the branch. A white sock protruded from the bundle. When Nick realized what he'd just found, he sprinted to his car, and snatched the radio hand piece.

An hour later, that section of the highway had been cordoned off and the area was swarming with law enforcement vehicles and personnel. Nick watched as the bundle was removed from the tree and slipped into a clear plastic evidence bag. He couldn't believe what he'd discovered. And while taking a piss at that. That part he kept to himself – it was nothing an officer of the law should be doing.

He drove back to the office as soon as he was no longer needed, mind racing. Maybe this would provide new evidence and that poor sucker LaVassar would get out of jail. He'd been feeling more and more like LaVassar wasn't the perp. Felt it in his gut. He couldn't wait to tell Matt about the find. And Kay. Maybe he could finally get some sleep tonight. It was apparent that somebody undressed Jennifer Williams right there that night. *How come we never thought to look up when we were searching?*

Chapter 27

PRESTON'S FIRST REACTION to the news about the clothing bundle was a desperate need to tell Cindy. He left a message on her voice mail. "Call me. News about the case. Call as soon as you can." He didn't need to leave his name or number. She'd know.

He ran to his car, having a hard time keeping to the speed limit on the way to the jail.

"LaVassar," he practically shouted at the desk clerk. "Bring him out. I'm his attorney. I need to see him right away." He paced the tiny meeting room until Gary was escorted in, handcuffed and shuffling through leg chains.

Jesus. Why do they have to do that to him? He shook off his disgust and motioned Gary to sit down across from him. A flash of curiosity chased the glumness from Gary's face when he noticed the grin Preston couldn't keep off his face.

"I have good news," Preston announced the moment the guard backed away and Gary sat down. "There's been a break in the case. They found a bundle of the victim's clothes tied way up in a tree right there at the scene. A trooper found 'em today. He was just wandering around out there and spotted something." He paused to catch his breath.

"Are there fingerprints?" Gary asked, leaning forward across the table, hope shining from his eyes.

"We don't know yet. We don't have lab results yet. But I wanted to tell you. If there is, you're off the hook, right?"

Gary's chair clattered to the floor as he jumped up. The guard took a quick step toward him in alarm, then stopped in confusion when he noticed the men's excited demeanors. Preston gave a reassuring wave to the guard.

Gary's voice rose. "Yes! God, I hope there's prints or something. I wanna go home so bad. I can't stand it. Maybe I'll get out!" His face shone with relief and hope.

At this reaction, Preston no longer had the slightest doubt about Gary's innocence. It was obvious the man had confidence that prints or any other clue or DNA from today's find would exonerate him. His response to this news proved to Preston that Gary had no fear of whatever the bundle would provide in the way of evidence. *I have to get him out of here, He's innocent. He doesn't deserve to be in here.*

"I'll call Cindy right away," he assured Gary.

NICK RUSHED THROUGH his paperwork and hurried home to Kay. "We got something on the murder case," he called as soon as he entered the kitchen.

Kay looked up from the sink, dropped the carrot from her hand, and rushed to him. Her wet hands covered his cheeks as she pulled his face to her and kissed him soundly on the lips. "I'm so glad, Sweetheart," she crooned. "Oh, Baby, now maybe you can sleep tonight."

Nick sighed. *She knows I haven't been sleeping. I didn't know she was that aware in the night. And she just kept it to herself until I was ready to talk about it. I'm so lucky to have her. I love her so damn much.*

"Kids get off the bus in about a half hour, right?" he asked with a gleam in his eye.

Kay nodded and turned back to the sink. "We're having tater tot casserole and candied carrots. I'm just putting the casserole in the oven and getting the carrots on."

She gave a yelp of surprise when Nick stole up behind her and molded himself against her, pushing firmly against her. Without a word, she dropped the peeler into the sink, turned, and snuggled herself back at him, wrapping her arms around his neck. "Mmmmm," she whispered. "What's up?"

"You know what's up," Nick grinned, pushing his wife back against the counter.

"God, I love you," Nick murmured.

"Me you more," Kay answered with a smile, beginning to unbutton her blouse.

By the time Andy and Natalie flew in the door, coats flapping, backpacks thudding onto the entry floor, their mother, cheeks still flushed, was setting plates on the table and their dad was paying bills in the den.

Chapter 28

THE MINUTES DRAGGED for Preston while he waited for Cindy to arrive at the jail. She'd given a squeak of delight at the news of the discovery of the bundle of clothing and left work early to rush into Anchorage, eager to rejoice in the good news with her dad. By the time visiting hours would be over at six, they'd need to eat. And he'd have the chance to explain about last night.

When Cindy rushed in breathless, anxious to see Gary, Preston escorted her into the visitors' room after a quick touch to her shoulder. Cindy hardly seemed to notice, but Preston savored the sweetness of her breath. His heart quickened.

It was great to watch Cindy and Gary discuss the possibility of his release. Lab results would certainly reveal he had no connection to the clothing found in the tree. Neither took much notice of Preston while they talked, but he didn't mind. He loved the way they interacted with quick sentences and eager words. It was obvious they loved each other and he felt happy to be the bearer of good news and to be with them. Their chatter about Gary's release warmed his heart. When the buzzer sounded to end visiting hours, Gary strode away with newfound confidence and hope in his step.

Cindy turned to Preston. "Thank you, Preston." Her words were clipped, almost cold. She slipped her arms into her jacket and turned away from him toward the door.

Preston's heart hammered. "But dinner. How about some dinner?" he managed to croak.

"No, thanks" Cindy answered, turning further toward the door.. "I have a long drive and I have to be at work first thing in the morning. And Daisy."

"Please," Preston begged. "Just dinner. You have to eat. I want to talk to you."

Cindy gave a reluctant shrug. "Okay, then." She avoided his eyes.

Ten minutes later, they were seated at an Italian restaurant. Hungry, thirsty, agitated, Preston quickly ordered red wine and a basket of garlic bread, desperate for the distraction of food. At last, he had Cindy sitting across from him for an intimate dinner. Finally, he could explain. She looked gorgeous, her eyes sparkling in the candlelight. The soft mounds of her chest tormented him. His thoughts tumbled.

"What?" he answered to Cindy's curious voice. "Pardon?"

Eyebrows drawn together in puzzlement, she repeated, "I asked when you think Dad might get released." Her words held an odd and distant tone.

Preston had to draw a deep breath before he could speak in a normal voice. "Oh, sorry. I don't know what to expect about timing on a possible release. I'll talk to my boss in the morning and find out how it goes when something like this happens."

"Sure. Okay." Again her words lacked warmth.

"Cindy, I want to talk to you..." Preston began. "I want to ..."

"No. Don't." Cindy's words were harsh. "If you bring up last night, I'll walk out of here. Right this minute. I mean it." Her eyes blazed and her chin lifted. "Just leave it alone."

Preston gulped. This was a new side of Cindy. There was no doubt she meant what she said. He couldn't let her walk out. He swallowed hard. "Okay."

The meal was over quickly, with only spurts of awkward small talk to pass the time. He walked her to her car in the frosty night. She slipped in without touching him, pulled the door shut, and drove away without a backward glance.

Preston stood in the parking lot, unable to move. His heart actually hurt. He bent over for a moment, easing the pain. While he drove home, agonized, through the complete blackness of the mountain roads, Preston realized he was experiencing the famed darkness of Alaskan winters. His low spirits matched it.

GARY AWOKE AFTER the first solid night's sleep he'd had since being put in his cell a month ago. He stretched, and slipped his feet to the cold floor, and muttered, "Thank God they found those clothes in the tree. It felt damn good to finally be able to sleep like this. Now I can get back to my life."

He stepped into the hated jumpsuit and pulled it up his thighs, thoughts tumbling. *Can't wait to wear real clothes again. And see Daisy. She's gotta be wondering where the hell I've been. Now Cindy can go back to her apartment. I'll get my job back and be getting more union hours so I can keep my benefits and pension. They might have the foundation laid at the hospital by now, and we can start on moving dirt for the parking lot.*

He ate heartily at breakfast since the cold scrambled eggs actually tasted okay this morning. Even the orange juice, thin as it was, had good flavor this time. Feeling hope and enthusiasm for the first time in many weeks, his spirits remained high even as he reported to the laundry room for his day's duties. Finally, he would get outa this hell hole and be able to go home.

Chapter 29

PRESTON'S SPIRITS REMAINED low as he arrived at the office ready to dig into his work for the day despite his troubled, nearly sleepless night. He had to get this case over with. Had to get Gary out, fix things and be able to be with Cindy.

First was a stop at Frank's office, where he entered at his boss' wave.

"We got a break in the Wasilla case yesterday. Did you hear?"

Frank shook his head, and Preston explained the discovery of the bundle of clothing in the tree.

Franks' eyes lit up. "Good," he answered. "We needed progress. The national media's starting to nose around. They're still calling it '*Wasilla's Frozen Lady.*' The tabloids are nosing around now, too."

Before he could say more, Preston interjected, "So can we get LaVassar out? How do we do it? How soon?"

Frank looked at him, brows lifted in surprise. "Hold on. He's still the primary suspect. The prosecutor's not gonna let him off just like that. The judicial officer already imposed conditions of release and they're inviolate. We can't get him out so easily this time. Maybe not at all. We'll need results from the lab on those clothes before anything happens. And the report on that bloody fingerprint by her lip isn't back yet. Could be a week or so, even if something new develops or this evidence shows it was someone else. Takes a while to get evidence examined and the reports filed. Then, getting a prisoner released takes a few days, too. Better not jump the gun here."

Preston's heart sank at these words. Not yet? Not right away? How could they continue to hold Gary? "But," Preston began, "if the results come in and eliminate him, can't LaVassar get out?"

"No, it doesn't mean he'll be released immediately. He's been arraigned. There are steps that need to be taken. It'll be a while. "

Seeing Preston's face, he softened. "Okay. Okay, I'll call O'Brien this morning. See what I can do. You really believe that the LaVassar guy's innocent don't you?"

"Completely," Preston answered. "He didn't do it. I'm sure of it. The guy doesn't deserve to be in jail. And he's having a pretty hard time."

"All right, then," Frank answered. "I'll call O'Brien and see what we can set in motion for immediate release when the evidence clears him. Meanwhile, keep on it. That bunch of clothes doesn't mean the case is solved. Even if we get prints or a strong clue, there's work to do. Lots of it." He shrugged. "Go to it. Keep on it. We don't have enough yet."

Preston left Frank's office dreading what he had to do next. He snatched the pile of messages and faxes from his inbox and glanced through them, but couldn't concentrate. He had to go see Gary.

Gary took the news about not being released right away hard. As soon as he realized what Preston was telling him, he ordered, "Tell Cindy to move back to her apartment right away. I can't have her doing that drive every morning and night this time of year. And keeping the fire going is too much for her. It's too dark and dangerous when I'm not there to keep the driveway plowed out. That highway gets damn icy before the plows get to it. I don't want her on it every day. Have her beg her boss to let her keep Daisy at the kennel."

"Ah, Gary. One more thing." Preston hesitated. "They just discovered a bloody partial print next to the victim's mouth. You didn't touch her, did you?"

Gary's face paled. "Oh, shit. I wiped her lip off...aw, crap. I'll never get out." He turned away abruptly and signaled the guard to unlock the door. Without another word, he left the room, back rigid.

Preston shook his head, sighing. He couldn't bear the thought of telling Cindy all this over the phone. He walked back to the office oblivious of the wind that clawed at his bare head and hands. Dejected, he opened the folders on his desk and tried to concentrate on the paperwork required to keep his other cases going. The day dragged. He worked through lunch without feeling hunger. When the clock finally read four, he could go. He hurried to his car through a blustery wind, hardly feeling the tiny pellets of stinging sleet that pecked at his face. He had to see

171

Cindy and catch her before she started the drive to the cabin. He dialed her number with trembling fingers, dreading what he had to say.

He felt a flash of panic when she answered. "Hey, it's me. Will you still be at work if I get there in an hour or so? I need to see you."

With a trace of curiosity in her frosty tone, Cindy answered, "I'll still be here by five. Come to the kennel, please."

"I'll be there as soon as I can. I'm leaving Anchorage now."

"Is everything all right?" Cindy asked, her words now laden with worry. But Preston swiped his phone shut as if he hadn't heard.

He drove, distracted and unmindful of the sleet battering his windshield and coating the highway with freezing grey sludge. He pulled up to the kennel an hour later, still not knowing what words he would use.

Cindy hurried through the snow to meet him, cheeks rosy with cold, her colorful wool hat cocked a bit to the side with the tassels hanging unevenly. "What's wrong?" she asked as she approached the driver's window, brows knit in an anxious face.

"Hi. Get in," Preston answered, pointing to the passenger side. Cindy slipped in, bringing a burst of cold air, pulled her thick knitted mittens off and turned to him, curiosity playing across her features.

As soon as she slammed the door, Preston reached for her, but she slid out of his reach. "What is it?" she asked, her voice as frigid as the frost on the windows.

"Your Dad won't be getting out right away." His voice caught on the next words. "My boss says it'll take time to get all the legalities taken care of. And that's only if the prosecution agrees. There's a chance they won't if another suspect isn't already in custody. Public opinion..." Preston trailed off at her expression. "And they just found a fingerprint by the victim's lip. Your Dad just told me he forgot that he wiped a bit of blood off her lip that night."

Cindy's face contorted, her eyes filled and she twisted away toward her door. Preston knew he better tell her everything right away. "And your Dad wants you to move back to your apartment right now. He said to see if you can keep Daisy here at the kennel."

"How's he doing?" Cindy asked, voice breaking.

Preston watched as she gathered herself. "Not very well," he answered.

"I'm not going to move back. I'll stay at the cabin as long as I need to. I need to keep it going for when he gets out." Cindy retorted. She finally looked at him, blinked away her tears and tipped her chin up.

Preston could see determination blazing in her eyes and in the set of her shoulders. She was so tough. Most women would just fall apart at news like this. But she was ready to keep fighting.

Preston leaned against the driver's window and took a deep breath. "Well, you can stay if that's what you decide. But, maybe you should think about how this is the only thing your Dad can control right now, under the circumstances. If he'd feel better that you're not way up there at the cabin alone and driving back and forth every day, maybe you should consider his wishes. At least he'd know you're listening to him. He wouldn't worry so much about you if you're in town close to work. And it wouldn't be such a long drive every time you need to go into Anchorage, either."

A flash of uncertainty crossed Cindy's face.

"I'll help you move back tonight. You can't do it all yourself. Let me help, please." Preston added, sensing a lessening of her resistance. "We'll go right now and get it done. Then tomorrow you can tell him. At least it'll be something to pick him up a little." He waited.

Cindy gave a slight nod. "Well, okay then. I suppose you're right."

"Let's go then," Preston said. "Let's get it done." He reached for the ignition key.

It was midnight by the time they finished carrying Cindy's belongings back up the steps of her apartment building. They'd worked silently and quickly at the cabin, awkward with each other, being careful not to touch. They finished by loading a puzzled Daisy into Preston's car for the ride back to Wasilla.

While they unloaded, Daisy skittered from one end of Cindy's small apartment to another, exploring, sniffing, and twirling at their feet. She finally squatted on the rug inside the front door and whizzed.

"Oh no!" Cindy yelped. "No!" She scurried for a rag.

Daisy hung her head and slunk off to the farthest corner of the living room. After tossing the rug into her shower, Cindy began a frenzied scrubbing of the tile. Preston watched until she abruptly stopped moving the rag and sank onto the floor into a dejected heap. When her shoulders began to shudder and he heard small sobs, he knew the situation had finally caught up with her.

He crouched down beside her and pulled her into his arms. "Hey, it's going to be all right," he murmured.

"No, it isn't," she cried with a furious twist away from him. "No, it won't be all right. I can't keep Daisy here. It says in the lease that pets aren't allowed. And Bob doesn't have room for any more dogs at the kennel. It's full. Anyway, Daisy couldn't spend winter days tied up with the sled dogs outside. It would be way too cold for her and she's too old."

Cindy hiccupped and wiped a sleeve across her face. "Even if Bob says I could keep her at work, there's no place where she can be warm and safe. And I'd have to leave her alone there overnight. It won't work."

Cindy turned to him, tears flooding her cheeks now. "And Daddy. He was so happy to be getting out. Now he can't!" she wailed.

"Hey, it's gonna be all right." Preston helped her to her feet. "We'll get your dad out. Remember the bundle of clothing? That could be the new lead. The troopers are working hard on this. So is an investigator. And so am I. We're interviewing the Ritter woman again tomorrow. And I think we should be looking at the husband again, too. I'll get your Dad out as soon as possible, I promise."

Cindy leaned toward him and finally made tentative eye contact. "What about Daisy?"

"She's coming home with me," Preston answered, surprising himself. "My landlady has two dogs of her own. She said I could have one, too. So I guess I have a dog until we get your Dad out."

Cindy drew back, eyes wide with hope and surprise. "You'd take Daisy?"

"Sure. No problem." Preston gave a shrug, hoping to hide how astounded he was at himself. He'd never had a dog and didn't have any idea how to take care of one. But, at the relief that shone from Cindy's eyes, he vowed to figure it out.

He loaded Daisy into his Jeep and left quickly, sensing this was no time to confront Cindy about personal issues. She had all she could handle without him pushing her to understand anything else right now. There'd be time, and he'd make it soon. At least, she'd seemed happy about him taking Daisy. At least he was able to maintain this much of a connection for now.

On the dark freeway back to Anchorage, a delighted Daisy sat upright in the passenger seat, nose pressed to the glass. The open bag of dog food behind the driver's seat gave the Jeep an unfamiliar odor. Preston rubbed the whiskers on his chin and marveled at how Alaskan this all felt. Despite how uncomfortable he and Cindy had been with each other, it had felt good to be with her.

Chapter 30

HIS PHONE CHIMED just as he was unlocking the apartment door. He shooed Daisy inside and wrestled it from his pocket. A familiar "Hellooooo," greeted him.

"Hi, Mom," he managed. "I was just walking in the door. Can I call you right back?"

"Sure, Dear. We'll wait here by the phone."

Preston dropped his jacket and briefcase on a chair, filled a bowl with water and set it on the floor. Daisy began lapping immediately, drips slopping from her lips onto the tile. Preston winced, then smiled at the friendly dog that seemed to be adapting at once to her new surroundings.

He took a deep breath. His parents. Great. Just great. Better get it over with. He punched in their number.

"Well, how's it going? Victoria said she'd talked to you. What's been going on?" his father boomed.

"Fine, Dad. The big murder case is consuming me and I have quite a few other ones, too. I'm keeping busy and I really like my apartment..."

Just then Daisy gave a loud woof and scrambled against Preston's knees.

"What was that?" His mother's voice. "What was that funny noise?"

"It's a dog, Mom. I'm taking care of someone's dog." Preston's breath came hard.

"A dog, son? Whose dog?" His father's voice cut in.

"Oh, a friend's. I just brought it home today," Preston answered, heart now racing. Why couldn't he tell them it belonged to his client? A murder suspect? Why hadn't he told them about Cindy yet? Because their first questions would be about her family, her education, her job, and how he met her. Their reaction to his interest in a woman with a mother who had abandoned her, an incarcerated father, a six month veterinary technician certificate, an occupation as a sled dog handler, and a childhood in a remote cabin could very well result in them landing at the Anchorage airport tomorrow.

He tried to change the subject. "Well, what's new there?"

"Nothing much," his father's voice was curt. "Anything else going on, Son?" Gordon had an uncanny knack for knowing when Preston wasn't being forthcoming. And it was apparent that this call was really to ask him about Victoria. They'd heard about his reaction to her call and were waiting for him to bring it up.

Preston spoke into the uneasy silence, "Everything's fine. I told Victoria I'd call her back and I will. I better go and get the dog taken care of. I'll be sure to call next week, okay?"

His mother's voice was voice too bright. "All right, Son. Call if you need anything. Are you eating enough? Will you be home for Thanksgiving? I'm going to make that special cornbread dressing like always. Let us know your flight time when you get it...and, well, Victoria will still be here. She doesn't leave now until December..." Her voice faltered.

Heat rose to his face at the subtle pressure. "I doubt it about Thanksgiving, Mom. There's so much happening here. I'll talk to you next week, okay? Bye, Dad." He swiped his phone shut in annoyance.

It buzzed again immediately. "Preston, this is your father. You don't hang up on your mother."

"I didn't."

"Well, it seemed like it to us. What's going on there? We expected you to be making plans to come home by now, with this Alaska thing out of your system. I'm not willing to hold a position in the firm for you indefinitely, you know."

Defiance roared in Preston's ears. "Then don't."

Gordon's voice dripped with disdain. "I can't believe my son is talking to me like this." The phone went dead.

Preston slammed his phone shut and whipped it onto the sofa. He stomped to the kitchen, grabbed a beer from the refrigerator, pulled the tab, and gulped it down. Daisy watched, ears cocked, eyes questioning.

Relaxing a bit when she nuzzled against his leg, he reached down and patted her soft head.

Chapter 31

PRESTON'S FEET DROPPED onto something warm and furry when he slid out of bed the next morning. Daisy looked up serenely, took her time moving out of his way, then lifted her hind end into an arc and stretched out as long as she could. She gave a leisurely yawn. Preston smiled. It was kind of cool to have a dog.

He'd been surprised at how easily Daisy adapted to his place last night. He'd let her out for a few minutes, and she returned promptly after doing her business. She'd roamed the rooms, then settled with a heavy sigh on the throw rug by the front door, falling asleep within minutes. He hadn't even heard her come into the bedroom during the night.

Preston opened the front door; Daisy dashed out, squatted in the brush across the driveway, and rushed back to the door. He scooted out to the car for the forgotten bag of dog food, but it was frozen into rock-hard pellets, so he set a bowl of water on the floor by the kitchen sink and held a piece of bread down to her. She lipped it from his hand, gobbled it down and looked inquiringly for more. He gave her another piece. That would have to do for now. Her food would be thawed by the time he got home. Maybe he'd have to come home early to let her out.

Daisy nuzzled against his knee while he put his jacket on and he reached down to give her head a friendly pat. "You be good now. I'll be back before you know it." He escaped, surprised at the longing to go along he read in her eyes. Maybe he'd take her for a walk when he got home. Let her get out and run a little, spend some time with her.

His thoughts turned to the day ahead. *What had happened with the clothing bundle? What the investigator had been doing? And what was up with the Ritter woman by now? It was time to focus on the part Dan Williams might have played.* Charged up, ignoring anxiety about the bloody fingerprint, and determined to accomplish something for Gary, Preston hurried to the office.

Before he'd been at his desk checking his in box more than a few minutes, Frank stopped by and announced, "Hey, Mills. I talked to O'Brien late yesterday. They won't budge on releasing the suspect in the Williams case. Feel they better keep him in custody to minimize public outcry. So until something else breaks, he stays. Sorry."

Preston nodded acknowledgement. "Okay. Thanks. But I'm going to keep working on getting him out quickly. I have to tell you – they just found a bloody fingerprint next to the victim's mouth. LaVassar said he wiped away a bit of blood and forgot to tell us."

"Jesus. That guy's his own worst enemy. Don't do anything about it until we're forced to. The reporters are gonna have a field day with this. Don't let this interfere with your other cases. Jenkins called yesterday. His mother just died, but he has to stay there and wrap up her affairs. Might take another couple of weeks. So, you're staying on this with me."

He turned to go, then whirled back. "Oh, yeah. You've been seen with LaVassar's daughter, up in Wasilla. You heard what I said about her, right?

Preston averted his eyes and gave a brief nod. "Yes, Sir. I heard you. I understand."

"Well, dammit. I mean it. I hear any more about you and her, and you're fired. It could cost us the case." Frank stormed off.

Preston leaned back to his desk, brows scrunched, stomach churning. He'd been deceitful with Frank about Cindy. He'd stay on this case, all right. It wasn't fair for Gary to still be incarcerated. But Cindy. How could he do without her? And now she was acting so distant, hurt and angry. He ached for her.

Preston left a message for the troopers and reviewed his notes for the afternoon's defense of the woman with marijuana in her car. He'd be able to get the slob off, as best he could tell. Feeling helpless and frustrated because he couldn't do the same for Gary, he punched in the troopers' number.

"Preston Mills here. Have the clothes been identified as belonging to Jennifer Williams?" he asked when he got through to Nick. "And wasn't your office supposed to set up an interview with the Ritter woman? What's the status on all this?"

"Yeah, the clothes were hers and the Ritter interview's scheduled here today. She may not show, though. She really protested about having to be involved. We had to threaten to subpoena her before she agreed. I wouldn't be surprised if she obtains counsel and refuses to cooperate."

"Thanks, man," Preston answered. The phone clicked shut in his ear.

Chapter 32

PRESTON'S CLIENT STRODE out of the courtroom with a belligerent swagger a mere fifteen minutes after her marijuana case was called. She'd been right about improper grounds for being stopped. Preston couldn't believe how easy it had gone down. She'd mouthed a brief thank you to Preston before shuffling down the aisle between the benches, a greasy ponytail of grey-streaked hair swaying behind her.

"Won one, but it sure doesn't feel very good," Preston mused under his breath as he gathered up his papers. Now he could hurry on out to Wasilla.

He called Dr. Williams' office and learned that the dentist had a break between patients at two-thirty. Preston asked the receptionist to schedule his investigator in for a short meeting relating to his wife's case. He picked up Mike and sped northeast out of Anchorage knowing the timing would be close. When he realized it might be after six by the time he made it back to the apartment, he decided it would be best to call his landlady to explain about Daisy and ask her if she'd let Daisy out a few times during the day.

"I thought I heard a dog down there," Karen answered when he told her why he was calling. "Sure, I'll let her out. What's her name again? Daisy? Yes, I can do that. No problem."

Preston hung up relieved and grateful to be able to focus completely on the interviews with Elizabeth Ritter and Dan Williams. He watched Mike walk into the dental office and waited, starting on the sandwich he pulled from his briefcase.

Mike hustled back out to the car and settled into the passenger's seat twenty minutes later. He related how a perky receptionist displaying dazzling white teeth had escorted him into Dr. Williams' private office.

"It was a nice office, a computer monitor on the desk with X rays of teeth, cardboard cases of toothpaste stacked in a corner and a huge window that framed the butte," Mike reported. "The leather chair I sat in felt cushy and expensive. He must be doing pretty well. When we shook hands, I noted a flicker of concern that the guy tried to hide. He asked if I was the attorney for my wife's killer."

Preston bristled. Killer? He held his temper and took a deep breath.

Mike went on, "But before I could answer, the dentist said he had only about five minutes. His next patient was here early, but he agreed to see us since we called and were probably on the way already. I guess the troopers plan to talk to him later today, too. He had to keep on schedule to pick up his son from daycare on time so he was pretty impatient. He kept squirming around in his seat like he couldn't wait to get rid of me."

"So he's showing no obvious signs of grief or sadness?" Preston asked.

"Not that I could tell," Mike began. "He answered my questions, but he was just bristling with impatience. He almost yelled at me and asked 'What else? I've been through all this with the troopers. Is there something new?' He kept looking at his watch."

Mike continued, "I asked if his wife said anything about going anyplace else after the kitchenware party His answer was just a rude shake of his head, kind of disgusted like. I said we needed to ask him to make sure she didn't have plans to go anywhere else that night. He was sure. When I told him she went to the Buck Shot Saloon with her friends, he acted shocked."

Mike told how Dr. Williams had turned away and stormed to the window, shouting. "Jennifer didn't go to bars! Never! It wasn't like her. She wouldn't have done that!" He'd turned, face crimson. When Mike didn't respond, Williams raged on. "That guy LaVassar did it! I hope they put him away for life." Words dripping with bitterness, he'd slammed into his desk chair and spun it away, shoulders heaving.

Preston and Mike realized the dentist hadn't even asked if there'd been any progress on the case. Why would that be? Afraid to make a mistake?

Chapter 33

PRESTON'S PHONE VIBRATED as he settled into his desk back at the office. He flipped it open. Victoria. His breath caught. Well, might as well get this over with.

"Hi, Victoria," he answered, trying to keep his voice calm. His heart stuttered. This wouldn't be an easy conversation. He swiveled his chair away from the bustle around him and cupped his hand around the mouthpiece.

"Preston. We need to talk." Victoria's voice came through calm and forceful. It was a tone he'd never heard from her before. "What's going on? Your mother called. She was crying. She said your dad is threatening to cut you out of the will and investments. What's happening with you?" Her words dwindled into a sob.

Victoria had never cried in front of him. She'd never caused him any trouble. They'd hardly ever fought or disagreed about anything. Preston was taken aback by a nearly overwhelming sense of homesickness and guilt. She'd been so easy and pleasant and available, and had fit perfectly into his life. To his surprise, a vision of her smooth perfect body in his bed caused his stomach to tighten. Now she was crying. And what was that about the will?

"Vic," he managed to croak. "I don't know what to say. I'm sorry. Very sorry. None of this is your fault."

"Preston?" Her tone was plaintive. "What's happened to you? To us?"

In the awkward silence that followed, Preston realized that the phone connection lacked the split second delay typical of cross country cell phone transmission. In a flash of panic, he croaked, "Vic? Where are you?"

There was a long silence, then, "I'm here. I just landed at the airport in Anchorage."

Preston gasped. "You're in Alaska?"

"Yes. Your Dad had an airline ticket delivered to me yesterday and even arranged a car service to take me to Logan this morning. You know how he is."

Preston, stunned and speechless, whirled from his desk, gripping his phone.

"Can you come and get me? He arranged my arrival at the end of the work week so you wouldn't have to miss work. I came in on Delta. I'm on my way to baggage claim."

Rage grew, nearly overcoming Preston. They were still doing it to him. He sucked in deep breaths. "I'll be right there. Look for my red Jeep."

If not for the glossy blond hair covering her shoulders, he wouldn't have recognized Victoria when she exited the baggage claim. She wore a red and black plaid shirt hanging loose outside jeans and leather boots that laced halfway to her knees. The straps of a camouflage backpack hung over her shoulders and she wore a matching ball cap. Everything looked brand new, like the tags from L.L.Bean should still be hanging on each item. He fought the urge to laugh. This was a ludicrous attempt to fit into his life. She'd never worn such an outfit. Then empathy hit him. She was trying so hard.

He thrust himself out of the car, grabbed her bag and back pack, tossed them into the back of the Jeep, and turned to hug her. She nestled into his arms as if she belonged. "I missed you," she murmured.

She still smelled clean and citrusy and her eyes were bluer than he remembered. She was beautiful and the embrace felt so familiar, so easy, so comfortable. An unsettling and surprising homesickness overcame him. Brick houses, oaks and maples lining wide avenues, the sounds of Boston traffic, the exuberance of the crowd at the stadium when the Red Socks beat the Yankees, clam bakes and bonfires at the shore.

He pushed himself back from her embrace, shock, anger, and frustration chasing these feelings away. "What made you come?"

"It was your parents, mostly. They thought I'd have the best chance of making you listen to reason. And, to tell you the truth, I needed to see you. I leave for Africa in a few weeks and I just had to see you before I go. We have to talk."

At her words, Preston's anger rose. They were all doing it again. Running his life.

He settled Victoria into the Jeep's passenger seat. "Are you hungry?"

"A little," she answered.

Of course. His father would have bought her a first class ticket so she'd been wined and dined and comfortable all the way. He defiantly pulled into the Seafood Gallery parking lot. It would be noisy, it was a bar, it was far from fine dining. It was where he wanted to be.

Victoria's eyes grew wide when they entered. He avoided looking at her and led her to a worn and scarred wooden booth, their feet crunching over peanut shells that littered the floor.

"Two Alaskan Amber. And halibut cheeks to start," he ordered when the waitress approached.

Victoria's face scrunched with puzzlement at this uncharacteristic behavior. "Preston?" she began.

A growing knot of rage filled Preston's stomach and his breath came hard. "When do you go back?" he asked, barely able to keep his voice normal.

Eyes beseeching him for explanation, Victoria answered, "It's an open ended ticket. We thought, well, we hoped, well, maybe you'd come back with me..." Her voice dropped in confusion and she looked down, as if afraid to meet his gaze.

Preston studied her. *How dare they send her to bring me home?* The waitress interrupted his thoughts, sliding their beers off her tray and plunking a plate of deep fried halibut cheeks onto the table between them.

Victoria looked at the plate, mouth turned down with revulsion. She reached for her glass and took a tiny sip, unaccustomed to drinking beer. She didn't belong here. She never would. Preston grew sure of what to do.

"Well, Vic, this sure is a surprise."

"I know," she answered, her voice wavering and unsure.

"Actually, it's not going to work. Having you here. I can take you downtown to the Captain Hook. It's one of Anchorage's finest hotels. There are flights back East every day."

Victoria's face reddened. She pushed back in the booth in consternation. "What?"

"Yeah. Well, I'm pretty angry about this. You and I never really talked about why I needed to come here. And this just proves it. I felt smothered and controlled by all three of you."

Victoria's expression crumpled.

Preston went on, emboldened at how good this felt. "There's no chance I'll be going back with you. Go on off to Africa like you planned. And you can tell my parents I'll come back when and if I feel ready. I like it here. I'm happy here. I'm on my own."

Tears leaked down Victoria's cheeks. She turned her face away to side of the booth, ever careful to avoid showing emotion. Of course, it wouldn't do to embarrass herself in public. She wasn't real, like Cindy.

Preston grew ever more defiant. "And, to tell you the truth, there's someone else."

Victoria shrunk into herself at these words. Voice barely audible, she raised her tear-filled eyes and asked, "Someone else? Already?"

"Yes." Preston had a twinge of guilt that quickly passed. This was the way to handle Victoria and his parents. Be bold. Be honest. It felt good. "So I'm taking you to the hotel. They'll have a shuttle to the airport tomorrow. I'm sorry it has to be this way. I'm sorry, Vic."

The ride in the Jeep to the hotel was made in complete silence. Victoria let herself out of the car, standing rigidly aside while Preston unloaded her bags, She turned away from him without a word. As Preston watched the bellhop carry Victoria's bags in, his heart soared with relief and pride. He'd done it. He'd taken a stand. Whatever the consequences, he'd be fine. He headed home to Daisy.

Chapter 34

PRESTON GRABBED THE folder Barb handed him when he walked by her counter, skimmed the words of the prosecutor's report, and rushed into Frank's office.

"We just got the report on the Wasilla case, the clothing bundle. They found only the victim's prints and one set of her husband's on a vinyl belt. No other prints. No bloodstains."

Frank looked up. "Did the troopers interview the Ritter woman?"

"Yeah, the report says they had a real hard time with her. She was belligerent and uncooperative from the first moment and apparently one of the toughest people they've ever interviewed. She wouldn't admit to any confrontation with the victim at all this time. And she told him somebody misunderstood if they thought there was a problem between her and the teacher. What a bunch of BS that is." Preston shook his head in disgust.

Frank leaned across his desk. "And?"

Preston answered, "Their investigator wrote that he thinks she could be capable of just about anything, she's that personality type. He couldn't get anything at all out of her. It's obvious she's stonewalling because the principal and the husband relate similar stories of the confrontation between her and Jennifer during the parent teacher conference." He paused and shrugged. "She threatened to get a lawyer if anyone bothers her again. She's a definite suspect, I think. There's motive, even though it's pretty bizarre.

"How'd it go with Mike and the dentist?" Frank asked.

"Tough, too" Preston said. "He bothers me. He doesn't seem to be grieving. At least not that we can see. He's pretty reserved. He was reluctant to talk to Mike and didn't even ask about progress on the case. I have a funny feeling about him. He isn't acting like a guy whose wife was just murdered."

Frank shifted in his seat and spoke. "We need to wrap this thing up. It's been four weeks. You're still talking about three suspects here. One in jail. The other two uncooperative. If we don't narrow it down in the next three days, O'Brien will go forward with prosecution of LaVassar, I'm sure. That's how O'Brian operates. Just wants to convict somebody and get it over with. So we either get LaVassar off the hook or he's going down." He glanced toward the blinking light on his phone, then back to Preston, "Oh, what about that fingerprint?"

Preston grimaced. "It was only a bloody smudge with a partial fingerprint. We're waiting to hear for sure."

"So he touched the body. Have you asked him about it?" Frank's words were gruff with disapproval.

"LaVassar said he forgot about doing it. He was pretty shook up that night." Preston spread his hands. "He's not doing very well right now. He's having a hard time being incarcerated. This is a rough break for him, especially since he's innocent."

Frank shoved his chair back and got to his feet. "Yeah, well. It's getting tougher all the time." He gestured at the door. "I have a hearing in twenty minutes – can't be late. The public is still up in arms about this murder, you know. And this fingerprint thing doesn't look good. Take another good hard look right away at Doc Williams and the Ritter woman. Let me know anything you find out right away. We're running out of time. O'Brien's a bulldog when he grabs onto something. He'll be moving fast on this. Especially with the media coverage. Anything to make himself look good."

He grabbed his briefcase and walked toward the door. "Not looking good, Mills."

Preston turned to the paperwork on his desk. A fleeting vision of Victoria boarding a plane crossed his mind. He shook it off, but couldn't quite eliminate the glimmer of worry about how he'd handle the inevitable response from his parents. Oddly, he was certain it would go his way. This feeling of strength and control filled him with confidence.

Chapter 35

AS THE AFTERNOON dragged on, all Preston could think of was his need to talk to Cindy. He rushed out of the office to his car at four and swerved north onto the Glenn Highway.

Her green Subaru was parked in her apartment building lot just as he hoped. He ran up the stairs to her door and rapped sharply. "It's me," he called.

"Preston?" Cindy called out, then opened the door. A fluffy yellow bath towel wrapped her head turban style. She drew her white terrycloth robe tight across her front and tugged the belt into a knot. "I just got out of the shower." A few drops of water clung to the freckles on her nose. "What...?"

Preston stepped in. "Can I come in?"

"Preston. Why are you here?" She stepped back, face hardening. "How's Daisy? What's up?" She reached up with both hands to adjust the towel.

"Daisy's doing fine. My landlady's gonna let her out. She slept on the rug right by my bed last night. She was perfect."

Cindy allowed a reluctant smile to cross her face. "Well, watch out tonight. She'll be right up in the bed with you if you don't stop her," She drew back, avoiding his eyes, and hunched her shoulders defensively.

"Sorry I didn't call before driving out. I just finished meeting with my boss and thought I'd take a chance that you were home so I could fill you in on what's happening with your Dad."

She moved back so he could enter. He stepped through the door, swallowing his dread. "They found that partial bloody fingerprint by Jennifer Williams' lip. It looks like it could be a match to your Dad's." He swallowed and went on, "It's made things worse."

Cindy blanched, but Preston continued, determined to get it all out. "The clothing bundle showed only fingerprints belonging to Jennifer and her husband on the belt. Nothing else. No damage or lost buttons or rips. Nothing out of the ordinary. There was absolutely no sign of violence. Investigators interviewed the Ritter woman from the school incident, but she's real hostile and would hardly talk to them. She threatened to get a lawyer if anybody bothered her again. I'm sure she's lying, so she's not off the hook."

He paused. Should he tell her about Dr. Williams? Yeah, better tell her everything. She'd done great so far. And he trusted her.

"There's more," he said. "But it's confidential so you can't say a word to anyone."

Cindy gathered her robe tighter around herself. She backed further away from Preston, mouth tight, head bent, refusing to look directly at him. "Okay."

He went on. "It's the husband, Dan Williams, the dentist. He isn't acting like someone who's just lost a wife. He doesn't seem to be as upset as you'd expect under the circumstances."

"I go to him," Cindy said, she tipped her head up, finally meeting his eyes. Her voice held a hint of excitement. "He's my dentist."

"Really?"

"Yeah. I've been going to him since he started there, maybe five years ago now. I haven't ever needed much, just cleanings and checkups, but he always seems real nice. That Patty at the front desk is great, too. She's been there forever. She even recognizes my voice when I call."

Preston pondered this. If Cindy thinks the guy is okay, that was important. Maybe Dan Williams was just handling his grief in his own way.

"But once...well..." Cindy began.

"What?" Preston asked.

"I heard him lose his temper in the next room. There was a little kid who was yelling about not wanting to get a shot. I was waiting in the chair in the next room. All of a sudden there was a big crash and I heard someone, I'm pretty sure it was Dr. Williams, storm past my room. Then Patty went in there and got the kid and took him out to his mother in the waiting room. I couldn't hear everything. But it sounded to me like Dr. Williams lost it and threw a chair or something. Then he came in to check my teeth a few minutes later. His face was kind of red, but he just acted normal." She drew a deep breath. "I forgot all about that until right now. I think he has a temper."

Preston raised his eyebrows. This put Dan Williams in a new light.

He turned his attention back to Cindy. "Hey, are you okay? With the news about the clothes and fingerprint?"

Cindy sighed. "Not really, but I have to be. It's pretty bad, isn't it?"

"Yeah, it's incriminating for sure. We didn't need this. He has a good explanation, though."

The tension in the air between them bristled at what was unsaid.

Cindy finally spoke. "Well, Dad does have an explanation." Her voice wavered and Preston could see the effort it took for her to act as if nothing was wrong between them.

"Are you all settled back in here?" he asked, knowing there was more he should say, struggling to figure out what words to use. How should he explain why he'd rushed from her bed at the cabin?

"Yeah, it was easy. I'd hardly been gone," she answered through an awkward pause. "I need to go back up to the cabin and drain the pipes though. Maybe this weekend."

"I'll help," Preston said. "Let's go Saturday, okay?"

"Well, maybe." Coldness had crept back into her voice.

She stepped further back into the apartment, challenging him with a defiant, unfriendly glare. Her freckles stood out clearly and her eyelashes glistened with hints of dampness. She'd never looked more appealing. Preston fought his thoughts. She hadn't been expecting him and wasn't even dressed. He wanted to rip that robe off her and unwind that towel instead. Take her all wet and fresh. Make her need another shower. He scolded himself. *You maniac. You can't be thinking of doing her every time you see her.* Frank's warning flashed through his mind. Then Cindy's face when he'd rolled away from her in the bedroom at the cabin.

"I better leave," he managed. "I have to stop and pick up some stuff and then get back to feed Daisy and let her out. What's your schedule tomorrow?"

Cindy took a step back. "It's Friday. John said I can take off early every Friday until this thing with Dad is over. I usually stay a little late the other days to make up the time. So, I'm going to drive in to Anchorage and see Dad tomorrow." Her voice had a flat tone he'd never heard from her before.

Preston took a deep breath. "How about if I come to the jail a little after five when visiting hours are almost over? I can fill you both in on what happened during the day. We might as well go ahead and ask him about the fingerprint. I'm sure it'll factor into what happens tomorrow."

He felt heat and shame and discomfort burn up his neck when Cindy dipped her head, refusing to meet his gaze.

She pulled further back into the room, assuring no contact. "You better go," she said, turning further away. "Thank you for coming to tell me all this me. Go now." She motioned toward the door. "I guess I'll take your help with the pipes tomorrow," she added over her shoulder, voice laden with reluctance

He ran to his Jeep, gulping the crisp evening air, hopeful. She'd agreed to spend time with him. Tomorrow they'd be together again and he'd finally be able to explain.

When he reached home, Daisy wagged her whole body in greeting and snuffled against his knees the minute he got through the door. He let her out, then stood on the steps in the frosty night watching her as she roamed and twirled in the nearby bushes and did her business. The colored lights of Anchorage glittered below. The waters of the inlet, framed by jagged dark mountain peaks in the distance glowed a deep burnished crimson, holding fast to the waning rays of the sun. A shimmering incandescent moon hanging low over the roofline behind him caught his eye when he turned to go back inside. Stars glittered across the vast black canopy of the Alaskan night overhead. Peace and contentment overcame him while he guided Daisy back into the apartment. He felt at home and content, living his dream. Then he remembered his parents, and Victoria, and, most importantly, how he had to make things right with Cindy. He frowned, neck and shoulders tightening with frustration.

Chapter 36

GARY WASN'T HAVING a good night. After that last miserable year behind bars, he'd vowed to never be here again. He'd felt sure he'd be out pretty fast on this charge, but now it looked like he'd been wrong.

He couldn't make himself get out of bed to leave his cell for supper. When the chow buzzer rang, he just burrowed back into the stiff smelly covers of his bunk, desperate for relief from the constant clamor of his surroundings.

To his cellmate's inquiry about supper, he merely snarled, "Leave me the hell alone. Get outa here."

"Up yours," the man had shrugged.

Gary fumed. How he hated living in this crappy little room so close he could smell his cellmate all the time. Hated having to live with somebody he didn't even know. And he could hardly force down those so called meals. *Couldn't they at least keep the milk cold? Who in hell can drink piss warm milk? And I want a cold beer. Would it kill 'em to serve a beer now and then?* He felt more than ever like a caged animal.

He tossed in his bunk, almost gagging on the smells drifting up from the cafeteria. *It smells like that goddamn sauerkraut and sausage again. They'll have that crappy white bread and the dry yellow cake they call dessert, too.* He wanted out of this miserable place. He longed to be home and fry up some moose steak with Yukon Golds and onions. Let Daisy lick the stuff outa the frying pan when it got cooled off. Daisy loved that. He missed his dog. He mashed the pillow again and struggled to get comfortable in the narrow bunk. Tears began to stream down his cheeks. He rolled onto his back and within seconds huge sobs he couldn't control overcame him. Screams that sounded like they were coming from someone else followed, "Let me outa here! Let me out! I gotta get out! Let me go home!"

He jumped from the bed and rushed to grip the bars. "Let me out! Let me out!" he hollered from the depths of his being. Uncontrolled agony poured from his throat and he could no longer stop hysterical shrieks. "Help! Help! Let me out! Help!" He banged his head harder and harder against the bars. "Let me out! Let me out!" Then blackness closed in. He didn't feel himself slide to the floor. He didn't feel the prison medics roughly roll him onto a stretcher.

PRESTON WAS SHOCKED to see Cindy waiting in the lobby of his office building at eight the next morning. Her agonized face told him something was very wrong.

"Cindy! What are you doing here? What..?" He rushed to her and caught her as she reached for him.

"I got the call at six thirty this morning. I rushed right here. They say he's in the hospital in Anchorage."

"What! Your Dad?"

"Yes!" Cindy wailed. "He had some kind of a breakdown last night and he hasn't regained consciousness. So they called me." She buried her face in her hands. "He's in the emergency room at Providence."

"What happened?"

"I don't know. They just called and said I should come as soon as possible. Something about signing papers for treatment. But I came to get you first." Cindy turned agonized eyes to Preston. "I'm scared. Will you come with me?"

"Sure, of course. Just let me run up and let Barb know I'll be out this morning. Stay right here."

Preston dashed up the stairwell, too impatient to wait for the elevator. Within minutes he was back at Cindy's side. "Here. Come with me. I'll drive."

They rushed the few blocks to his car and sped to the hospital. Cindy remained silent on the ride, hunched against the passenger door, her face white. Preston drove hard, running yellow lights, heart racing. *What the hell? What happened to Gary? Did he just freak? That's probably it. Since he heard he won't get out right away, he must've lost it.* They screeched into the hospital parking lot and half ran to the main entrance.

The white-haired woman in the information booth looked at a list and pointed down a corridor when Preston spoke Gary's name. "That way. Take the elevator to the third floor. See the nurses at the first desk."

He could hardly keep up with Cindy as she rushed ahead of him. At the nurses' station, she breathed, "LaVassar? Gary LaVassar?"

The nurse looked up. "LaVassar?" She checked computer screen. "Oh, yeah, admitted from the ER..." She hesitated, "Room 380. On the left at the end of the hall."

Preston noticed the flash of contempt the nurse couldn't quite hide. She was obviously aware that Gary had been admitted from the jail. Preston swallowed his anger. *So she thinks of us like dirt because we're here for a prisoner. This whole business stinks. No wonder Gary lost it. He's been treated like this for months now.* Preston hoped Cindy hadn't noticed the nurse's attitude.

He followed Cindy into room 380 where Gary lay still and pale, bloody abrasions on his forehead, covered by white sheets, a faded green gown covering his shoulders and chest. An IV snaked into a gauze bandage on his hand. Dark shadows made hollows beneath his closed eyes.

Cindy walked to the bedside and leaned down. "Daddy?" she whispered. A slight flutter of his eyelids indicated that he heard her.

"Daddy. Wake up. It's me. Wake up." Her voice was stronger this time. She grabbed his hand and stroked it.

Gary's eyes struggled to open. His mouth moved but no sound came out.

A nurse entered. "Are you family?" she asked. "We need next of kin. Is that you?" She glanced at a chart in her hand. "He's sedated, so don't expect much in the way of response." She looked pointedly at Preston. "Family?' she repeated.

While Preston nodded, Cindy turned from her father. "Yes, I'm his daughter. They called me this morning. What happened?"

"The doctor will have to explain. He'll be here on rounds between nine and ten. We have paper..."

"But what happened?" Cindy interrupted, her voice shrill. "Why is he here? What happened?"

The nurse gave Cindy a calm, patient look. "As I said, the doctor will have to explain. Now, if you'll please come out to the desk, we have forms for you to sign." She made a brisk turn on her heels and left the room.

Cindy turned to Preston.

"Let's go out to the desk and look at the forms," he said. "Maybe we'll get a clue about what's happened. She's not gonna tell us, that's for sure."

Cindy gave a lingering glance at her father and then followed Preston to the nurses' station. The forms were standard admission and insurance paperwork, and he nodded to Cindy to fill out and sign them. As soon as that was done, they hurried back to the room. By now it was nine o'clock.

"I'm staying right here until we see the doctor," Cindy said, her voice decisive. Preston knew it would be fruitless to argue. He pulled the single chair close to the bed and settled her into it before he leaned against the windowsill.

Cindy resumed her position at her father's side and again bent over him. "Daddy, I'm here," she murmured.

Gary lay silent, not moving, not responding at all.

The doctor who strode into Gary's hospital room appeared to be in a hurry. He studied Gary's still form for a moment and glanced at his clipboard before turning to Preston and Cindy, his voice curt.

"I'm Dr. Hall. Are you family?"

Cindy answered, "Yes. What happened? Why is he here?"

"He had a psychotic episode last night. He was brought in comatose about midnight when the nurse at the jail infirmary hadn't been able to rouse him for five hours. We're keeping him sedated since the report said he'd been screaming and pounding his head on the bars of his cell before he lost consciousness. We didn't want to take any chances of that behavior recurring until we get a definitive diagnosis and a treatment plan in place."

Preston could see that Cindy was too surprised to respond.

The doctor turned to study Gary again. "Is there any history of this? Prior episodes?"

"No. Nothing." Cindy managed. "He's never done anything like this. Why didn't someone call me last night?"

"I don't know," the doctor responded with impatient flick of his hand. "Do you have an idea of what may have precipitated it? It says here that he's been incarcerated for the past month or so. Any way he could have obtained drugs or alcohol? Is a he a user? Is there any family history of behavioral or mental disturbances?"

Preston could see Cindy growing more upset by the second. He stepped forward. "I'm Preston Mills, Mr. LaVassar's attorney. This is his daughter, Cindy LaVassar." He looked at Cindy for permission to continue.

At her nod, he went on. "Mr. LaVassar became despondent when he found out he'd have to remain in jail longer than expected. It happened a few days ago. He thought he was getting out, but that changed at the last minute. To the best of our knowledge, he shouldn't be in jail at all. And he wasn't using any illegal substances."

"I've never heard of anybody in the family having a nervous breakdown or anything like that," Cindy added in a shaky voice. "He's innocent. He shouldn't be in jail."

"I'm his defense attorney," Preston said. "We believe he's innocent. This has been very stressful for him."

The doctor stepped toward them, his demeanor softened, his tone now more kindly. "Isn't he the suspect in that woman's murder up in Wasilla?" When Cindy and Preston both nodded, he added, "Everybody wonders if he's actually the one did who it. A lot of people think he's just the passerby who found the body."

"Well, they're right," Preston answered. "So this crisis for Mr. LaVassar appears to be the result of stress."

The doctor looked down at his clipboard for a moment. "I think you could be right, this might be a direct response to stress like that. I'll see what I can do to keep him here in the hospital and out of jail as long as possible. Do you think there's danger of him bolting or having another episode if we wean him off the sedation?"

"I don't think so," Preston answered. "Can we explain it to him as soon as he wakes up? When will that be?' He glanced at Gary's still form. "I think if he understands that he doesn't have to go right back to jail, he'll settle down. He got pretty agitated at being locked up."

The doctor pursed his lips. "We can begin by weaning him off the medications today. By tomorrow morning, he should be lucid. I'll be doing rounds again this same time tomorrow. Why don't you try talking to him and then we'll discuss it when I'm back here in the morning?" The doctor gave Cindy a sympathetic glance. "Can you be here in the morning, Miss LaVassar?"

"Yes, I'll be here," she replied. "Thank you."

The doctor lifted Gary's eyelids, felt his pulse, made some notes, and left.

Cindy rushed over as soon as he was gone and bent to her father. "Daddy? It's me. I'm here. It's gonna be okay." Gary's right hand gave a barely discernible wiggle and Cindy squeezed it in return. "I'll be here with you all day, Daddy. Tomorrow we'll be able to talk with you. We have a plan."

At Preston's insistence, Cindy left for the cafeteria, promising to eat a good meal since she would stay with her father all afternoon while Preston went back to work. He planned to pick her up for an early dinner and then return to sit with Gary until visiting hours were over. Neither spoke of the unfinished business between them.

Chapter 37

PRESTON'S AFTERNOON FLEW by. His phone flashed often on a desk now covered with files, papers, notes, and messages. He'd grown much more confident about procedures in the Alaska legal system and had wrapped up over twenty misdemeanors in his first month on the job.

Frank had been out of town on a case in Juneau all week, so Preston hadn't had a chance to discuss Gary's defense, but one of the messages Barb took for him set a meeting with Frank for first thing Monday morning.

I'm gonna go after Dan Williams like he won't believe, Preston vowed. *He's the one. That sonofabitch did his wife and now is letting somebody else take the rap. Well, he's not getting away with it. I'm doing it for Gary. And for Cindy. Williams might be clever, but I'm going to figure out how he did it.*

After picking Cindy up in Gary's room, Preston helped her on with her jacket, an awkwardness between them preventing actual touch. She agreed to stay at his apartment overnight to avoid the long dark drive back out to Wasilla. The arrangements were made with minimal conversation, all the focus being directed at Gary's condition.

Daisy bounced up, tail whipping, when Cindy accompanied Preston through the door of the apartment. Cindy nuzzled Daisy and stepped outside to watch her while Preston turned on lights and hung up their coats.

As soon as she was back inside, Preston began. "Ummm. Cindy, about out at the cabin. I can explain."

She dipped her head, refused to look at him, saying nothing.

"It's my boss. He noticed that we had something going, and he ordered me to cool it with you. He said a relationship of any kind with a client or his family could compromise the case. And, well, I didn't want our first time to be when you were so vulnerable. I knew you were worrying about what I'd think of the cabin. And you were still so worried about your Dad. I wanted us to remember it as...well..." He hesitated. Were these the right words?

Cindy raised her gaze, face softening. "So that's it? We shouldn't be seeing each other unless it's related to the case? And you were being considerate of me? That's what it was?"

"Yeah, I wasn't sure how to explain it that night. It kind of took me by surprise, what we were doing. I worried that I might be taking advantage of you – you've had so much to handle since we met." He looked away. "And well, I had some unfinished business in my life, too. But I've taken care of it."

He wavered, unsure of her reaction. At her nod, he went on. "Right then, I realized that what we were doing was a big deal. I know I blew it by leaving so abruptly like that. I'm sorry."

"So is it wrong, me being here now?" Cindy turned worried eyes to him.

"I'm sure it is. But I don't care. Nobody knows. Nobody has to know. We have to stop being seen together until the case is over, but we should be able to manage that, don't you think?"

"I guess so. That's what it was, then? You were worried about all that?"

He reached for her and drew her close. "You know how I feel, don't you? You're what I think about as soon as I wake up every day and last thing before I fall asleep at night."

Cindy pulled back a bit and smiled into his eyes. No words were needed.

He half carried her to the bedroom and laid her gently on the bed. Their clothes were on the floor within minutes.

Much later, Cindy grabbed a corner of the sheet and covered herself, giving him a tentative and bashful look. It was the sexiest and most beautiful sight Preston had ever seen. Her face was flushed with lovemaking, the creamy skin of her shoulders and the leg that peeked from the sheet glowed in the moonlight, damp tendrils of hair clung to her cheeks and neck. She'd been a tiger, much to his surprise. A powerful feeling of satisfaction and ownership filled his senses. He felt an astonishing return of arousal and rolled away from her to hide it.

"Cindy, you're amazing," he breathed through a smile.

When he reached for her, she snuggled over to mold against him. He pulled the sheet across them both and kissed her forehead. She fit perfectly in his arms and smelled so good. He sighed with pleasure at her fragrance and as her velvety body nestled against him.

They slept little that night. Preston knew his life had been forever changed. He had his partner. He would never be without her. He had no doubt about her feelings, either.

Daisy awoke him with snuffles at his shoulder as the first bluish light of morning teased the edges of the window shade. Preston rose and padded through the living room to let her out, barely opening his eyes until she scurried back inside from the dim, foggy morning.

He returned to his bedroom where Cindy lay curled in the middle of the bed, a twisted sheet covering her shoulders and outlining the curve of her hip. A dainty ankle and foot peeked from the bottom of the sheet. She was sleeping deeply. He contemplated her form. God, she was beautiful. He stood for long moments admiring the woman in his bed, hating to wake her, wishing she could be there every morning. He wanted to slip that sheet off her and make love to her. Start with her toes and work up this time.

Preston shook his head to clear it. Stop it, you sex obsessed jerk, he told himself. We have to get to the hospital early. He turned away from her with reluctance and walked to the kitchen, banging the cupboard door a little too loudly while getting the coffee and talking to Daisy who had followed him into the kitchen.

When he returned to the bedroom, Cindy was out of bed and gathering her clothes. Her naked body caused Preston's heart to thunder. He gulped. "You can have the shower first if you want."

Cindy nodded a bit self-consciously, crammed her clothing tight against her chest, and scurried for the bathroom.

An hour later, as they headed down the mountain for the hospital, Cindy breathed an awestruck, "Wow! Look at this view! The morning sun lights up the city down there like it's on fire!"

Preston glanced over at her. "Yeah, I never get tired of it. Every day it's different. I can't believe the view from up here. Lots of times, there are moose right on the road, too. And my landlady said there's been a lynx in the yard lately. This is the greatest place to live." He hesitated. "And, Cindy? Well, I love having you in my life."

There was an awkward silence. He kept his eyes on the road. Had he said too much too soon? Had he scared her off? Preston's face burned. He finally dared glance over at Cindy.

She looked back, her face serious. "I love you, Preston Mills," she whispered. A bashful look followed her words and she dropped her eyes.

Preston's heart skittered. He drew a deep breath of joyous relief, suddenly overcome with emotion. He pulled to the side of the road and shifted into park.

"Cindy, I love you, too," He breathed and reached for her.

He buried his face in her curls as he pulled her to his chest, crushing her against him, jacket and all. Her arms crept up and she returned his hug. They stayed locked together, neither saying a word, not moving at all. They finally pulled away from each other, goofy grins spread across their faces.

"Well, we better get to the hospital," Preston managed, trying to calm his breathing. Cindy settled back in her seat and refastened her seat belt, face glowing.

Frank's warning skittered through Preston's mind. His parents' faces followed.

Chapter 38

GARY WAS AWAKE when they entered his room. "Hi, Honey," he croaked, his voice slurred. "Hey, Mills. Morning, you two."

Cindy dashed to his side. "Daddy, you're awake. Good. How do you feel?"

"Like I've been run over by a truck," he answered. "What' going on? I can tell I'm in a hospital, but why? What happened?"

Preston stood back while Cindy explained. She held her father's hand, explained what happened, and reassured him about not having to go right back to jail.

Gary shook his head. "Don't remember freaking out. Don't remember nothin', really. Is this Saturday then?" He hesitated. "Does this mean something's wrong with me? With my brain?"

"No," Preston stepped forward. "The doctor will be in soon and he'll explain better what happened. You'll be okay. You might get to stay here a while."

Gary's face relaxed while he settled back into his pillow.

The doctor entered the room and explained Gary's stress-induced psychotic episode and shared his plan to keep Gary under observation for at least another week. It meant a transfer to another wing of the hospital, as well as appointments and interviews with mental health professionals. As soon as Gary expressed thanks and his promise to cooperate, the doctor left to set the transfer in motion.

Cindy decided to stay all day with her dad, and Preston felt the pull of the case. "I'm going to go into work," he said.

"But it's Saturday…" Cindy began.

"I know. But you'll be busy getting your Dad transferred to the other wing. I'm anxious to get working on the case. I'll be checking out Dr. Williams more thoroughly. The sooner I find something, the sooner this will be over for you." His tone of voice left no room for argument.

Cindy smiled acknowledgement and Preston was soon at his desk researching everything he could find about Dan Williams. Grew up in Fairbanks. Went to the University of Alaska Fairbanks for his undergraduate work, then to the University of Washington for his dental degree. Married Jennifer while both were students there. Moved back as soon as he graduated. Started his practice five years ago. No criminal record in Alaska or Washington.

Okay, then. Nothing out of the ordinary there. Preston decided he better get up to Wasilla and start talking to people who knew Williams. The weekend could catch the neighbors at home. And maybe it would be easier to talk to Williams himself when he wasn't under pressure at his office.

He made a quick call to Cindy to tell her his plans and she agreed to stay with her dad until Preston got back into Anchorage. It went unspoken between them that Cindy would be staying overnight again.

NICK WAS BOTHERED by the case, too, motivated to move it forward even though it was his day off. He decided to take Kay's car in to have the studded tires installed. It meant a wait at the tire shop since he didn't have an appointment, but it would give him time to be alone and think. Sometimes a change of environment spurred new ideas.

"See you in a while," he called to Kay. "Need anything picked up on my way back?"

"Yeah, milk. And a cake mix. Chocolate. I'm making cupcakes for Natalie's class. Thank you, Baby," she turned from the sink and smiled her thanks.

Nick stood for a minute before walking out the door. Kay's hair shone with highlights in the patch of morning sunlight that streamed through the kitchen window. She looked extremely sexy in those grey sweatpants that hugged her rear that certain way. He was a lucky man. Nick fought off an urge to pull her away from her kitchen duties and take her up to the bedroom. He shook his head, stepped into the garage, and dropped into the driver's seat of Kay's car.

Getting the tires changed meant a couple of hours on the hard plastic seats in the waiting room of the tire shop. He pulled his jacket close against the chill of the dirty, concrete-walled room and tried to pick something interesting out of the messy heap of grubby newspapers that lay atop a pile of tires serving as an end table. Greasy car magazines were his only other choice. He tried to shut out the clangs and racket from the shop on the other side of the waiting room's glass door.

All Nick could think about was the Williams case. *Did Elizabeth Ritter murder her kid's teacher? Or did Dr. Williams do in his wife? Was LaVassar really just a passerby?* Nick didn't feel confident that LaVassar did it, even with this latest fingerprint development. There had to be something else to it. Something they were missing. He needed to focus on the Ritter woman and dig deeper into Dr. Williams' life and past.

His cell phone rang a moment later and he listened to Matt report that the suspect was at Providence. After hearing the details, Nick was even more certain that LaVassar wasn't the one who should be behind bars.

Although Nick looked forward to the weekend ahead, he knew he'd be working on the case in his mind the entire time. So he couldn't help stopping into the office to grab Elizabeth Ritter's file on his way home.

He slipped down to his desk in the den that night after Kay and the kids were asleep to study the sparse information in the pages. Based on his experience with Elizabeth Ritter at the first interview and the reports of the investigators that followed, he concluded that she could be capable of the crime. She had motive. LaVassar didn't. That's what bothered him. He couldn't wait to get back to his desk Monday morning, wrap up as much as he could on his other cases, and begin to examine Elizabeth Ritter's life in detail. He slipped back into bed, mind made up on the plan, and snuggled against Kay's warm back, but sleep didn't come easily.

Chapter 39

NICK HAD A hard time concentrating on the boys sprinting up and down the field at Andy's soccer game. He'd spent the last three hours of his workday on the Williams case and couldn't get it out of his mind. He hardly heard Natalie's little voice, "Daddy? Can I have money for popcorn? Daaaaddy! Are you listening?" until it became indignant.

"What? Oh, sure, Sweetie. Here." He handed his daughter a dollar. "Stay where I can see you when you go to the stand. Remember?"

He watched his daughter bounce away. Why couldn't he get this murder investigation out of his mind? He could hardly think of anything else. Maybe it was because it had made him realize how terrible it would be to lose Kay. He reached for his wife's hand. "I love you, my wife."

Kay tore her attention from the boys on the field, eyes wide with surprise. "Me, too, my husband" she answered. After a moment, she turned to him, eyebrows raised in question. "Is that murder case still bothering you?"

"Yup."

"Then go. Go to work. The kids and I can get a ride home with the Andersons. Go if you need to."

Nick bolted off the bleachers, hurried to the car, and was soon at his desk powering up his computer for a search on Elizabeth Ritter. A half hour later, he decided to call Preston. He probably shouldn't call a defense attorney, especially at this time of day, but this was important. At least he could leave a message if Mills didn't answer.

Preston picked up on the first ring, to Nick's surprise. "Mills. Trooper Kerrans here. Hate to bother you so late in the day."

Preston interrupted, "I'm still at the office. I'm trying to make some progress on LaVassar's case. He's innocent."

"I found something on Elizabeth Ritter," Nick said. "She has a record. Assault. Twice. Once as a coed at Notre Dame and once for an altercation in a restaurant in Seward."

"Assault? Convictions?"

"Yup. Cases both went to jury trial at her insistence, but she lost both times. She gave quite a beating to her dorm roommate in '96, and then slammed a waitress across the face with a plate a couple years later down in Seward. The cases were slam dunk wins for the victims."

"No shit?"

"Yeah. Hard to believe, huh? And get this. She has a degree in chemical engineering from Notre Dame. Does that say anything to you about poison?"

"It sure does. You know LaVassar broke down the day before yesterday? A psychotic episode at being locked up. He'll be in the hospital for at least a week. You'll have reports on it Monday. He's pretty happy with the situation, being out of jail. I want to have someone else in custody by the time you bastards succeed in slamming him back in."

Nick's grin came through the phone. "I'll follow up on this Ritter angle then."

"Thanks, man. I know you didn't have to call me."

"I have to do the right thing. But this is just between us," Nick replied and hung up.

Preston hustled to his car, buoyed by Nick's call, and merged onto the freeway, headed for the Williams' neighborhood in Wasilla. The news about Elizabeth Ritter's criminal history surprised him and tilted suspicion toward her, but he wasn't ready to let Dan Williams off the hook.

Preston parked a few houses away from the address and studied the neighborhood. Large, recently built homes with freshly landscaped yards sat widely spaced along both sides of a cul-de-sac. Clean, late model vehicles, mostly SUV's, filled the driveways. Three boys pounded back and forth beneath a basketball hoop at the house next to the Williams.

A sudden, loud rap on his side window startled Preston. He whipped his head around to see a dark-haired clean-cut man leaning toward him, eyebrows raised. Preston lowered his window.

"Can I help you?" the man asked, a glint of suspicion in his eyes.

"Oh, no. I'm okay," Preston managed, still trying to catch his breath from the unexpected knock on his window.

"Looking for someone?" the man asked.

"I'm Preston Mills with the Public Defender's office. Working on the Williams murder. Just trying to get a sense of the neighborhood."

"Oh." The man stepped back. "Okay, then. We kind of check on cars we don't recognize around here. Especially since it happened. We're all pretty nervous. You understand." He stole a look into Preston's back seat. "Got some ID?"

Preston dug a card out of his billfold and handed it out the window. "Sure. Here you go." He waited while the man examined the card.

The man handed it back toward Preston. "Keep it," Preston said. "In case you or somebody else thinks of anything. Anything at all. We're checking every lead, no matter how insignificant it might seem."

The man slipped it into the pocket of his jeans. "Well, I guess we can talk to you." He waited, now clearly uncomfortable. "What do you need to know? I thought you had a suspect in custody. Laveese, something like that? The construction guy who found her?"

Preston pushed his car door open and stepped out. "Yeah, but he hasn't been convicted. The case is still open. We're looking for more information. Especially about Jennifer's activities that night. Did you know her?"

"Sure Well, my wife Amy knows…knew her better than I did. Amy does daycare for Tyler, Dan and Jennifer's son. Amy's the one who had the kitchenware party that night. She's been really affected by all this. She and Jennifer were pretty close, living right by each other and all. And then the babysitting…" his voice trailed off.

"Is your wife home?" Preston asked, trying to keep the eagerness from his voice. This wouldn't be smart, doing an interview himself. He'd make himself a witness in his own case. Better call Mike.

The man turned to look at the house behind him. "Well, yeah. Amy's home. I suppose she'll talk to you. Chuck Bartell." He offered a firm handshake then and began walking up the sidewalk. Preston dug out his cell phone and dialed Mike as he followed. "How soon can you get out to Wasilla?"

"I'm already in Wasilla. At my sister's. What's up?"

Preston explained and hurried after Bartell.

"Amy?" the man called out, pushing open the front door. "Where are you, Sweetie? Come in the kitchen. Someone's here."

He led Preston through the house to a large, bright kitchen and motioned him to a chair at the table. Within seconds, a petite woman appeared at the kitchen door, brows lifted in question. She looked at her husband.

"Amy, this is attorney Preston Mills from the Public Defender's office." A flash of agony crossed Amy's face before she stepped forward and reached a hand toward Preston.

He rose and shook her hand. "I'm pleased to meet you. Our investigator is on his way. He'll be here in about ten minutes. Are you willing to talk to him?"

Amy stepped back, eyes wary, and looked at her husband. He moved to her side and put a protective arm around her waist. "It's okay. I think we should talk to him. I know you already talked to the troopers, but anything we can do to help, we should. It'll be okay."

He turned to Preston. "She has a hard time talking about Jennifer. It's hit her pretty hard."

"I'm sorry," Preston offered, with a smile of sympathy. "I'll send the investigator in as soon as he gets here. I'll ask him to try and keep it short. I appreciate you taking the time. We need all the help we can get on this."

His words seemed to calm Amy. She pulled away from her husband and settled into a chair across from Preston. Placing her hands on the table in front of her, she spoke, "Why can't you ask me the questions?"

"I'm the defense attorney and I wouldn't be able to testify as a witness to your statements, so Mike from our office will do it," Preston said. "Mike will need to hear everything you can tell him about Jennifer's activities, feelings, problems, whatever you know."

Amy thought for a minute. "Okay. I'll wait." She looked to her husband for confirmation and he nodded.

AN HOUR LATER, Mike slid into the passenger's seat of Preston's car, jostling the laptop Preston had been focused on while he waited. "Well, apparently Jennifer Williams attended the Kitchen Ease party that night, but she left before it was over. She wasn't feeling well. Said her head hurt and she had a really bad stomachache. They were right in the middle of things so she let herself out. They never dreamed they wouldn't see her again."

Mike shrugged. "Amy Bartell cried the whole time she was talking to me. Jennifer was her best friend and she's taken care of little Tyler ever since he was born. She said Jennifer was a really nice person. They can't believe anyone would kill her. Amy knew Jennifer and Dan fought a little. About another baby. About money. But nothing out of the ordinary. They have no idea why she was murdered and left out there."

Chuck Bartell knocked on Mike's side window, Amy at his side. "We have your card. If Amy thinks of anything else, we'll call you. And we'll ask around the neighborhood, too. Everybody talks about it all the time. That guy's still in custody, isn't he? The one who found her that night?"

"Yes, he is," Mike answered through the partly open glass. "He's actually in the hospital at this time. There's one more thing, though. Did Jennifer Williams leave the party here that night? Maybe early? With a few of the others? Just for a short time?"

Amy blanched and stole a frantic look at her husband. He turned in surprise at her expression. "Amy? Why is he asking that?"

She pursed her lips and looked at the ground. "Yeah, we left at seven. Jennifer and I and Lisa. We went to the Buck Shot for a quick drink. Kind of as an adventure. We'd told everyone else the party started at eight."

Her husband's gasp was audible. He took a step toward her. "What? Amy!"

She refused to look at him and began nervously twisting her hands. "We thought it would be something new to do. We ordered Cosmopolitans, like the *Sex and the City* girls do. We were back here by a quarter to eight. I know it was stupid. Then Jennifer felt sick and went home about an hour later." She began to cry. "It happened that same night. I feel so guilty. So does Lisa."

Preston spoke to the stricken couple. "Please call Mike if you think of anything else. Anything at all."

He pondered Mike's information on the drive back to Anchorage. So Jennifer had been to the Buck Shot and then felt sick that night. And Jennifer and Dan Williams fought about adding to their family and about finances. This was new information and could be another direction to take the investigation. Marital troubles. The women being out at a bar the night of the crime.

Chapter 40

ELIZABETH RITTER ARRIVED precisely on time Monday for her meeting with the troopers. She entered the room in business attire, hair lacquered into a helmet, demeanor making it obvious she didn't want to be there.

Nick began. "We're here to eliminate you as an involved party in the Jennifer Williams murder. For your own good, we have to record this and read you your rights."

He pressed the record button, introduced himself, Matt, the investigator, and their boss, O'Brien, and read her rights to her. While he talked, her face reddened and she started to protest. "No. I don't have to…"

Nick broke in, "Your name came up, as you know, after reports of an altercation with the victim at Valley Elementary regarding your daughter, who was Mrs. William's student. Am I correct? Our investigator said you weren't cooperative with him, that's why you had to come in."

Elizabeth turned toward him with a forced smile. "Okay, Okay, then. Yes, I had words with Mrs.

Williams at my daughter's conference. I'm sure the principal told you I was in his office about it, too. But it was nothing. Nothing. Certainly not any reason to bring me here." She pursed her lips and stared haughtily back at Nick.

His anger rose. "Do you understand why we have to keep you in the loop? You're the only person we've found who had any motive, however slight, to do such a thing." He returned her challenging look.

Elizabeth glared at him. "I am not involved. Do you understand? There was no motive. I'm NOT involved." Her face had grown pinched and white, her eyes too bright.

"Do you have a degree in chemical engineering?" Nick asked.

Elizabeth gave a jerk, "Yes. What does that have to do with anything?"

"Jennifer felt sick the night she died. We're looking at poisoning. Know anything about poison?"

"Of course not." Her eyes burned into Nick's. "I highly resent this line of questioning. I shouldn't even be here. This meeting is over. My attorney is Brad Knight." She shoved back her chair and stalked from the room.

The men sat in silence until they felt sure she was out of the building.

Nick got up and closed the door. "Well. That was interesting. It looks like we'll have to go through Knight for anything else."

"Has the coroner been looking at poison?" O'Brien asked, rearranging his pudgy belly over his belt.

"Yeah. That's about all he's had to go on," the investigator said. "When I got nowhere with Ritter, I talked to the coroner. He's sure she was killed elsewhere and then placed beside the road. He's doing every test he knows. He can't find a wound or an injection site anywhere, though. There was nothing identifiable in the analysis of the stomach contents. The tissue hasn't tested positive for any well-known substance. If it was poison, it was administered very cleverly." He shrugged. "It looks like a lot depends on whether the coroner can find anything."

"Do you agree we should keep Ritter as a suspect even if we can't talk to her anymore?" Preston looked around the table.

"Without a doubt," Nick answered. "I'll look into her background some more. We have to check out the dentist, too. Has anybody been on that lately?"

"So we have two other suspects, huh?" O'Brien scratched his head and rubbed his hand through the rough brown beard that covered his cheeks and chin. "What's everybody's take on the guy in custody? LaVassar is it?"

"I'm not so sure," Nick admitted. "No motive."

O'Brien pulled his bulk up straighter in his chair. "We gotta have somebody in jail. Public outcry. This case is dragging out too long. We need a conviction. LaVassar had opportunity and no real alibi. He lied to us. There's his fingerprint on the victim. He was at the same location as she was that night. LaVassar has a record. I think he's the one. The rest of this is just pissin' in the wind…"

Nick spoke up. "I want go see the coroner myself. I think he's the one who'll find the key to this."

THE CORONER LISTENED to Nick's ideas about Jennifer Williams and responded. "I just can't find anything. This one baffles me so far. I really think it was poison, but I don't know what or how." He paused to polish a hand over his bald head. "Tell me again everything you know."

The man's eyes brightened when Nick finished. "You say she wasn't feeling well the night it happened? She drank at a bar? Her neighbor said she left the party early with stomach problems and a headache? Do you know her activities to the minute that day?"

"Well, not to the minute. I guess it was a typical Friday. She taught all day, then went home. She had pizza with her husband and son before she went to the neighbor's for a kitchenware party. She snuck out to a bar for a quick drink with two other women and drank the same thing her companions had. That's it."

"I need more. What she ate and drank for breakfast and lunch, too. What she had for snacks. Who ate lunch with her. What medications she took that day, even aspirin. Exactly where she was every second of that day. Find that out, will you? I think the key will be in there."

"Okay," Nick replied, thinking hard. He had to go back and see Dr. Williams. He dialed the dental office and insisted on another meeting with Dan Williams.

Chapter 41

THE NEXT DAY, Preston asked Mike to follow him out to Wasilla for another interview with Dan Williams. When they arrived, the perky receptionist instructed them to have a seat in the waiting room. Pouty voice heavy with annoyance, she reserved her blinding smile for the patient who checked in just after them.

Preston slipped into a chair in the waiting room while Mike explained to the receptionist that his coworker would be waiting. Preston wanted to observe as much as could by himself, and sensed a nervousness in her when he noticed her frequent anxious glances in his direction. He remembered Cindy's tale of the temper displayed by Dan Williams toward a problem child patient.

Mike was finally ushered into Dr. William's office by the reluctant receptionist and the dentist blew in, impatiently checking his watch. "Again? What's up? Anything new?" He asked, leaning against the edge of his desk.

"The coroner needs more detail on your wife's activities the day it happened," Mike began. "Everything. I need everything you can tell me. What she ate, where she was every minute. Anything unusual..."

Dan interrupted. "I've been through all this with the troopers. There's nothing new I can tell you. I don't have time for this again. I have to get back to my patients." He glanced toward the door.

"Fine, then. I'll call you into the station for a formal statement."

"Oh, all right," Dan answered with a groan. He walked around his desk, flopped down into his chair and poked a button on his phone. "Patti. Hold calls. Tell Mrs. Nelson there'll be a bit of a wait. See if you can reschedule my last patient. I'll be in a meeting for a while here and I can't be late picking up Tyler." He turned to Preston. "Okay. What exactly do you need to know?"

Dan Williams assured Mike that it had been a typical day for his wife as far as he knew. They'd talked briefly in the morning before she left for work. He saw her drink a cup of coffee with an envelope of hot chocolate mixed in like she did every morning. He didn't recall her eating anything else before she left the house. He had no information on her activities at school. She usually took her own lunch in a little kit, but he couldn't remember for sure if he'd seen one by her purse on the counter that morning. She hadn't reported anything unusual during supper that he could recall. Supper had been pizza since she had that party to go to at the neighbor's.

"I picked up the pizza so she could get Tyler on time after her appointment. And that's it. We ate supper. She had milk, so did Tyler and I. There were some leftover brownies but I can't remember if she had any. Tyler and I did."

Dan paused, his eyes far away. "Now that I think of it, she didn't eat very much. Said she didn't feel very good. Upset stomach. I forgot all about that." He looked up, eyebrows raised. "I forgot she felt kind of sick that night."

When Mike didn't respond, Dan continued, "She cleaned up the kitchen and looked through the mail that was on the counter. Then she left for the party a little before seven. It was just over at Amy's so she walked. She said she'd come home early if she didn't feel any better. I fooled around with Tyler and we watched TV until I put him to bed around eight. I fell asleep pretty quickly after that and didn't realize Jennifer wasn't home until morning. I totally forgot she felt sick that night. Is that important? She seemed okay at her appointment." His eyes had darkened with worry.

"Her appointment?"

"Yes. She was having a root canal. My only time to do it was late Friday afternoon. Usually I take off early Fridays, but I had an emergency crown prep that morning, and then I spent the afternoon catching up on paperwork. We had her come in after she got out of school that afternoon. I forgot all about it until now."

A flash of alarm crossed his face. "Should I have told you that earlier? It was no big deal. She broke a tooth on a piece of popcorn a couple days before and it was such a deep fracture that we had to do a root

canal. A whole cusp broke right down into the pulp."
He paused. "She was fine while she was in the chair.
She almost fell asleep, I remember now. We laughed
about it afterward, how she could fall asleep whenever
her feet were up and she didn't have to do anything."

Grief flashed across his features and he took a deep
steadying breath. "I did the initial procedure and then
Patti filled the canal temporarily with gutta percha -
that's routine until we're sure the tooth has settled
down and we can put in the final filling. It was just a
typical root canal. Then I left to pick up the pizza and
Jennifer was going to get Tyler. Patti said she'd close
up since we were here kind of late, so I took off. I can't
remember anything else at all that wasn't an ordinary
day."

Dan Williams looked down at his desk for a long
minute and brushed away tears. Uncomfortable and a
bit surprised at the display of emotion, Mike rose and
stuck out a hand.

Williams stood, too, his face blotchy. "It's hard," he
managed. "I miss her so much. And Tyler...he asks for
his mommy every day..." his voice broke. "Let me
know if..." He turned to the window and buried his
face in his hands, shoulders shaking. Mike stole out
and headed for the waiting room.

Patti looked up as he passed the reception desk.
"Will you need to see him anymore?" she asked in a
disapproving tone. "You can't just call when you're on
your way like this; we need time to fit you in. It makes
it hard for him if you don't come when he's got an
opening in his schedule. Call me first if you need to

meet with him again." Her tone was proprietary and she stared at Preston and Mike with reproach.

Whew! Where did that come from? She's so uptight and bossy, Preston thought. He shook the feeling off and led Mike out to the parking lot. "Well?"

Mike related what he'd heard and added, "I was really puzzled by the display of grief and emotion I hadn't expected to see. What a change."

They headed next for Valley Elementary. Preston wanted Mike to talk to the principal himself so he could tell the coroner he found out everything first hand. But the principal insisted he had no new details about Jennifer Williams.

"I haven't thought of anything I didn't already tell the troopers," he apologized. "I wish there was something more, but there isn't. The confrontation was simply an upset parent with a problem. Although, I must admit, in all my years, I haven't seen too many parents go ballistic like Mrs. Ritter did."

On the drive back, Preston made a quick call to Frank. "There's a new development on the Williams murder. The victim felt sick and had a dental appointment, the day of the crime. There's a new player, too, I think. The receptionist at the husband's dental office caught my attention today."

"Okay," Frank replied. "Let's go over it tomorrow. We have to move forward. O'Brien's pushing for a trial date. He's not gonna give us much more time. Mostly because the public's clamoring. Looks like LaVassar's on the hook unless we come up with something fast. Did you hear about the Ritter woman?"

"No, what?"

"Barb brought me a fax an hour ago. Ritter's attorney informed us that she'll be unavailable and all communication has to go to him from now on. She flew out last night to the Lower Forty Eight. Took her kid with her. For the holiday season she said."

Preston's mind spun in the shocked silence that followed until Frank spoke again. "The holiday season. Already. It's still November. Did anyone limit her activities? Set any conditions?"

"Not that I know of."

"Well, we sure as hell should have. She's a clever one. Now she's gone. We dropped the ball on this one, Mills."

Preston couldn't answer. He cursed under his breath. "Damn! We should have known. Should have predicted this." He pounded the steering wheel in frustration. A suspect was gone. Maybe they could extradite her. He wondered what the procedure was for that here in Alaska. He had to tell Cindy and decided to stop at the dog yard before heading home.

Chapter 42

WINTER DARKNESS WAS falling fast by the time he reached the kennel, even though it was only four-thirty. It'd been totally black on the mountain roads by the time he drove home from work the past few weeks, too, and there weren't any street lights so high up in the mountain neighborhoods.

He pulled into the parking lot, turned off the ignition, and noticed Cindy at the far end of the dog yard. She was leaning over a dog, rubbing its shoulders while its tail whipped back and forth in a frenzy of delight. Preston couldn't tear his eyes from the contours of her body as she bent.

Cindy stood up, looked in his direction, and gave a wave before starting over. "Hi," she greeted him as she reached his window. Her cheeks were flushed with cold beneath a blue stocking cap and her breath shot a quick plume of frost onto the air between them. She was breathing hard. It reminded Preston of other times she'd breathed like that.

"Are you done soon?" he asked.

"Yup. I was just finishing up."

"Can you go into Anchorage with me? We can stop and see your Dad."

A charge flashed through the air between them. Spend Friday and the weekend in Anchorage. Stay at his apartment. Spend three days together.

Cindy answered without hesitation. "Okay, but should we drive separately? So we won't be seen together? I really don't want to do anything that might damage Dad's case. And your boss would be pretty mad, wouldn't he, if he found out?"

Preston sighed. She was right.

But before he could reply, she went on. "Dad can talk on the phone right there at his bed now, so that sure is nice. He says it's boring but way better than jail. He had to talk to a psychiatrist today. He said it was a waste of time and he sounded kind of irritated because the doctor kept harping about booze. But he sounds okay."

She went on, a feisty gleam in her eyes. "And yes, I'd like to come into Anchorage. Let me grab my things and I'll follow you."

"Naw. Come with me. We'll be careful. We'll go into the hospital separately. Not eat out. I can bring you back Sunday night or early Monday. Most likely, I'll have business up here anyway." Great. A whole weekend with her. At his place. She'd be in his bed in the mornings. They could have breakfast together. Do lots of things together. He blushed. The hell with Frank. They'd be careful not to be seen together. He'd take the risk.

Cindy gave a naughty grin filled with promise. A flash of jealousy surprised him. Who else had she grinned at like that?

THEY FOUND GARY sitting in a crisp, clean hospital robe and black slippers in the day room of his ward. A stock car race filled the screen and he didn't notice them until Cindy slid into the chair beside him and nudged his arm.

"Hi, Dad. How are you?"

Gary reached over and drew her close for a hug. "Good. Real good, Honey. Food isn't bad. At least not compared to where I came from," he grinned. "Hey, Mills. Thanks for all you're doing. Keeping Daisy and all. And gettin' me out of there, especially."

Preston dipped his head in acknowledgement.

"Any news on my case?" Gary asked with an anxious frown. "We gettin' anywhere?"

"There are some new developments we're still working on. I can give you a complete report in a few more days. What does the doctor say about keeping you here?"

"Guess they think I have some problems. Some "stuff to work on" the psychiatrist says. He said I'll be here at least another week. Fine with me. But it's not like bein' home." He shrugged. "Hey, what about Daisy? How's she doin? God, I miss her."

"Daisy's doing fine at my place. She's a good dog," Preston answered.

Cindy and Preston walked ten feet apart through the darkness to the parking lot, their attention drawn to twinkling white and blue lights that covered trees and buildings all over the city. Above the glittering city, thousands of stars dazzled the black sky. Not even the Christmas displays in the Lower Forty Eight had ever come close to this splendor.

Seeing Preston's awe, Cindy called over to him. "City of Lights, we call it. Helps with the dark winters. It's pretty, isn't it?"

Preston's heart warmed. Cindy going home with him. Daisy waiting there. Nearly overcome with happiness and a desire to get home to his snug apartment. He fought off a troublesome spark of jealousy. He hadn't been her first. Cindy had been with another guy. Why had she never mentioned someone else? Who? Why couldn't he bring it up to her?

"How about we pick up a pizza?" he asked, pushing those thoughts from his mind.

"Sounds good," she replied, eyes shining with reflected light. She scurried to his car after he was in, and slipped quickly in beside him, ducking her head.

WHEN HE OPENED her car door in the apartment driveway later, a shaft of moonlight shone directly onto her face, illuminating it. Preston paused at her beauty, then looked up, pointing to the moon. Cindy followed his gaze and both stood, mesmerized. A silvery half-moon hung above them.

Cindy smiled up at him. "How beautiful!"

"Yes." Preston answered. "Like you."

He took Cindy in his arms and kissed her, enraptured. They stumbled through his front door, entwined. Daisy scooted out between them, returning a quick moment later, tail wagging furiously. Preston scooped some food into Daisy's bowl, never letting go of Cindy. They moved as one down the hall toward the bedroom. Preston half-heartedly mumbled something about the bed not being made, but the taste of Cindy's lips made him eager to nibble. She became the only thing he could concentrate on.

This time, Cindy teased him, taking her time undressing while he waited beneath the cool sheets.

The bedding had been kicked into a tangle by the time they finished. A shower together brought new pleasures. Slippery soap, clean wet kisses, the soft lush body pressing back at him brought a giddiness Preston had never before experienced.

Preston was padding to the kitchen for a glass of water with a towel wrapped around his waist when strange greenish lights bouncing across the living room walls caught his attention. He walked into the room and looked out. He called to Cindy. "Come quick. Look! I think it's the northern lights!"

Cindy appeared at his side, tucking a shirt into her sweatpants. "Oh! Let's grab coats and mittens and go out in the yard. It's always best looking north!"

Preston snuggled Cindy close against him in the numbingly cold night air of the yard. He wrapped his arms around her from behind, cradling her to keep her warm. For the next half hour, they stood pressed together, watching the show that danced across the black sky of the northern horizon. Shivering, twisting beams of white and gold and green flooded the sky, lighting up the landscape and mountaintops. Curtains of undulating light tumbled and whirled, illuminating half of the sky. Monstrous spears of glowing green changed to crimson and then shimmered and danced, arching across the sky. Brilliant dancing lights flitted randomly, whirling, glowing white before transforming into zinging rays of red. Preston was awestruck.

Finally feeling the deepening cold of the night, they returned to the living room. "Hey, where's Daisy?" Cindy asked. The dog was nowhere to be seen and didn't answer their calls.

"Did she get out when we had the door open?" Preston asked.

"I don't think so. We would have noticed."

Just then, a small scraping noise drew them to the bedroom. Finding only an empty room, Preston bent down and peered under the bed.

He laughed. "Here she is. I bet she was scared of the lights. Come here, girl. Come on, good girl."

He coaxed a reluctant and trembling Daisy from under the bed. Cindy rushed over to comfort the fearful dog and soon had her squirming into her embrace and wagging her tail. While Preston watched, he realized he had never felt such tenderness and love and contentment. Cindy was the one. Never mind anything else, not Frank, not his parents, not Victoria. He turned away to hide tears of raw emotion that threatened to choke him.

Chapter 43

NICK WATCHED THE AURORA display that night, too. His bedroom window faced north and since he was such a light sleeper, he often woke to the dancing lights across his bedroom walls. The show was so spectacular this time that he roused Kay.

"Hey, Baby. Great northern lights. You asked me to wake you up when they're this good."

Kay shook off sleep, rolled from under the covers and joined him at the window, tugging a sheet around her bare shoulders. He wrapped his arms around her to ward off the chill as she leaned back into him, drawing on his warmth. They stood without speaking while the aurora display flashed and flickered across the sky.

"Thanks for waking me. This is beautiful. Are you still having trouble sleeping?" Kay finally asked, her voice husky in the darkness.

"Yeah."

"The case?"

"Yup. I just can't put it to rest. Some of us don't think we have the right guy in custody and it looks like he's gonna have to go to trial. The sucker won't have a chance. Even with a jury. There's been too much publicity already and too many other things not in his favor. Somebody has to go down. If it's him, I think we'll be convicting the wrong man."

"And you can't pin down why you think it's someone else?"

"Nope. Just a gut feeling."

"Well, then, why don't you think outside the box? What if it was someone you haven't even suspected before? Who was in her world that would have wanted her dead? For any reason you haven't even thought of yet? There has to be a motive out there somewhere."

"Yeah. That's what bothers me most, I guess. No real motive. The guy we arrested didn't even know her. He had had no connection to the victim except finding her body. Well, and being in the same bar earlier that night. But nobody saw them even look at each other. As far as we can tell, he had no reason to do such a thing."

"Have you guys looked at a possible affair? Either the victim or her husband? Or some kind of trouble from her past, like long ago, that you don't know about yet?"

By the time Nick drew the curtains tight and cuddled Kay back to sleep, he had a plan. They needed to look harder at the victim. That's what had been bothering him. Kay was so wise. And warm. He fell into a much needed deep sleep, holding his wife close.

THAT PLAN HAD been implemented by the time O'Brien called Nick into his office the next afternoon.

O'Brien leaned back heavily into his huge leather chair. "Whatcha got? Long enough now for that LaVassar to be just sittin' around. I'm filing our request for a trial date on him tomorrow."

"You might want to wait," Nick replied. He had awakened rested, charged and motivated this morning and had been at his desk since six. "I have new information on the victim and her husband. I talked to some neighbors over the weekend."

"I thought you were off on the weekend," O'Brien interrupted.

"Yeah, but I was around that neighborhood for my son's tournament, so I went over there. I guess the Williams did a fair amount of arguing. Loud enough for others to hear. And I talked to the neighbor who does daycare for their kid. She's the one who had the party that night, too. I got some interesting stuff from her. She told me Jennifer Williams wanted to have another kid, but the husband kept saying no. Apparently, they fought a lot about money, too."

"So you think we should be looking at the husband?"

"Yeah. For sure."

"Well, then. Bring him in again for questioning. Let's get moving on this. Today. We don't want that defense attorney discovering this and ambushing us at the last minute. And I sure as hell don't want to look like a fool for holding the wrong man this long. Make this your priority." O'Brien's face had grown ruddy. "Let's get this thing put to bed."

NICK WAS TAKEN aback at the tone of Dr. William's receptionist when he called.

"No, he's with a patient. You can't speak with him right now. I'll have to take a message," she said, her tone short and dismissive.

Nick snorted. What's with her? Must have rough Monday mornings. Well, she's not in charge here. "This is Alaska State Trooper Nick Kerrans. I will speak with Dr. Williams. Now. Go bring him to the phone."

"I told you. Our policy is that he can't be interrupted with phone calls when he's with a patient," she argued, her voice snippy, hostile.

In the silence of the next few seconds, Nick bristled. She was directly challenging him. Who did she think she was? "Tell him I'm on the phone."

"No. I will not break policy. He is not to be disturbed."

Nick slammed the receiver down. He motioned for Matt to follow him as he passed his desk. "Bring your jacket and badge. We're going to Dr. Williams' office." He stomped to the patrol car.

Matt hustled into the seat beside him as Nick started the engine. "What's up?"

Nick explained while they covered the two miles to the dental office. Still steaming, Nick pushed open the glass doors to the suite and strode to the desk. He flashed his badge. The receptionist's eyes grew wide with surprise.

"Trooper Kerrans. We talked earlier. I need to see him."

The receptionist reared up behind her counter, slapped open the appointment book and glared at Nick, "I told you to make an appointment. All of you are interrupting his schedule too much. He gets behind."

Her mouth puckered in disapproval and she crossed her arms across her jutting chest. Her eyes flashed with challenge while Nick stood momentarily astounded at her belligerence. He turned to Matt who was watching the exchange with astonishment. It was apparent that this young woman was not intimidated at all by law enforcement.

They heard Dr. Williams call out," Patti? What's up out there? Is there a problem?"

"Yes, sir," Nick called back. "Alaska State Troopers to see you." He shot a threatening look at the receptionist, whose face had mottled deep red. She turned and stormed away down the hall behind her.

Dan Williams strode past her with a puzzled look as she tore around him. He turned. "Patti...?" But she ignored him and disappeared. He turned to Nick. "What's this about? Aren't you the one I talked to last month?"

"Yes, sir. We need to talk to you again. I tried to set something up but I couldn't get anywhere with your receptionist by phone. Patti, is it?"

Williams nodded, concern and confusion playing across his face. "I have an hour free at noon. Will that work? Can it be here? If I drive into the station, it'll take up some time. I have a one o'clock patient."

"Can you cancel it? We'd like you to come in. Noon would be fine."

Williams nodded. "I'll be there. What's this about anyway? Something new come up? I told the suspect's attorney everything last week when he was here. "

"We'd prefer to discuss it at the station," Nick replied. "See you there."

Back in the car, Matt let out a whoop. "Man! That Patti would give the Ritter woman a run for it in a bitch contest!"

"She's over-reacting," Nick said. "I don't like it. She's too damn hostile for the situation."

Chapter 44

PATTI'S ADDRESS TURNED out to be a tiny, wood-sided house with white paint begging to be recoated. Vintage storm windows, their green painted frames flaked bare by the seasons and glass clouded with age, clung to the siding. A withered flower garden skirted the unpainted block foundation and wilted yellow grass that hadn't been mowed for a final time peeked from the edges of the snow-covered yard.

Preston parked across the street and studied the house. What kind of woman would live here, what was she really like, was this house where she grew up? While he watched, a white-haired woman opened the front door and let out a miniature, fluffy black dog that scooted for the shrubs along the fence. She glanced curiously across the street at Preston while waiting for it. Patti's mother? Maybe she'd talk to him. Preston opened the car door and started across the street.

"Mimi!" the woman called, growing alarmed as he approached. "Mimi! Get in here. Right now!"

"Are you Patti's mother?" Preston called from the edge of the street.

The woman's eyebrows shot up. She took several cautious steps back into the house. "Mimi! Get up here!" This time the little dog scurried for the steps and disappeared into the doorway behind her.

"I'm an attorney working on the Jennifer Williams murder case," Preston called to her. He might be compromising the case by being involved in doing an interview himself. *What the hell. This disregard for protocol must be what being in Alaska does to people.* He stepped toward her, wiping a flash of Franks' disapproving face from his mind.

The woman looked at him, eyes wary, lips puckered in confusion.

"I'm checking some things out. Looking for any clues that might help. Your daughter works for Dr. Williams, right?"

This time the woman's look was less fearful. "A lawyer, you say?" she asked in a throaty voice. A smoker.

"Yeah. I'm working on the case with Dr. Williams," Preston said, surprising himself.

"Oh, yeah, okay then. Patti works for him. She's been there 'bout four years now."

"Can I talk to you for a minute? Just to clear some things up?"

"I suppose," the woman replied. "You might as well come on in then." She backed up a few steps and motioned him in. "You got a card or something?"

She studied the card Preston handed her. "Public Defender. That's where you help folks who can't pay, right?"

Preston nodded. His answer seemed to please her.

She looked him full in the eyes now. "I'm Gladys. My auntie had a public defender once. Nice enough man. Helped her get off a hit and run. She never did it. It was somebody else's car, they found out. But she was real happy with how he helped her. So, what do ya need to know?"

A flash of conscience whipped through Preston's mind. The old woman didn't understand that he might be looking for evidence against her daughter's employer. Well, that was her problem. He'd get whatever information he could.

He quickly gained Patti's mother's confidence with a reassuring smile. She settled in a rocking chair after motioning Preston to the shabby orange and brown plaid sofa, seeming eager to have a willing listener.

She reached down, scooped Mimi into her arms, cuddled her dog, and began. "Well, my Patti's been with Dr. Williams for a little over four years now, like I said. He treats her real good. She even babysits their little boy for them... well, him." She paused to gather herself. Preston realized Gladys was one of those people who will just go on talking as long as they have someone willing to listen. Perfect. Let her roll. He turned eager eyes to her and she began again, basking in the attention.

"Such a tragedy. His wife. Patti was real broken up about it. She stayed with little Tyler the day of the funeral so Dr. Williams could take care of things without worrying about the little one. Patti's brung the little guy to see me a coupla times before when she's been babysittin' him. And she stayed at their house last year with him for a whole week while they went to Hawaii."

Gladys continued with a proud lift of her chin. "Them people think the world of Patti. She does everything at the office. Runs the desk. Does the books. Even assists with patients when the other gal ain't there. She can do everything. Doc depends on her."

Preston looked at his watch. He had to leave in a few minutes to be back at the troopers' office by noon. "Can I ask you a few questions?"

"Sure." Gladys smiled at her new friend, revealing brown stained teeth that leaned against each other like crooked fence posts.

"How did you and Patti hear about Jennifer?"

"Oh, somebody called the next morning. We was just shocked. Patti was a wreck. Bawled her eyes out. Couldn't hardly talk. I had to make her tomato soup and toast twice. That's her favorite when she doesn't feel so good, but she hardly ate any. Just moped around. Then Monday, she went in to the office real early and called all the patients to let 'em know not to come in. She took care of it all for Doc."

Gladys turned self-satisfied eyes to Preston. "My girl would do anything for Doc. Anything."

A chill overcame Preston at her words. "I have to leave for a meeting now," he said. "Thank you so much. You've been wonderful. And you should be very proud of Patti. You raised a fine girl. Does she live here with you?"

"Yup. Been here all her life. She's big help to me. My older daughter's married so now it's just the two of us."

"Do you mind if I look around the outside before I leave?" Preston asked.

"Oh, sure. That's fine. And come back again anytime, young man. Have you met Patti?" she asked with a sudden gleam in her eye. Her eyes flitted to his left hand.

"Yes, at the dental office. On the case," Preston assured her and hurried to the door. "I just need to take a quick look around and then I have to get to that meeting. Thank you again."

Gladys rushed to accompany him as he walked out the front door. He waved before turning the corner of the house into the backyard. Instantly, he noticed a shiny aluminum step ladder propped against the side of the decrepit garage. The ladder's feet rested atop mashed snow over matted grass. It was apparent it hadn't been there when the grass was last mowed or before the snow fell. *Why was a new ladder out here? The clothes bundle! How high up in that tree was it?* His breathing accelerated. *Why would a new ladder be sitting out here?*

It was difficult to keep his steps leisurely while walking around the other side of the house to the front yard. He wanted to run. To race to the station with this new information. He waved to Gladys whose face peered from the kitchen window and received a perky wave and enthusiastic smile in return. Her hair smashed against the smudged window and he thought he saw her give a wink.

Preston hid a shudder and raced down the sidewalk to his car.

Chapter 45

THE NOON MEETING with Dan Williams began right on time.

Nick spoke first. "We're recording this. There'll be a transcript ready for the PD later today. We asked you to come in to go over some new developments in the case. First, we've heard you and your wife were having some trouble that you haven't mentioned to us. Care to enlighten us?"

The dentist's face paled. "Like what?"

"You know. Disagreements about another kid. Money. Other stuff. You know what we're talking about. Don't waste our time here." He spoke up with surprising rancor. This mess was keeping an innocent man from his job and his home. It would make the troopers look bad if it went on much longer. "So, talk," he ordered.

Williams' gulp was audible. His mouth tightened. "I have the right to have an attorney present. I think I need to call my lawyer."

"Go ahead. Call him. Have him come on in. We'll wait." Nick's voice grew cold with authority.

Dan Williams wilted, "Okay. Okay. I don't need him. Will you be recording this?"

"Yup," Matt answered and pushed the recorder's button. "You have the right to remain silent. Anything you say can…"

"I know. I know. I waive 'em," Williams responded.

"I have to read 'em to you in their entirety," Matt said and completed his spiel. When finished, he added, "Go ahead. Just tell us everything. Save us time asking the questions. We already know how it was between you and your wife."

With a look of resignation, Dan Williams explained how he and Jennifer had moved back to Wasilla after his graduation from dental school. Their plan was to both work for five years to get established financially before starting a family. How Tyler happened had been a mystery to him. Jennifer must have missed a pill. Having a child early made their plan tougher to stick to, but they decided to keep on track. But then when Tyler turned two, Jennifer began harping about having a sibling for him so the kids wouldn't be too far apart to be friends.

"I didn't agree. I wanted to stick to our plan. I still need a couple more years to get the practice as profitable as I want. She was stubborn about another baby, though. Yeah, we did argue about it. And sure, we fought about money, like everybody. I didn't think we should just go ahead and have another kid right away or we'd never get ahead. Daycare alone for Tyler runs almost as much as our mortgage. We didn't agree about it. But it wasn't bad enough between us that I'd kill my wife. My God!"

Williams turned agonized eyes to the other men. "I'd never hurt Jennifer. She was my wife. I loved her. We were working through it. Every marriage has its problems, you know that, don't you? We loved each other..." His voice broke. "She was Tyler's mommy. We'd bought the house. We were working hard at our jobs, making it fine." His voice trailed off and he looked across the table in desperation. "Surely you don't think I killed Jennifer?"

In the silence following his words, nobody met his eyes.

Finally, Nick spoke. "Tell us about your practice. Employees. Finances. Everything."

"Well, I'm finally making money," Williams said. "You can look at the books. Or have someone audit them. I have nothing to hide. I'm clean that way. It should be a real good living about another year from now. I have my equipment almost paid for now, even the Panoramic X-ray machine. It would have been only another year or so until we could afford another baby." His gaze drifted off. Everyone waited in silence.

He gave a sigh. "I don't know what else to tell you. My receptionist Patti's been with me for almost five years now. She was my first full-time employee. She did everything in the early days. I trained her on the job and she was quick to pick it all up. Last January, I added Denise. She's my assistant Monday through Thursday. A good employee, too. She came out of the assisting program at UAA. She's pretty bright." He raised his palms upright. "That's all. I don't know what else to tell you."

"This Patti. She was extremely protective of you when we've tried to see you. Why's that?"

"She was?" Williams asked in surprise. "How so?"

"Pretty hostile, actually," Nick said.

"Really?"

"Yeah, to say the least. What's her relationship with you? She gives the impression that she's very important in your life. Does she do more than work in the office?"

Williams' eyebrows shot up in surprise. "How do you know that?" When nobody answered, he went on. "Well, she's been babysitting for us ever since Tyler was born. Like when we go out. And when we went to Hawaii for a week. Tyler adores her. We always felt confident that he'd be well cared for when he was with Patti." He turned to Preston, face scrunched and eyebrows knit. "What makes you ask about her?"

When the men around the table just looked back at him without speaking, Williams continued in a troubled voice. "We had Patti over for the holidays last year. She's almost like family now. She brought her mother over, too. Jennifer counts..." he choked.

There was an uneasy silence while Williams composed himself. "I don't like where this line of questioning is going. I'm getting uneasy. Maybe I should call my attorney."

"Sure. It's your right. But this is enough for today anyway." O'Brien heaved himself to his feet. "Let's call it a day. Have your attorney call me directly so we can set up a follow-up interview on this within the next few days." He extended a pudgy hand to Williams. "You're free to go. You've been a great help."

After Williams left, O'Brien turned to the others. "Well?"

"The wrong man is being held," Nick answered. "We're gonna look more and more like fools the longer we keep him. It's the Ritter woman, Williams, or this Patti; maybe some combination of the three. We better release LaVassar." He met O'Brien's startled gaze. "You're wrong about LaVassar."

For the first time, he detected a shadow of doubt flit across O'Brien's face. Then the big man shook his head, turned away and left the room.

PRESTON DROVE THROUGH the drive up window of the McDonalds on the corner and downed the burger and onion rings before heading back to Anchorage. He was hungry, and fired up. His mind raced. The ladder was finally a break in the case. Gary's ordeal might be coming to an end.

He picked up his messages with a brief nod to Barb and started on the three new folders that had appeared in his message slot. *What? Jeff Griffin again? I thought he was in jail. Now what's he done?* He shook his head in frustration while he read. *Theft from a liquor store? The idiot. I guess if you want to get caught, that's how to do it. They have cameras all over the stores. It says here he was positively identified on one. Now I have to find him and defend him again. What a waste of taxpayers' money. He probably wants to go back to jail now that the December weather is starting and the nights are so long and dark. He probably wants a warm bed and three meals a day he doesn't have to scrounge for. What a waste of my time. I better see if they're still holding him. And his court date is tomorrow already. God.*

Preston left his desk at five thirty, feeling weary. He dialed Cindy. "Hi. How'd your day go?"

At her soft reply, he closed his eyes. "I'm totally beat, too. Guess we know why after the weekend, huh?"

She giggled. "Go home to bed. I can't stay awake another minute, either. I'm already home and I'm making some soup and then heading for my pillow."

Preston said goodnight and headed for home. Home. That sounded nice. He felt too worn out to even think anymore while he drove up the now familiar twisting turns to his apartment. He let Daisy out, watched her prance around the yard, and then warmed a leftover burrito before collapsing into bed. He nestled into Cindy's pillow until sleep claimed him.

Chapter 46

PRESTON RUSHED INTO Frank's office without an appointment the next morning and reported yesterday's findings about Dr. Williams and Patti, and the ladder.

Frank's eyes lit up. "Go get 'em, Mills. I'll authorize Mike to work right by your side full time until further notice. You can't do the interviewing yourself, you understand that, don't you?"

Preston gave a guilty nod. "Yeah. I do. Sorry. I just went ahead since the old lady wanted to talk. I didn't expect it to happen that way."

"Don't do it again, hear me? We might get away with it, but let's not push our luck. Make a demand to the troopers for search warrants for the dental office and for the dentist's and the receptionist's houses."

He pushed back from his desk and rose. "Nab that ladder, too, right away. Might have some residue left on the feet that would put it at the crime scene. Get right on it. Looks like we have something concrete to go on. Don't go it alone again. I mean it. I didn't figure you for a maverick. Knock it off! Keep Mike with you at all times, got it?"

"Can we be present for the all searches?" Preston asked. "I don't trust the troopers to do it as well as we would. I'll keep Mike with me."

Frank thought for a minute, then punched his phone button. "Okay. Fine. You've already blown it by talking to the mother and I don't like it. We're gonna discuss it when this is over." He scowled, then shrugged. "But we need progress and we have the right to observe the troopers when they search. I'll call O'Brien myself right now for that document. Mike has to stay with you every minute on this. Every minute, understand me?" He waved Preston out of his office.

Preston located Jeff Griffin who was still in custody, but knew it would be a waste of time to try to get a story out of him. The ten o'clock hearing went just as expected. Griffin met Preston's eyes only briefly after being led handcuffed into the courtroom. He shook his head when Preston walked over and asked if there was reason to appeal the charge. He promptly pled guilty to attempted robbery, was sentenced to six months, and accompanied the uniformed guards out, looking strangely satisfied. Preston was out of the courtroom within a half hour.

Copies of the search warrants for Dan Williams' office and home and Patti's house lay on his desk when he got back to the office. Under them lay a court order allowing the defense's investigator and attorney to inspect evidence and observe the searches. There was also a message from Mike, saying he was ready to head for Palmer as soon as Preston needed him.

Chapter 47

PRESTON AND MIKE pulled up in front of the house shared by Gladys and Patti, hoping the lack of the presence of a trooper wouldn't pose problems down the road. Preston's mind raced while Mike parked behind him. He needed to grab that ladder first thing. He asked Mike to remain in the car and headed up the cracked sidewalk to the house. This time, Gladys opened the door at his knock so quickly that Preston knew she must have watched them pull up.

"Hi, Gladys. Preston Mills. Remember me from the other day?"

She smiled in recognition. "You're back so soon. Do you have more questions? Come on in. I can put the coffee pot on."

She smoothed the baggy, pilled black sweater that drooped over her hips. Loose tan slacks hung over the grubby brown slippers rimmed in fake fur. She smiled coyly, exposing a missing tooth in the corner of her mouth that he hadn't noticed before. With great effort, Preston kept himself from recoiling.

"Come on in," she repeated.

"Ummm. Well. I have a colleague with me. He's out in the car." Gladys glanced out. "Oh. Well, sure, then. He can come in, too."

"Thanks. But we're here on official business. He's an investigator from Anchorage who works with me. We have a warrant. A warrant to search this dwelling and grounds."

Gladys' eyes widened. "What? What for? What does that mean, a warrant?"

Preston thrust it at her. She grabbed it, scanned it and handed it back too quickly to have absorbed what it said. She stood searching his eyes, obviously confused.

"Gladys. You have to step back. The investigator and I will be going through the house and yard. This piece of paper allows us to do that."

Anxiety and fear replaced her confusion. "But...but...why? Why do you hafta do this? What's wrong?" she stammered, eyes now wide with dismay.

"It relates to Jennifer Williams' case," Preston explained as kindly as he could. "It's really nothing to worry about. You're not in any trouble. We'll be done as soon as we can. We're doing several searches. You're not the only one. Please step aside." He waved Matt in.

"Start on the inside. I'll do the yard." Preston instructed as he reached the front door.

Gladys stood back in the entry with a bewildered expression. "I'm calling Patti," she mumbled and rushed away while Matt moved into the living room.

Preston hurried around the corner of the house. The ladder was still there. He sprinted to the ladder, took some pictures of it, then raced back to his car to pull on a pair of sterile gloves. He swung the ladder over his shoulder, and to his relief, the Jeep's hatchback allowed him to slide the full length of the ladder all the way in across the headrest of the passenger's seat.

He turned back to the yard. There was nothing of interest along the front and sides of the house. The shabby garage was unlocked, empty except for a grass-caked red lawn mower, two rakes with dilapidated wooden handles and a tarnished metal scoop shovel. The packed dirt floor gave off a strong musty smell and the unpainted studs that made up the walls showed years of dank, accumulated dust. A single high window, nearly opaque with smudged dust and cobwebs, gave off only enough light to show Preston that the building was empty and apparently rarely used. He returned to the house.

Gladys, her mouth now hard and tight, met him at the back door. "Patti's on her way home. She'll be here any minute. She said to keep you men out of the house." Fear and hostility chased each other across her features.

"Sorry, but we have the right to be in here. This warrant gives us the right. We're going to keep on with our work," Preston said. "I'm sorry, but you have to let us do this. It's the law."

Gladys backed away, reluctance obvious in every move. "Well, if the law says so. But Patti will be here any minute." She continued to stand by the kitchen door, eyes now filled with betrayal and accusation. She clutched Mimi to her chest. Preston followed the sound of the investigator.

"Got the ladder," he said when Mike looked up at him.

"Good. It may be the only thing we go away with. There's not much here. The house doesn't even have a basement. The walls and ceilings look undisturbed and the floors haven't been touched for a long time, that I can tell. There's really no place to hide anything. I already went through the dresser drawers in both bedrooms. Nothing out of the ordinary there. Same with the closets. Will you help me roll up this living room carpet? The place is so small and simply built, that's about the only thing left."

As Preston and the investigator began to roll up the shabby piece of moss green shag carpet, a mist of dirt dropped steadily from it. Preston felt his eyes watering and sneezed hard.

"God. It's filthy," Mike mumbled, wiping his eyes. "Whew!"

Just then, the front door opened and Patti stormed in. "What the hell are you doing here?" she raged, flinging her purse on a chair. "You have no right to be here!" She stood with hands on hips, glaring, waiting for an answer. Preston got up and brushed the dirt from his hands.

"We're just finishing. We have a search warrant that was signed by a judge this morning. Please calm down. We're just following every possible lead on the Jennifer

Williams' case. We're almost done here. There's nothing to…"

Patti interrupted, "Let me see that warrant." Preston handed it to her. She studied it briefly and thrust it back at him. "You shoulda called me. You got my mother upset. You can't just barge in on an old lady like this." She paused for breath and studied Preston. "You're one of them that's been at the office, aren't you?"

When Preston nodded, she continued, "Well, you shoulda called me about this. You've scared my mother half to death. Who do you think you are? Get out of here right now!" Her face had grown red and her eyes blazed with hostility. She sucked in several hard breaths and took a threatening step forward.

Preston ignored her and turned to Mike. "Let's finish with the carpet."

The investigator crouched to continue rolling up the filthy rug.

"Did you understand me?" Patti yelled. She stamped her foot in their direction. "Get out of my house! Now! I'm calling the troopers!"

Preston turned his back and bent to help with the rug. A second later, a thick cloud of flying dust blinded him. Patti had stepped onto the carpet roll and kicked it as hard as she could right into his face. Preston leaped up, choking, eyes burning and watering. He wiped at them desperately.

Mike spoke. "Here, man. Follow me to the kitchen sink. We'll rinse you off." Preston grabbed blindly for Mike's arm and stumbled behind him to the kitchen.

"Over here, put your head under the faucet. Right here. Splash lots of water."

Painful minutes later, Preston fumbled for the towel the man handed him and wiped his face. The towel stunk of grease and old food. Preston managed to open his burning eyes and take several deep gulps of air.

Mike's concerned face was the first thing he saw. "Let's get out of here. She's crazy. We can send a team back."

Now enraged, Preston swiped at his eyes again and looked across the room to where Patti stood bristling with defiance at her mother's side next to the refrigerator.

"Now get out and don't come back," she ordered.

"No. We will finish our search now. You stand back. If you say another word, I'll file charges against you for assault and obstruction of justice. You stay away from us and keep your mouth shut! We're going to finish! And the troopers will be coming in to do a search like this, too."

He heard gasps from all three before motioning to his colleague. "Let's get it done."

Mike followed him past Gladys and Patti, who stood aside in shocked silence.

When the men finished rolling up the carpet, it was obvious that the grimy floor beneath it had not been disturbed for many years. They unrolled the carpet back into place and without a backward glance or another word, Preston led the way out the front door, leaving it standing open.

"Okay, Mike. Let's hit the dental office next. Follow me."

He noted a glimmer of surprise and admiration in Mike's eyes before sliding into the driver's seat of the Jeep. The ladder partially blocked his view through the passenger window, but he didn't care. Having that ladder was important. He hoped Patti was watching and hoped she noticed her ladder in his car. Bitch! He gunned the accelerator and shot away from the curb.

Chapter 48

PRESTON BRUSHED HIMSELF off as best he could in the parking lot of the dental office. Mike stepped over from his car and swatted the dust off Preston's shoulders and back.

Preston finished by ruffling his fingers through his hair and looked to Mike. "Okay?"

Mike grimaced. "You'll do." He shook his head. "I can't believe she did that to you. Bet a shower would feel good, huh?"

It was a relief to see an empty receptionist desk at the dental office. Preston felt even better when a trooper walked in just in time to join them.

When Preston called out, "Dr. Williams?" Dan popped his head out an operatory door. "Be right there."

He walked out to the desk a long minute later, curiosity and alarm playing across his face. He spoke first to the woman sitting on the other side of the waiting room. "Mrs. Evenson, Jake will be finished in a moment. He did fine. Denise will bring him out as soon as the sealants have finished setting up."

He motioned Preston and Matt to follow him and led the way to his private office where he turned and faced them with a questioning look. "Patti took off in a huff a while ago. Something about you and a search warrant. What's going on?"

"Yeah, we do have warrants. For her home, and yours, and this office," Preston replied. "We'll start here right now."

Williams' eyes widened. "Search warrants? For here? Right now? What for? What's going on?"

"There's a new lead. We can't say more right now. We'll be as quick as we can. Go ahead with your normal activities. But we'll need to get into every room here."

"Wait a minute. Let me see that." Williams studied the document Preston handed him. "Do you have to do it now? I have patients scheduled all day. What will they think? Can't it be rescheduled for Friday afternoon or the weekend?"

Preston shook his head. "Nope. You have no choice but to allow it and be cooperative. We'll be as unobtrusive as we can. Nobody needs to know what's going on."

At Williams' look of dismay, Preston added, "We'll start with the empty patient rooms and let you know when we're through with the first one. Maybe you can move into it and then we'll get to the rest. We should be done and out of here in a few hours. We apologize for the intrusion, but it's necessary to the progress of the investigation."

Preston could see that Williams was upset and felt a flash of sympathy for him. But it quickly passed and he directed Mike and the trooper into the first empty treatment room. It was past three by the time they finished and Preston became aware of sharp pangs of hunger. He'd been expecting Patti to return and was braced for another confrontation, but to his relief she didn't show up. The phone buzzed many times during the afternoon, but apparently a machine was picking up the calls.

"Let's go," he said to Mike. "Should we pick up something to eat?"

Mike gave an eager, "Yeah. I'm starving."

Dan Williams didn't look up from his patient when Preston stuck his head around the door frame. "We're out of here. We'll be heading over to your house next. Can we get in?"

Dan answered without turning around, his tone sullen. "The door is open on the side of the garage. I'd appreciate it if you don't mess things up too much."

Preston visited the men's room at the sandwich shop and noticed his face was still smudged with a bit of carpet dirt. He bent over the sink and splashed warm water over his face, bumped soap from the dispenser and scrubbed his neck and ears, then did a thorough job on his hands. He dried off as best he could with the stiff paper towels and joined Mike at a table where his sandwich waited. "Ok, I feel better." he said.

Mike shook his head, "Can you believe she did that to you? That was just plain crazy. She kinda scares me. Is she a suspect?"

"You bet." Between bites of sandwich, Preston filled Mike in on the latest developments of the case. "And my boss says you're on this with me until we're done."

"Okay. I have a sister here in Wasilla. I think I'll stay overnight with her to save the drive back to Anchorage. It looks like we might be facing some long hours. That's fine with me. If you think the wrong guy's in jail, let's get him out."

Preston drove to the Williams' house, heartened by his new partner's attitude and work ethic. But along the way, he grew frustrated again. He had to get Gary out before he had to leave the hospital and return to a jail cell. They had to find the real criminal. He was sure now it was Patti. She probably wanted to step into Jennifer's shoes. But he didn't think she was capable of pulling it off alone. Especially being able to conceal the cause of death so well, move the body, and leave no clues at all. So there had to be someone else. Maybe Dan Williams. Maybe not. It sure wasn't her clueless mother who helped her. So who was it?

He realized, too, how valuable Trooper Nick's cooperation had been, and marveled at being part of a team like this. The arresting officers were supposed to be his opponents. But Nick hadn't formally enforced the discovery rules or made Preston go through the process of written requests for every bit of information. The only thing Preston could think of to explain the cooperation was that Nick had his own doubts about who the real murderer was. He decided to warn Nick about Patti. Nick needed to know what she did before he went over there. He reached for his phone and punched in Nick's number.

NICK LISTENED IN silence, then said he needed to tell O'Brien how Patti had reacted to the search warrant. He had just stepped out and down the hall toward his boss's office when he heard a woman's agitated voice at the front counter. He changed direction, curious.

As he came into sight of the reception area, the woman pointed a finger at him and screeched, "Him! He's the one! I gotta talk to him!"

Nick blanched, caught his breath, and hustled over behind the counter. "Dave, I'll take this. Come on back. Patti, is it?"

The clerk at the desk shot Nick a grateful look.

Patti's rant finally wound down fifteen minutes later. Nick continued to sit quietly to make sure she was through. He was glad Mills had called before she got here or he wouldn't have known what was going on. Well, Patti was screwed. He wouldn't let her hinder the defense. Based on this behavior, Patti was definitely overreacting if she was innocent.

"Anything else you want to tell me?" he asked, trying to hide his feelings. Crazy broad. Expecting them to go after the Public Defender for her. He figured Patti was too dumb to even realize she was a suspect. She had herself in a major snit because someone dared challenge her and the dentist.

"Well, no. I guess that's all," Patti replied with a puzzled. Look. "What are you gonna do? He can't do this to us. I want him arrested. Right now."

Nick suppressed a smile. Dumb chick. She had no idea what was going on. He'd see what he could get out of her since she came in voluntarily. "Are you willing to give a statement?

"Yes, I sure am."

"We need to record it and I have to bring in my partner."

"Fine. Fine. Whatever."

"Excuse me just a minute while I get him." Nick hurried to their office and motioned to Matt. "Quick. Bring the recorder to the small conference room."

Matt drew back in surprise, then jumped up, grabbed the recorder and followed him.

"Okay. This is Matt. He'll be handling the recorder."

"You have the right to remain…" Matt began.

"Hey! Wait a minute. I'm not the one…" Patti cried in alarm.

"No, no," Nick said in a soothing tone. "This is standard. We have to do it for everybody on a case. Recording statements is a legal requirement. Don't worry. Just hear him out and then we'll start. It's nothing at all to be concerned about."

Patti looked at him in confusion. Nick smiled the most reassuring smile he could muster.

"Okay, then." She smiled back and answered affirmatively in a clear voice when Matt finished reading her rights.

I cannot believe how dumb she is, Nick thought. This is gonna be a piece of cake. He gave Patti another smile and began. "Dr. Williams says you've been close to the family during the past few years. They've depended on you. Tell us about it."

Patti sat up straight, bristling with pride. "Yes, I run the office for Dan. And I'm the number one babysitter for Tyler, too. He's so cute. I just love the little guy. And I have a key to their house so I can get the mail and water the plants whenever they're away. They depend on me, that's for sure." She beamed. "I'm like family"

She prattled on. Matt met Nick's eyes. Dan? On a first name basis with her boss? Loves the little boy? Has a house key?

Patti's face grew flushed with pride as she went on bragging. "I take care of everything for Dan at the office. Everything. He would be absolutely overwhelmed if I didn't take care of things. Especially with Jennifer working full time."

Her voice faltered. "Well, did work full time." Her eyes shifted. She gave a quick shake of her head and continued. "I keep Dan's schedule on track and I handle the books, too. It's been looking up this year. We've had to pay for all the equipment, the office construction, all the supplies and stuff, ya know. It's been a heavy load moneywise for the past few years. But it's looking better now. Dan says we'll be making a lot more by this time next year."

Patti stopped to take a breath, and suddenly seemed to realize she'd been doing all the talking. "Well, what else do you need to know?" she asked, now looking a bit wary.

Nick pulled his chair close to the table. "Where were you the night of Jennifer's murder?" He looked straight into Patti's eyes as he spoke, challenging her.

She straightened in alarm. "What? Where was I? Why ask me that? Surely you don't..." She bolted from her chair, sending it scraping across the floor. "Whaddya mean?"

"Easy," Nick said. "Just routine. We have to ask this of everyone she knew. We've asked lots of people. You're way down on the list."

He noticed Patti relaxing a bit and went on, "You've been forthcoming. And very cooperative. I'm sure with you doing this voluntary interview, we'll be able to move on real soon. There's nothing to worry about. Just try to remember what you were doing that night." He gave a reassuring smile and caressed Patti with his eyes.

She blushed, sat back down, and thrust her chest out just a little. She smiled back at him with her blazing white teeth. "Well, I was home. Mom will vouch for that. I got home late for supper because I stayed and cleaned up the office after Jennifer's appointment."

"Jennifer's appointment?" Nick prodded. She was so easy.

"Yeah. She was having a root canal. For a broken tooth. We did it on Friday after she got off work. She had to leave by five thirty because she had some kind of a woman's party to go to that night. I think it was one of those ones where they sell expensive kitchen gadgets. It was at her daycare place, I think."

A quick flash of what Nick recognized as envy crossed her features. "I helped with her root canal because I'm the only one who works Fridays. I do some assisting, too. Did I tell you that?"

Matt answered this time. "So you helped with the procedure and then they left? That was it?"

"Yup. I went home. Stayed there all night. I don't go out much. Ma needs the company. If I go out, it's usually on Saturday night. Just down to the bar to listen to music and dance a little. I don't have a boyfriend right now."

She tossed her head and continued, "So I heard about Jennifer the next morning. My friend Shirley called me from the gas station. Everybody was talking about it. I rushed over to the house. Dan turned Tyler over to me right away and I brought him back to be with Mom and me for a while. So much going on there, you know. All the calls. And people coming to the door. Dan was beside himself. He was crying. Her relatives started getting there, too. It was a madhouse." Patti's gaze was now distant, immersed in memories.

"So Dr. Williams didn't call you? Your friend did?"

"Mmm Hmmm. And I went right over. I knew he'd need me." In the silence of the next minute, Patti seemed to realize she'd talked a lot.

Nick spoke, "Hey, Patti. Thanks for stopping in. You've been a big help."

"But what about that lawyer? The one who came to the house and tore it up? What are you gonna do?"

"We'll look into it for you," Nick promised with a vague nod. "We'll be in touch. We know where to find you."

Patti rose, apparently mollified and reassured by their attention and promises. Nick rushed to help her with her chair and showed her to the front desk. "Thanks again, Patti. Thanks for coming in. We'll keep you informed." Uncertainty and suspicion showed on her features as she turned to go, as if she suddenly wondered if she had said more than she should have.

Nick turned and fled down the hall before she could speak again. "What do you think?" he asked Matt who was gathering papers and unplugging the tape recorder.

"Dumb broad. I heard motive, for sure. And her alibi for that night – not really solid if you ask me. You think the dentist's involved?"

"I'm not sure yet. That's a tough one. Either they did it together, or he has an admirer who did what she needed to so she could step into the wife's shoes. Will you get that tape transcribed right away? And fax a copy to Mills at the public defender's office while you're at it. He's been upfront about this. I'm gonna do a little payback for him."

Chapter 49

PRESTON AND MATT were sifting through the boy's toy boxes on the second floor of the Williams house when they heard the rumble of the automatic garage door. Preston took the stairs down and greeted Dan Williams as he hung his coat in the closet.

Williams gave a curt greeting before asking, "How much longer do you need to be here? I have to go and pick up Tyler at Amy's and I'd rather he didn't see you here." His face was tight with irritation. "What'd you find at the office? Get anything for your efforts?"

"Can't say," Preston replied. "We should finish upstairs within the hour. We can stay out of sight if you want to bring your son in. We'll leave quietly when we're done."

"Just hurry it up if you can." Dan strode toward the kitchen and Preston heard the refrigerator door open, then the pop of a bottle cap.

He's not happy, Preston thought. He didn't act this rude before. He sure doesn't want us here in his house, that's obvious. Preston and Matt finished their search of the upstairs to the sound of the television from the living room. Not a thing in the whole house was out of

284

place or raised their suspicions and Preston felt a bit guilty when they stole out the front door.

"I'll talk to you in the morning," he said to Matt. "You're staying overnight up here, did you say?"

"Yeah, at my sister's. Where should we meet in the morning?"

"You know the café in the old hotel? How about breakfast at nine? It'll be starting to get light by the time we finish eating."

"Yeah. I know the place. See you there."

Preston's thoughts turned to Cindy. He needed to see her. Talk to her. This had been a rough day. He badly needed a shower and a change of clothes. He could do it at Cindy's.

Her eyes shot open wide five minutes later when she opened her apartment door to him, "Hey, hi." She frowned. "You're all dusty and dirty. And you have stuff in your hair. What've you been doing anyway?"

"Can I take a shower here? Stay the night? I have to be back here again early tomorrow morning. There's been lots happening and I'm beat. Do you have anything to eat? I'll talk to you after I get cleaned up."

Cindy stepped back. "Sure. Toss your clothes out the bathroom door and I'll run 'em through the washer and dryer. There's a robe on the back of the door you can use. The white terry one. Will leftover chili be okay?"

"That sounds great. I have to call Karen about Daisy, too."

An hour later, Preston sank into the rocking chair in front of Cindy's TV and pulled her into his lap. "Thanks. The chili was good. Did you make it?"

"Yeah. Dad taught me. It's his special recipe." She turned inquisitive eyes to him. "So, what's happening?"

Preston nuzzled her shoulder. "A new lead. Remember, this is just between us." Cindy nodded, snuggled deeper into his lap, and looked up. "Well, it looks like an employee at the dental office might be involved. Patti. Oh, you know her, don't you?"

"Yeah. She's the one who recognizes my voice when I call."

"Yup. Her. We interviewed her today. It sounds like she's way too personally involved with Dr. Williams. Or perceives herself to be, anyway. We confiscated a ladder from her backyard today that looked out of place. It could be the one used to put the bundle of clothing up in that tree."

Cindy pulled away and her mouth dropped open. "Patti? You're kidding. She seems so nice."

Preston explained the rest of the facts and Cindy listened, rapt. "She kicked the carpet right in your face? That's why you were so dirty? Man! I bet you were surprised. So now what do you do?"

"Turn the ladder in for inspection and analysis. Let the troopers know what's happening. Check Patti's alibi. I'm sure her mother will back up her story about being home that night, though. The mother's old and kind of odd, but she seems to like me for some reason. So I think I'll see her as soon as I can in the morning.

That's the plan." He turned his attention to Cindy's waiting lips.

It felt good to wake up in Cindy's bed the next morning. She lay curled, warm and soft, next to him and Preston cuddled against her for a few minutes, nuzzling her awake, before forcing himself to get out of bed. He had to be at the café to meet Mike by nine. He dressed while Cindy watched through half open eyes.

"Do you want something to eat? Toast? Coffee?" she murmured.

"No, thanks," he replied. "I have a breakfast meeting with Mike. Stay in bed. Thanks for the accommodations." He grinned "And everything else."

Cindy drew the covers up around her neck. It took every bit of Preston's willpower to keep pulling his shirt on. The sheet outlined her form, dipping into the curves of her body. What he couldn't see made her more appealing. He tore his eyes away and bent to pull on his socks. He gave a final yank to his sock, then dropped to one knee at the side of the bed.

"Cindy. Will you marry me?"

She gasped and bolted upright, clutching the sheet to her chin. "What?"

Preston waited a second, not daring to breathe. "Will you marry me?"

She slipped further beneath the covers and pulled them over her head. Preston heard small unfamiliar sounds. He rushed to the bed and pried the sheet from her face. She was crying.

Before he could react, Cindy reached up and drew him to her. "Do you mean it? Really?" she asked. She looked up at him through teary eyes. "Really? You want to marry me?"

Preston had never been so sure of anything. "Yes, I mean it. Will you be my wife? I love you, Cindy." He took a trembling breath, "I want you to have my children. And when I die, I want it to be in your arms." He paused, heart thumping wildly. "Will you?"

Cindy squealed and sat up. When the sheet fell from her breasts, Preston could hardly breathe. She was so beautiful. So perfect. *Please say yes. Please say you'll marry me.*

"Yes," Cindy said. "Yes, I'll marry you. I love you, Preston Mills."

Preston fell onto the bed beside her. "Cindy Mills. Sounds good."

His heart rattled like a machine gun. She would marry him. He'd get to have her as his wife. He drew her into his arms and kissed her sleep softened lips with tenderness.

"Thank you. I promise you'll never be sorry you said yes. I'll love you with all my heart. Always."

They remained entangled, not moving for long moments while the words of the past few minutes sunk in. Preston finally forced himself to rise from the bed. He'd never been happier or more sure of anything in his life.

Chapter 50

NICK POURED PANCAKE batter onto the electric frying pan and called toward the stairs. "Hey, Andrew! Natalie! Cakes are on. You only have thirty minutes before the bus comes."

Kids finally out the door, he turned to his wife. "So what's on your agenda for the day?"

Kay shrugged. "Laundry. Probably go get milk and a few other things. Why?"

"Oh, nothing," Nick answered.

But Kay didn't buy it. "Something's bothering you. You tossed and turned all night." When Nick didn't answer, she touched his arm. "Is it still the murder case? Is that it?"

Nick nodded. "Yup. I'm pretty sure we have the wrong man in jail. The defense attorney's working hard to get his client out. He really believes the guy's innocent. I think so now, too. It bothers me that we can't figure out who did it, though."

"Well, here, have some more coffee. Let's talk about it."

"Naw. I can't just sit around here. Let's go for a ride."

Minutes later, he was behind the wheel of Kay's car headed toward the snowy meadows and mountains that ringed the town. This drive always calmed him. Having Kay beside him and the whole day ahead felt good. Often, on winter weekend mornings, they loaded the kids in the car and were far out in this same countryside by the time the sky began turning faint pink and gold beyond the mountain peaks. On what Andrew called those "moose looking" trips, they held contests to guess how many moose they'd spot before they got back home. He knew this drive was what he needed to do today. Just Kay and him. Driving and talking.

He turned to his wife. "Okay. So if the suspect in custody didn't do it, then who did? The mother who had the confrontation with Jennifer Williams in the kindergarten classroom? The other person of interest is the husband, of course. So now everybody's looking at the husband. And his receptionist, too."

"Why?"

"Motive. The receptionist is apparently unusually close to her boss. And she's exhibited some pretty bizarre behavior in the past few days."

"Ooooh! There's a big one!" Kay exclaimed, pointing to a bull moose in the ditch ahead. Nick stomped the brake. The huge ungainly animal strolled to the middle of the road, then stopped and turned its wide rack in their direction. It stared directly at them for a long moment before continuing down into the ditch on the other side, rump bobbing. It stopped and looked back one more time with curious flat black eyes before beginning a clumsy trot across the frost-covered field.

Nick put the car back into gear. He'd never get tired of seeing wildlife like this massive moose. He'd read that some of the bulls weighed close to two thousand pounds and he marveled that their scrawny legs could be strong enough to support such a massive and awkward body. The sky beyond the mountains was now streaked with rose and yellow. This country always cleared his brain. And he had his beautiful wife beside him. Nick sighed with contentment. Now if only he could get this case wrapped up with the right guy, he could go back to his usual workload.

"So the focus is on the dentist and his employee now?" Kay asked, breaking his reverie. "What about that woman, Ritter, was it? Can she just take off like that? Run away from this? Can't you make her come back if you suspect she's involved?"

"Yeah, we can issue a warrant if she is charged. But we don't know where she is in the Lower Forty-Eight at present. The boss said we don't have enough on her right now to go that route. She walked out of the last interview after instructing us to contact her only through her attorney and was out of the state twenty four hours later. But she surprised us. We dropped the ball on keeping her here. She's still a possible suspect."

Nick explained the details of Preston's investigation of Dan Williams and Patti while Kay listened with rapt attention.

"When will they find out if the ladder was at the scene of the crime?" she asked.

"Well, they could match the vegetation as early as today. But even if the ladder can be placed at the scene, it won't prove Patti did it. She could claim someone else put it there. And there's still no cause of death. The medical examiner is pretty sure it was poison, but so far he can't pin it down to a certain substance. At this point, the victim was just laying nude and half-frozen out there, and nobody knows why. It's obvious it was a murder. I mean Jennifer Williams wouldn't have taken off her own clothes, bagged them, and strapped them way up in a tree, and then laid down on the shoulder of the road and just died. It doesn't make sense. So it had to be murder."

"The question is how," Kay said.

Nick turned to her. "Yeah. Once that's figured out, it'll probably explain why. But we had to pick somebody up pretty fast on this case. The public has been clamoring with near panic since day one. So we put LaVassar in the can, but I don't think he's our guy."

He shrugged, "It was our job to pick him up and turn him in as long as there was reasonable cause. We did that. Now it looks like his attorney is close to undoing the arrest. Then the ball will be in our court to pick up the right person. We have to be ready. We'll look like we're not doing our job if suddenly the suspect is freed and we don't have anybody else in custody."

Kay asked, "And, this attorney, Preston, is it? He's been kind of working with you even though he doesn't have to?"

"Yeah. He's a good guy. I think his strategy is to push us to look elsewhere so he can spring LaVassar as soon as possible."

"So you're positive it was murder and the killer is still out there?"

At Nick's murmur of assent, Kay continued," Well, then, suppose it was the Ritter woman or the dentist and his assistant. Shouldn't you guys be on it?"

By the time Nick and Kay, fifteen moose later, got back to the house, Nick was fired up to go after another suspect. As usual, Kay's thoughts made sense.

Over grilled cheese sandwiches at the kitchen table, he asked Kay, "So who do you think did it? What's your gut feeling?"

"I think you should look at that Patti. And make that Ritter woman come back. I bet it was one of them. And I'd push the coroner. Make him go over every speck of that body again. There has to be evidence if it was poison. It's the only thing that would explain why the victim was laying out there like that."

She paused and sipped her iced tea. "The women and the poison. Poison is a woman's weapon. That's what I think you need to focus on. And I think you're right to worry. You guys need another suspect in line for when that LaVassar guy gets out."

While they cleaned up the kitchen, Kay suddenly turned from the sink. "Why don't I go for a dental appointment at Williams' office? I'll use my maiden name. That way they won't connect that I'm related to a trooper, in case your name has come up. I can get a good look at both the dentist and that Patti. See how they interact. I'll ask for an appointment tomorrow since you said Patti told you they're there Fridays without the other assistant, right? I'll say I have a toothache so they might take me in right away. Maybe a fresh set of eyes on this would help. Want me to?"

She was on the phone within minutes and had an appointment scheduled. *Damn, my wife is smart.* He drew her to him. *Talking to her always helps.*

Chapter 51

KAY FINISHED FILLING out the new patient form and handed it across the counter to the receptionist.

Patti gave a dazzling smile, peering at Kay through eyes garishly outlined in black. "I'm Patti. Have a seat. We'll be right with you," She turned back to her computer screen.

Kay took a seat across the room and picked up a magazine, pretending to read while she studied the young woman. Patti's long hair looked home permed, judging by the frizzy ends. Her bangs had been backcombed into the style popular in high schools a few years back and a dark part down the center of her head spoke of the need to touch up the obviously fake blond color. The word 'tart' flashed through Kay's mind. Patti's lips, darkened by ruby lipstick, were pursed in concentration. She bent over the keyboard, the curve of her breasts peeking from a uniform top unbuttoned too far down. Definitely not a class act.

Kay looked around the waiting room. A floor to ceiling glass wall gave a view of the highway and the snowy mountains in the distance. A tall, unusual plant with dark green, leathery leaves dominated one corner of the room, looking almost like a young tree with its clusters of lacy, salmon-colored blossoms. The walls held tastefully displayed Alaskan prints. The upholstered chairs were a cut above those found in the typical dentist's waiting room. Even the magazines were current.

Soon, she heard Patti call, "Mrs. Brinkman? We're ready. This way, please."

The appointment was brief. After a quick adjustment of Kay's bite that they hoped would settle the bothersome tooth, they agreed to watch and wait before proceeding with further treatment. Kay sensed a subtle closeness between Dr. Williams and Patti. Words weren't even needed as they passed instruments back and forth. She felt a definite connection between them, but couldn't tell if it was simply the ease of a long term working relationship or if there was more to it.

When she reported to Nick at home, he asked, "But what if you had to choose? Was it all business between them? Or something more?"

"I don't know," Kay replied with a frown of concentration.

"But if you had to say," Nick pressed.

"Then, no. Not lovers," Kay finally decided.

"Anything else out of the ordinary?"

Kay shook her head reluctance, knitting her brows. "Not that I can think of right now. The office was really nice. Decorated well. The furnishings and equipment looked new and the art on the walls was good stuff, I think. There was a huge, unusual plant just full of really pretty, ruffled salmon-colored blossoms, along the waiting room window wall. Otherwise, nothing jumped out at me."

"Thanks, Babe. If anything else comes to mind, tell me right away, okay?"

Their attention was caught by a pecking of sleet at the kitchen windows and a sudden strong wind that rattled the glass doors of the fireplace in the living room.

"That wind gives me a chill," Kay said. She wrapped her arms around her chest and shivered.

"Want me to warm you up?" Nick asked, a gleam in his eye. Before she could answer, he stepped over and wrapped his arms around her, pinning hers to her body. She wiggled in mock protest before he dropped his arms and drew her against him, then breathed hot breath into her ear, causing her to give a tiny squeal. Half stumbling over each other, they made it to the bedroom and fell together onto the bed in a frenzied heap.

Nick soaped his wife in the shower later, enjoying sliding his hands along her smooth, slippery curves. He couldn't help becoming aroused again, and it was a long time before they turned off the hot water and stepped out. When Andrew and Natalie ran through the front door and tossed their backpacks on the floor an hour later, their mother was cutting apples for their afternoon snack.

"It's snowing, Daddy! Look! Let's get the snow machines out!" Andrew called. He and his sister didn't notice their mother's rosy cheeks or how their parents gazed at each other across the kitchen with lingering intimacy in their eyes.

Chapter 52

PRESTON DROVE TO Wasilla early Saturday morning with Daisy sitting upright in the passenger's seat beside him. It was a good time for the dog to have a visit home since he and Cindy planned to drive up and check on Gary's cabin. Preston agreed with Gary's suggestion that it would do Daisy good to see if anything was new in the yard and to be able eat from her own dish again.

He thought back to his call to Gary yesterday afternoon, with news about warrants being issued for other suspects, and regretted he hadn't been able to get definite news on a release date. Gary sounded more upbeat than he had for a long time and was becoming anxious to get out of the hospital. So when Gary had asked him to take Daisy home and go check the cabin over the weekend, Preston readily agreed and arranged to pick Cindy up by eight.

This morning he'd have breakfast with his fiancée. Fiancée. Funny word. It would be great when he could call her his wife. A flash of his parents' faces almost stopped him in his tracks. He was engaged and they didn't even know. How far away they seemed. He had to call them. Soon. It had been weeks since he sent Victoria back and he had ignored two calls from his parents. His stomach tightened. He shook off the feeling with an odd abandon and dashed up the steps to Cindy's apartment. He wrapped her in a bear hug, coat and all, when she opened the door.

"Should we eat on the way to the cabin?" she asked. "There's a little general store along the highway that has a café. They make the best waffles and the bacon is the thick, old-fashioned kind. Dad and I used to eat there all the time." A flash of hurt crossed her face. "Maybe we'll go there again as soon as he gets out. He'd like that."

"That sounds good to me," Preston agreed.

Cindy slipped out her apartment door ahead of him, betraying a trace of the odd shyness they'd felt with each other since the proposal. Preston watched as Cindy shooed Daisy into the back seat and then slid into the passenger seat. The red parka she wore set off her the caramel brown of her eyes and a ruff of silvery fur perfectly framed her face. He settled into the driver's seat and turned to meet her eyes.

A sudden need to know about her past love life overcame him. "Cindy, I need to ask you something." He drew a deep breath. Maybe it would be best to let this go. What if the subject offended her? Maybe he didn't even want to know. But then he'd always wonder.

"Well, it's about, about..." He gulped and felt his throat go dry. "About another guy. I know there must have been one." He gripped the steering wheel. There, it was out. He didn't dare look at her.

Her answer came out so quiet he almost couldn't hear her. "Yes, there was. Back in high school. Trent. He went into the Air Force right after we graduated..." She stammered. "He met somebody else. It's been over for a long time." She gave a sudden giggle and covered her mouth with her hand. "Are you jealous?" Her shoulders shook. "Are you?" She laughed out loud. "Yes, you're jealous!"

Preston fought off annoyance. "Well, sure. What do you suppose?"

He glanced over to see her eyes dancing with merriment. "I'm sorry I didn't tell you," she said. "It never occurred to me. So you've been worrying about that?"

"Yeah," Preston admitted, feeling relieved. "Okay. Yes, I was jealous."

"Well, just get over it." Her voice barely hid her mirth. "I love that you were jealous. Don't you know how much I love you? I'm all yours forever."

Preston turned the key and headed for the cabin, light-hearted and happier than he ever remembered. The headlights had to be on high beam to cut through the curtain of thickly falling snow, even though it was morning. A ghostly white world surrounded them in their own private cocoon of contentment as the wheels turned on the pavement.

"Well, then, what about you? You told me you took care of some unfinished business. Was it a woman?"

Cindy blurted out the question and turned her face to the window.

Preston's eyebrows lifted in surprise. "Yes. It was."

"From back East?"

"Yeah."

"Well, tell me."

"Victoria. She was the only serious girlfriend I ever had. For seven years, since high school. But I ended it when I decided you were the one for me." He glanced over at Cindy.

She turned inquisitive eyes to him. "Seven years? Wow! And it's over for sure?"

He nodded and the conversation ended. That's what he liked about Cindy. Direct talk, honest answers, then done. And she'd had a relationship with a high school boy and that was it.

BY SUNDAY AFTERNOON, he and Daisy and Cindy had enjoyed the general store café's bacon and waffles, spent an hour at the cabin, driven back to Anchorage, picked out a ring at a jewelry store on Fifth Avenue downtown, and hiked the Chugach Park trails near his apartment. They spent a lot of time in bed, and decided that the first Saturday in June would be a good wedding date. They headed back to Wasilla in comfortable silence.

Preston's cell phone rang just as they pulled into Cindy's parking lot and he heard Mike's voice. "Hey, Mills. Anything new on the Williams murder?"

"Yeah. Are you back in Anchorage?"

"Naw. I'm still in Palmer at my sister's. She needed a babysitter so I stayed with my nieces yesterday. Frank told me to keep working with you on this as long as it takes. Overtime and all. Have you been working?"

"Sort of. I've been doing a lot of thinking and I'm sure we should go talk to Patti and her mother again. Tomorrow late afternoon so Patti will be home from work. Okay with you?"

"Sure. But you better watch out for flying carpet dirt." He chuckled. "How about meeting at the café parking lot tomorrow, say at nine again? We can review what we have, stop at the coroner's and see if he's made any progress. Hey, guy. Drive carefully. This snow is that slick, slippery kind. They say the Glenn Highway's really bad. I hear there's been about fifty cars in the ditches between here and Anchorage."

NICK AND MATT spent the weekend on duty due to the blizzard. Tow trucks were out in force. A woman in a station wagon collided with a moose near the flats in the early morning darkness. Although the moose crushed the car's grille and hood, it had been a small enough animal that it didn't break through the windshield. The woman had been lucky to walk away with only a bruise on her forehead. The moose was killed on impact. After the troopers arranged for pickup of the animal by volunteers for the Wasilla food shelf, they spent the rest of the day patrolling the slippery streets, windshield wipers beating ineffectively at the thick, relentless snowfall.

Mountaintops that had been only frosted with snow now stood draped in white. Patches of dark green spruce crawled part way up the slopes, their branches drooping under mounds of snow. The town's lawns and streets were covered in thick layers of undisturbed white now, too. Citizens, wary of the dangers of dense snowfall like this, respected the storm by staying in, so there was very little activity on the streets. The hours on patrol dragged for Nick and Mike and by late Sunday afternoon they were anxious to get out of the car and away from the silent white world that surrounded them.

Nick pulled up in his driveway at dark and stopped the car for a moment, enjoying the sight of the glowing windows and familiar outline of his house. His home. His family. His wife in there making supper. He sighed with pleasure and pulled into the garage. As soon as he opened the kitchen door, the aroma of pizza blasted him. *Oh, yeah, it's make your own pizza night.* He wondered what the kids would put on theirs this time. He smiled at the sight of his bustling family setting the table for supper.

Kay turned to him, her eyes bright. "I thought of something. About the case. Something that might be important." She glanced at the kids whose attention had been caught by her tone. She looked back at Nick. Later, her eyes signaled. Nick dipped his chin in acknowledgement.

"Daddy, what case? What does Mommy mean?" Andrew asked.

Nick remembered their vow not to discuss his work in front of the kids. "Oh, Mommy and I talked about a problem I had at work the other day. It's nothing, though," he reassured his son. "What'd you put on your pizza this time? Not apples again, I hope."

It was a very long hour before Nick and Kay could sneak up to their room while the kids loaded the dishwasher.

"What?" he asked as soon as he shut the door.

"Remember I told you about the big plant I noticed in Dr. Williams' waiting room? I think it was an oleander. They're poisonous, extremely toxic to humans and animals. I've never seen one in Alaska before."

Nick's heart skipped. He interrupted. "You mean that could be the poison?"

"Maybe. When I worked in the greenhouse in North Carolina during high school, they had a lot of 'em. There are lots of different colors of blossoms. Pink, red, white, and yellow, but I always thought the salmon colored ones were the prettiest. That's the color that was blooming on the one in the waiting room at Dr. Williams' office. I think that's why I noticed it, but I didn't think about the poison then. I remembered about the oleanders this morning while I was folding laundry. We didn't sell those plants to families with children or pets because even a tiny lick on a leaf can kill." Kay stopped for breath, her eyes bright. "That plant looked new. Kinda shiny and lush for Alaska. Maybe they knew about what oleander could do. I think Jennifer Williams might have been poisoned with oleander."

Nick caught his breath. *God. Maybe she had figured it out. That's why the coroner hadn't been able to trace it. Who would ever think of oleander in Alaska, much less know it's poisonous?*

"Way to go, Babe. Good thinking. You might have figured out the clue we need. I love you, my woman. You're the best."

Kay beamed. Nick punched Preston's number into his cell phone and passed the information on.

NICK COULDN'T SLEEP after the call. Anxious for morning, he tossed and tangled the blankets. Finally, he went down to the kitchen for a can of beer and drank it down while looking out the living room window. An enormous milky moon illuminated the shards of distant mountains that thrust upward into the black sky. The yard and trees shown bright in the eerie moonlight. He was scheduled to have tomorrow off, but this couldn't wait. A growing excitement gnawed at the pit of his stomach while he waited out the long dark hours.

Chapter 53

PRESTON COULDN'T SLEEP that night, either. He snuggled against Cindy, absorbing her scent, enjoying the warmth and softness of her body against his, but he couldn't fall asleep. The room glowed with moonlight that crept in along the sides of the shades in Cindy's bedroom. Cindy's curls shone in the pale light and her steady breathing comforted him, but he couldn't escape into sleep. He'd been stunned by Nick's call about the plant in Williams' waiting room. He couldn't wait to go to Patti's house again. There had to be more they could find out there.

This time, Gladys was unfriendly, almost hostile, when she opened the door to Mike and him. Before Preston could even greet her, she spouted, as if the words had been rehearsed, "My daughter Lizzie said we don't have to talk to you. She's on her way back to Alaska and she said to tell you to talk to our lawyer. She said we don't have to say a word to you or those troopers that came here, or anybody else." She stepped back from the door smugly and crossed her arms across her chest, chin raised in defiance. Mimi crouched behind Gladys' ankles, growling faintly.

"Okay," Preston answered, trying to hide his surprise. Playing a hunch, he added quickly, "I appreciate all you and Patti have helped us with so far. We have new information. I wanted to tell you, but..."

Curiosity replaced the animosity on Gladys' face. "New information?"

"Yes, but we better go if someone said you're not supposed to talk to us." He held his breath.

"Well," Gladys said. "Patti's gone to get Burger King to pick up some supper. She'll be right back. I 'spose she'd want to hear new information." She hesitated. "I guess you can come in and wait. But don't be asking me anything. Wait 'til Patti gets back." She reached down to gather Mimi into her arms, then stood aside and motioned Preston and Matt in.

Preston smiled at her, doing his best to look reassuring. "Thank you."

He took a seat beside Mike on the sofa. Before them lay the rug Patti had kicked in his face. Preston's eyes watered at the memory. He looked at Mike and caught a glimpse of a fleeting tight grin that told him Mike was thinking the same thing. Preston thought of Gary in his hospital room at Providence. He thought of Daisy leaping joyfully from the car when they'd brought her for a visit to the cabin yesterday. He thought of Cindy's worry about her father. He turned to Gladys.

"How have you been?"

"Just fine, thank you," Gladys answered primly and straightened her back, chin jutting out further. She stroked Mimi with nervous movements. Preston waited. Remember what the professor said. Wait them out. Let the silence go on so long that they have to break it.

"Well, Lizzie's coming home. She told us we shouldn't say a word. And to tell you to talk her lawyer. Said you'd have his name and number."

"Lizzie? Her lawyer?" Preston asked.

"Yes. My older daughter. She lives here in Wasilla but she's been gone to Portland to her in-laws for a while. Now she's coming home. When we told her all you law people had been around, she said she better come home now. She doesn't want us involved in this mess."

Gladys looked like she wanted to say more, but then pressed her lips firmly together, as if remembering her instructions. Preston gave her another warm smile. Keep her talking.

"Is Lizzie older than Patti?" he asked.

Gladys hesitated, evaluating the question. Apparently deciding it was merely small talk, she replied, "Yeah. She's ten years older. Got a college degree in the Lower Forty Eight. Smart one of the family. Chemistry or something. She's married now and has a little girl. Courtney."

Preston stifled a gasp. Courtney. Wasn't that Elizabeth Ritter's daughter's name? He took a deep calming breath and smiled again at Gladys. "You must be very proud. Did she marry a local guy?"

"Yup. Thomas Ritter. He owns apartments and buildings all over town. And in Anchorage, too. Lizzie doesn't have to work, he does so well. She's good to us.

I prob'ly wouldn't make it on my social security. So Lizzie helps out. And Patti brings home her paycheck, too. That's how I've been able to keep this house. Sure don't wanna go into one a' them old folks' homes."

Preston could hardly breathe. Patti and Elizabeth Ritter were connected, they were sisters! Ritter had a degree in chemical engineering. It took brains to get that. She would be clever enough to know about a poisonous plant. And helping her little sister was probably a way of life for her. If she'd been involved with her sister's plan, that would explain the instant hostility Ritter had shown to law enforcement, and her flight to the Lower Forty Eight.

Preston practically jumped up. "Well, we can't wait for Patti any more. We have another meeting." Mike turned startled eyes to him.

"Let's go," Preston said, still trying to calm his breathing. "Thanks for your time, Gladys. Will you tell Patti we'll see her another day?"

"But...but, the new stuff you had to tell us?" Gladys stammered as she rose hastily from her recliner.

"Later. We'll talk with you later. Good-bye." Preston jogged out the door, Mike at his heels. Now it all was beginning to make sense. Patti and Elizabeth Ritter were sisters who were in cahoots. Who'd have guessed? So they were in cahoots on the murder. He spilled out his conclusion while he and Mike rode back toward the troopers' office.

"But the cause of death? How'd they do it?" Mike asked.

"I don't know yet. But now we know about the poisonous plant. And we know who to look at. We'll get 'em."

Preston dropped Mike off and sped to the Lazy Dog Kennel, elated. When he finished telling Cindy about Elizabeth Ritter and Patti, her eyes were bright with hope. "So Dad will get out soon?"

Preston nodded. "Yup. I'm sure we'll break this quick and get him out. Maybe with this new evidence, he can be released quickly. I don't know exactly how it goes, though. I'll ask Frank first thing in the morning. But don't tell your Dad yet. Just in case it can't happen right away. We don't want him to have to go through disappointment again."

Cindy bobbed her head in agreement. "And are you gonna tell the troopers?"

"Sure. Right away. And I'll have to contact the DA so he can drop the charges against your Dad. I'll also ask for an emergency hearing so we can get him out sooner than it would usually take. They need to know this. I just know they have the wrong man locked up. There are new suspects, new developments. I'll call the trooper on my cell right away. I have to let him know."

He gave Cindy a peck on the lips, then rushed to his car, charged. The drive back to

Anchorage flew by while Preston's thoughts bounced. When he told Frank about the sisters and the plant, Gary would get out for sure. But, how did they poison her and leave no mark on her body?

Chapter 54

PRESTON WAS AT his desk early Monday morning. He dialed Nick and wasn't surprised to get an answer on the second ring.

"I'm supposed to be off today, but I couldn't stay away after finding out about the plant," Nick explained. "We're having the coroner test for oleander. And the ladder had traces of leaves and earth that matched the woods where the clothes were found. So it can be placed at the scene."

"It all fits," Preston exclaimed. "We just have to figure out how they got the plant poison into Jennifer."

Preston watched for Frank to arrive and hustled into his office before his boss even sat down at his desk. The surprise in Frank's eyes was followed by admiration while Preston explained the latest developments. "Good work. Very good," he exclaimed, rubbing his hands together. "We'll get your man off. LaVassar, is it?"

"Yeah. How will it work? Can he get out today?"

"Hold on. The prosecutor has to do things properly at his end. I imagine he's heard about this by now. No telling what he'll do, though. He'll need definite facts before he signs off on releasing a suspect already in custody. A lot will depend on what the coroner finds. And the Ritter woman and that receptionist, maybe the dentist, too, will have to be picked up and booked. It's imperative that we keep this quiet until then so they don't get wind of it. Do your people understand that?" Frank's look was almost gleeful.

Preston had never felt prouder. This lawyer business was great. A fleeting image of himself in a judge's robe flashed through his mind. He longed to be with Cindy and share every detail. He couldn't wait to see the look on Gary's face when he found out he was finally going home. He almost danced back to his desk.

Soon, a scan appeared on his screen reporting that the process for the arrests of Patti Evans and Elizabeth Ritter had begun. Once alerted to the unusual plant poison, the coroner had identified a trace of oleander in the victim's tissue and was working hard to pinpoint the site of entry. He assured the troopers that he felt he'd have results within twenty-four hours. Troopers had already been dispatched to pick up the oleander plant from the dental office. Based on that, O'Brien had agreed to drop charges against Gary.

When Preston reported this to Frank, his boss looked up and barked, "So take the rest of the day off. You did good, Mills."

"What about LaVassar? Can I get him out?" Preston held his breath.

"For the moment, no. Not yet." At Preston's disappointed look, he said. "Okay. Okay. I'll call O'Brien up in Wasilla and see if he'll get the wheels moving. My best guess is sometime tomorrow. Check this afternoon, though, just in case. Go on. Get outa here. Take the day off. Got any hearings?"

"Nope. Two tomorrow, though. Thanks." Preston hustled to his desk, snapped his briefcase shut and informed Barb he would be gone for the day. As he walked by her, she smiled as if she already knew and waved him on.

In the daylight, Preston could see that the streets of Anchorage were bordered by mounds of dirty slush from the weekend storm. The city was coming to life sluggishly and street lights remained on, struggling to pierce the foggy, sunless day. Hesitant traffic snaked along and what few pedestrians there were scurried along next to buildings, shoulders hunched into collars. The surrounding mountains were invisible in the overcast mist. The city appeared empty to Preston without that backdrop.

An unexpected day to do as he wished took Preston by surprise. His thoughts turned immediately to Cindy, but she was working. He wished he could drive to the hospital, grab Gary, and just take him home. He reached his car, punched Frank's number and asked, "Hey, Frank, Mills here. Did you get through to O'Brien? Is there anything I can do to expedite LaVassar's release?" He hoped he didn't sound too anxious.

After a silent moment, Frank's gruff voice came over the line. "O'Brien said he heard you had something going on with LaVassar's daughter. We talked about this before. What's the deal?"

Preston gulped. "Sir, I can handle this. It's not a fling. It's well, it's…I can explain."

"So you still have a personal interest in this then," Frank interrupted. "I told you it's not ethical. Not smart. You know that. This disobedience could compromise the case. And then you did direct interviews yourself that make you a witness in your own case." He snorted. "You're challenging me. I didn't expect you to be a maverick. What the hell!"

Preston's throat went dry. How much did Frank know about Cindy? Should he explain that Cindy was his fiancée?

Frank went on, his tone scolding. "Cool it with her. Understand me? Things like that can blow a case in unexpected ways. We can't afford to screw up, especially now that this is so close to being wrapped up. "

"Yes, Sir, I understand," Preston replied.

"Well, then," Frank said. "I just hung up with O'Brien. He agrees LaVassar can be sprung. If it's that important to you, go ahead and give O'Brien a call. He'll cooperate. And, Mills, lay off it with the woman until this is buttoned up. Got it?"

"I'm going to marry her," Preston said boldly.

"Oh, God," Frank huffed a huge sigh, and hung up.

Preston's spirits couldn't be dampened. He called the DA's office and asked for O'Brien. Ten minutes later, he was on the freeway to pick up the motion to dismiss that O'Brien agreed to let him hand carry back to the court house and the hospital.

With papers in hand, he pulled into the kennel parking lot and tooted his horn. He spotted Cindy with her foot on a shovel at the other side of the dog yard. She looked up at the sound of the beep. He leaped from the car, waving the papers above his head and motioned for her to come to him. She hurried toward him, brows knotted in puzzlement. When she got close enough and recognized the huge smile on his face she broke into a run.

And when he called out, "Your Dad! We can go get your Dad!" her wide grin matched his.

"Now?"

"Yes. Right now."

"I'll tell Bob. I'll be right back." She tore toward the office.

Cindy peeled off her work jacket and they climbed into his car, grinning crazily at each other. Preston explained the latest developments while they drove to Anchorage. He left Cindy in the car at the courthouse curb while he hurried in to file Gary's motion and get a release order from the judge.

"Next stop Providence!" he chortled, flinging himself back into the driver's seat. Cindy glowed with happiness and snuggled close to him. She smelled of flowers and dogs and her hair tickled his cheek.

They hustled down the hospital corridor. Cindy spotted him first. "Daddy! Daddy!" she cried and broke into a run before he could heave himself up from the rocking chair by the window of the day room. He halted her mad dash as he lurched to his feet and grabbed her.

"Cindy? What? Is something wrong?"

"No! No! You're getting out. Right now!"

"What?"

"Yes! You're free! We have the court order. You can come with us right now. You're free! They found out who did it! You have to sign something at the nurses' station. That's all."

Gary's disbelief quickly turned to glee. He turned to Preston. "I get to go home?"

At Preston's affirmative nod, Gary grinned. "I'm free! I'm out. I'm out! Hot Damn!"

They headed up the mountain a half hour later to pick up Daisy. Preston flung open the apartment door while Gary was still climbing out of the car. Daisy began her usual dash to the bushes, then stopped in her tracks. After a shocked second, she launched herself at Gary and they fell in a heap in the snow, rolling over and over. Cindy and Preston laughed at the sight.

The ride to Wasilla included the drive-thru at Arby's in Eagle River where Gary ordered two super-sized roast beef sandwiches with horseradish so he'd have enough to share with Daisy. It was midnight before Gary and Daisy had been delivered to the cabin and settled in. Gary insisted that the place would warm up soon enough and practically shooed Cindy and Preston out the door.

"Go. Go. Leave me here. I just wanna be home by myself. There's still some food in the freezer, and it'll warm up in here in an hour or so if I keep the stove going like this. My truck'll start in the morning just fine. It always does. Gotta check the job site. It's the weekend, but I still wanna have a look at how far they are." It was obvious that he was very eager to be left alone.

On the ride back, Cindy asked, "Well, should we tell him now about the wedding?"

"Sure. Now he'll be able to give you away for sure. Let's tell him as soon as we see him tomorrow, okay?"

They grinned at each other, eager to share the good news. It was nearly two a.m. by the time they pulled into the parking lot of Cindy's apartment building and both had run out of steam. They fell into her bed and nestled into each other, exhausted by the day.

Chapter 55

PRESTON'S CELL PHONE melody woke him in the morning. He knuckled the sleep from his eyes and read ten o'clock on the screen while he flipped it open. "Preston Mills here."

"Mills. Kerrans. Elizabeth Ritter got back to town last night. We're gonna pick her and Patti up first thing Monday morning. We'll bring 'em in around ten or so. Do you want to be here for the interview? I know that's not protocol for us to let you sit in, but the hell with it."

"Thanks, man. Sure," Preston replied, fully awake now. "Is there any progress on how they got the poison into the victim?"

"Nope. The coroner's baffled. There's not even the tiniest injection site or any sign of a wound. He's gonna keep looking but he said he's been over every speck of the body many times and there's nothing. He's bringing in a forensic expert from Seattle Monday. Maybe a second set of eyes will be able to spot it."

"We really need that, don't we? Right now, we have motive for both women, the ladder placed at the scene, and the oleander. But we really need to know how they got it into her, don't we?"

"Yeah. I'll see you Monday morning early here at the station. It'll be a long wait over the weekend."

Saturday and Sunday dragged for Preston. He couldn't concentrate on TV and had little appetite. He puzzled the method of poisoning over and over, but came up with nothing.

EQUALLY FRUSTRATED, NICK wrapped things up at his desk Saturday just in time to walk the sidelines of Andrew' fifth grade football game, the last of the season. Even though he usually lost himself in the boys' intense, amateurish struggle on the field, he couldn't overcome the agitation that claimed him. How did they get the poison into Jennifer? How? He needed Kay's input again on this. Needed to run all this new stuff by her. Maybe he'd take her out for dinner to that new restaurant on Lake Lucille so they could talk.

He whisked his cell phone from his pocket and called home. "Hey, can you get a sitter? Or can we drop the kids off at Lynn's? Let's eat out tonight."

Kay answered, her voice eager with surprise. "Sure. Sounds great. By the time you and Andrew get home, I'll have it arranged."

Nick sat across the table, admiring his wife in the candlelight. She had whipped her hair up into some kind of a twisted knot that defied gravity, and brightened her face with lipstick and eye shadow and all the other stuff she kept on the bathroom counter. Through the floor to ceiling windows behind her a glimmering lake reflected the bare branches of shoreline trees in the moonlight. How could she look that pretty when he'd called her at the last minute? Her breasts were almost too big for the top she wore and he liked how they pressed against the fabric as if they wanted to escape. He could tell right where her nipples were. Nick felt a rush of heat and drew a sigh of contentment.

"So, what's up?" Kay asked, breaking his reverie. "Is it the case?"

Nick nodded and filled her in on the latest developments. "We just need how. How did they get that poison into her?"

Kay shook her head. "Boy, I don't know."

They sat lost in thought until the waitress interrupted them for their order. The Copper River salmon was perfect, the baked potatoes fluffy and hot, the service even better. As they walked to the car, Nick felt more calm and content than he had in a long time. Maybe it was a good thing to relax. Maybe something would come to him now.

Suddenly, Kay's voice startled him. "I got it! I bet I know! Of course. That would work!"

Nick jerked the car to the side of the road, stomped the brake, and turned to her. "You figured it out?"

"Yup. How 'bout this?"

Nick and Kay logged on to their computer as soon as they got home to verify her idea. Nick fell into bed that night and slept so hard that he didn't wake up until Andrew and Natalie's high pitched voices from the kitchen penetrated his consciousness. He rolled over in an empty bed to the smell of toast and coffee and the sight of the sun streaming through the window.

Chapter 56

THE LARGE CONFERENCE room at the troopers' office bustled with activity by eight Monday morning. Preston, Mike, Nick, Matt, and O'Brien gulped cups of coffee from cardboard cups while they fidgeted, watching the clock. O'Brien said not a word, only studying Preston through the awkward silence. It was obvious from his scowl that he objected to this arrangement.

A few minutes before nine, they heard agitated voices in the hall and rose to meet the uniformed trooper who escorted Patti and Elizabeth Ritter to the room. Elizabeth's face was set, her eyes hard over a frown. Patti's pale face was pinched with apprehension. They walked side by side without touching or looking at each other. Preston sensed deep hostility in Elizabeth's demeanor.

"I want our lawyer," Elizabeth demanded. "I want Brad Knight to be here."

"We read 'em their rights when we picked them up," a trooper said.

"Thanks," O'Brien answered. He turned to Elizabeth and Patti. "Go ahead and make your call.

Phone's on the wall there right outside the door if you don't have a cell along. You'll need a quarter or a credit card."

He leaned toward the men. "Let's read 'em their rights again into the record as soon as they get back in the room. Matt, recorder ready?"

When they returned from the hall, Matt addressed the women, "You have the right to remain silent. Anything you say…" When he finished, Patti nodded, but Elizabeth stood just inside the door in belligerent silence. She refused to say a word even when O'Brien told her it was mandatory that she answer out loud for the recording of the interview.

"Patti?' he asked.

"Okay. Yes, I heard," Patti murmured, her voice small. She hung her head, not looking at anyone. Elizabeth set her lips tight, still refusing to speak.

"Jennifer Williams' murder case. December 2, 2015." Nick finished the preliminary oral instructions and turned to Patti. He looked her in the eyes, ignored Elizabeth, and said sharply, "We know you did it. We know how you did it. If you cooperate, things will go easier for you."

Patti's face froze into a white mask of shock. She turned to her sister.

"Don't say anything. Wait for the lawyer. Wait for Knight to get here," Elizabeth ordered in a clipped tone, giving her sister only a brief sidelong glance. She turned from her sister's entreating gaze. "Stay silent."

"But they know…" Patti began.

"No they don't. It's a trick they use. Just wait for Knight to get here."

Patti met Preston's eyes, beseeching him.

He gave her a reassuring smile. "We'll help you," he murmured in a quiet and confidential tone, speaking just to her. "Your Mom will be comforted if she knows you helped us out. She'll be proud, and it'll go easier for you, too. Helping us out is the best way."

Elizabeth turned and shook her finger at Patti. "Don't listen to him! Just wait 'til I tell you to open your mouth!" She glared at her sister.

Patti sank into her chair and wrapped her arms around her chest in obvious dismay, looking bewildered and terrified. Preston felt certain he should keep pushing her. She was taking it hard, especially any reference to her mother. Maybe he could get her to break before the lawyer arrived. He ignored Elizabeth and gave Patti his most encouraging look.

"Look, you have the right to wait for your lawyer if you want to. It'll go better for you if you tell us about the root canal on Jennifer. Tell us if Dr. Williams was involved in placing the oleander in her tooth canal. It'll be..."

Elizabeth took a few steps forward, feet braced apart, hands on her hips. "Shut up! Stop!" Her face had turned deep crimson. "Patti! Don't say anything!" For the first time, fear flickered across on her face.

"But, they..."

Elizabeth slammed herself back into her chair. She raged at Patti. "Stop talking! Stop!"

But Patti appeared not to hear. She sought Preston's eyes. "How did you know? About the root canal? About packing the plant in her tooth?"

"You mean filling the canal with crushed oleander leaves instead of gutta percha? The coroner discovered and identified the material in her tooth and then toxicology reports showed it in her body. Was Dr. Williams involved?"

At this, Patti crumpled.

Elizabeth sat back, stunned.

"No, he didn't know about it," Patti began in a quavering voice. "He always lets me finish packing temporary fillings. He didn't know."

She covered her face with her hands and began sobbing. "Will you tell Mama I cooperated? Will you tell her?"

Preston heaved a sigh and met Nick's grin. Next stop, his fiancée. Life in Alaska was good. He punched speed dial for his parents. It was time to let them know they needed to get airline tickets for a June wedding.